Thank you for
supporting
Evernight Publishing
Happy Reading
:)
JD Blakeley
xo

Evernight Publishing

www.evernightpublishing.com

Copyright© 2016

Evernight Publishing

Editor: Jules Kafri

Cover Artist: Jay Aheer

ISBN: 978-1-77233-779-2

ALL RIGHTS RESERVED

7 AUTHOR ANTHOLOGY

BAD ALPHA

Manlove Edition

7 Author Anthology

Bully Boys by Nicola Cameron

The Alpha's Assassin by Doris O'Connor

Discarded Pup by Angelique Voisen

Yellow Eyes by Gale Stanley

Destined by L.D. Blakeley

Trouble by James Cox

Outlaw Wolf by Elizabeth Monvey

BULLY BOYS

Copyright © 2015

Nicola Cameron

Chapter One

Arthur Finter hunched deeper into his overcoat, letting the slightly worn collar act as a barrier between his ears and the wet October wind sweeping in from the Thames. Around him the city crowd bustled, busy as an ant's nest even as the day wore toward an end.

His day had been just as busy, and twice as exhausting. The law office of Burcham and Stowe was a small but well-respected one, and as the junior solicitor, Arthur was required to review the firm's more tedious paperwork. When he wasn't reading myriad wills, settlements, pensions, and other legal documents for accuracy, he was often sent out on tasks that John Burcham and Matthew Stowe decided were beneath their status.

Arthur made a point of shouldering his workload without complaint. He knew full well that keeping his nose to the grindstone was the only way he would ever see the addition of Finter to the firm's door plaque. So he tolerated the cheap set of rooms within walking distance of the office, and the long hours working well into the night, and the knowledge that he could be called upon at any time to "read over this will, Finter, and see if Mrs. Mablethorpe has decided to include her nephew William or cut him out again." When he was made a full partner in the firm, he told himself, *then* he could indulge himself in better digs, finer clothes, and all the accouterments of a successful solicitor.

The only benefit of his lowly position was that no one questioned his bachelor status. An orphan raised by a maiden aunt who was now deceased, he had no family connections that might appeal to a lady of quality, and his status as a junior solicitor at a small firm was prosaic at best. That he was somewhat shorter than the average, with an unremarkable face and an even more unremarkable bank balance, had also helped to keep him free of matrimony, much to his quiet relief.

Although lately Mr. Stowe had begun mentioning his oldest daughter Eleanora, a sharp-tongued spinster who spent the bulk of her time working for various good causes, as "a wonderful spouse for a solicitor, what with her upbringing and all, eh, Finter?"

So far Arthur had been able to avoid any meetings of a more personal nature with La Stowe, but it did worry him that advancement at the firm would also require him to take on Eleanora and her multitudinous causes.

But that was a concern for another time. For now he headed home to his spartan rooms, carrying a briefcase bulging with papers to be studied over a solitary dinner set out by his landlady. He hefted the case, estimating a good four hours of work to be contained in the worn leather sides. *Sooner started, sooner done.*

Head down against the wind, he didn't notice the crowd slowing around him until he bumped into the overcoated back of a man. He muttered an apology to the mutton-chopped man who turned and glared at him. "What's going on?" he asked.

"The Inns of Court Hotel has caught fire," the man said. "The fire brigade has blocked off High Holborn."

Arthur now noticed the flickering orange glow farther down the street. Fires were serious business in London, as they would be in any city that had once burned to the ground. The fire brigade would be hard at work making sure that the conflagration didn't spread.

The crowd was already starting to push back, looking for alternate ways around the blockage. Arthur ducked into a shop front, mentally remapping his route home. He would have to take a rather wide detour to get around the fire, getting him home later than usual. Not only would his dinner be cold, but it would take valuable time from his evening's work.

The alternative, to take a shortcut through the alleys, would get him home on time, possibly even earlier than usual. But that route ran the greatly increased risk of running into cutpurses, women of ill repute, and other unsavory types that populated London's backstreets. *But others will be going that way, surely? The riffraff won't try anything if they're outnumbered.*

His feet, weary after a day of running errands for Mr. Burcham, made the decision for him. Tightening his grip on his case, he squared his shoulders and headed into the entrance of a nearby alley.

****

Gunner Jones snarled as he punched and kicked at the trio of bully boys facing him. Across the alley Willie Campbell dealt with his own handful of scrappers, knocking them about with scarred fists the size of hams.

He was surprised it had taken this long for the Haymaker Gang to decide that they should muscle in on the Black Staffs' patch, launching their campaign with an ambush of the gang leaders far afield. As the alpha of the Black Staffs, it was Gunner's job to explain to the Hays their error, ideally with as much blood and carnage as possible.

He grabbed a Hay by his greasy hair, twisting and slamming the man's face into the alley brickwork. The Hay gurgled and went limp. Gunner let him drop onto the filthy ground, just in time to jerk out of the way of a knife thrust. He grabbed the thug's wrist and squeezed hard, feeling bones grind and crack in his grip. Grinning cruelly, he twisted, neatly popping the elbow out of socket. The Hay screamed shrilly and dropped to his knees, clutching his wounded arm. Gunner took aim and kicked him in the face, sending him sprawling into the alley dirt.

"Gettin' in yer exercise, Willie?" he called out.

Willie smashed a Hay in the gut, following with an equally heavy blow to the chin. There was a meaty crack and the Hay sank down, gargling blood. "Fine day for it," his beta said with a grunt. "Let's move it along, though. I want me supper."

"Right." Gunner glared at the last Hay standing. Gang muscle by the look of his thick arms and dull eyes. The Hay wouldn't go down easily. "Come on, then."

The Hay grinned, revealing strong white teeth that would have looked out of place on any other member of the London poor. Lowering his head, he charged at Gunner, shifting in mid-lunge into the stocky, muscular shape of a brindle and white bull terrier.

Gunner shifted as well, meeting the charge with jaws open wide. He snapped at the brindle terrier's nose, causing it to flinch, and used his momentum to knock his opponent sprawling. The Hay scrambled to all four paws and bit at Gunner's foreleg, forcing him to jump back.

The dogfight continued for a few brief, vicious moments until Gunner saw an opening. Using his powerful hind quarters, he drove forward and slammed his head into the brindle terrier's jaw, forcing it up. He clamped his own jaws on the thick throat and bit down hard, ignoring the Hay's pain-filled howl. Ripping back, he felt the flesh in his jaws tear free. The brindle terrier's scream died in a wet, bubbling sound.

Spitting out the mouthful of blood and flesh, he shifted back. The dead brindle terrier shifted as well into the naked Hay, sightless eyes staring at the slice of sky visible from the alley. Gunner hawked and spat bloody saliva on the corpse.

"And stay off our patch," he added for the benefit of the other Hays.

Willie stepped up, handing him his clothes. "All right, then?"

"Yeah," Gunner grunted, pulling on his clothes. "Arseholes, all of 'em. They should know better."

Willie shrugged. "Better off dead, if you ask me."

"Too right—" Gunner broke off, sniffing. Beyond the usual olfactory nightmare that was a London alley, he could smell the Hays, fresh blood and sweat, piss and shit from the new corpse—

—and something that was absolutely impossible. He glanced around and saw a man in an overcoat and hat clinging to the edge of a wall, staring right at him.

****

Arthur had heard the dogfight before he'd seen it. He'd assumed it was simply two curs scrapping over food or a fertile bitch and intended to step quickly past the beasts. Instead, he walked into a scene of bodies sprawled around the alleyway. A stocky man with salt and pepper hair stood off to one side watching the canine battle.

As Arthur watched a handsome Blue Staffordshire bull terrier had gotten its teeth into the throat of a larger brindle terrier, cutting off its last howl with a jerking tear. The dead dog sagged to the ground, and then....

Arthur's calm, logical brain went into shock. There was no way he could have witnessed the dead terrier transform into a dead man, or the Staff into a quite living one. Not only living, but quite possibly the most handsome man Arthur had ever seen, with coal-black hair, piercing blue eyes, and a body as lean and muscled as one of the Elgin marbles at the British Museum. Blood smeared the man's mouth, however, just as it had the Staff, and he carried the dog's rangy aggression in his human stature.

The graying man stepped up, offering clothes. Breath clogging in his throat, Arthur tried to make himself move while his unlikely Adonis dressed. He would return to Red Lion Street, take the safer route to his rooms, and do his utmost to forget that he'd ever seen anything like the carnage in the alleyway—

Adonis's head came up as if scenting something. He turned and stared directly at Arthur, blue eyes glittering in a blood-smeared face.

"You. Come here," he ordered.

Arthur gasped. Gentlemanly scrapping and fisticuffs were one thing, but facing down a bloodthirsty werebeast—no matter how handsome he was in human form—was something else altogether. He turned and stumbled back up the alley.

He hadn't gotten more than a few yards before something slammed into his back, knocking his hat to the filthy alley floor. A thick arm wrapped around his throat, cutting off his air. He dropped the briefcase, clawing desperately at the arm, but it was adamantine.

"Calm down, pet," he heard the werebeast croon in his ear. "It's all right."

The arm tightened around his throat and dark blooms appeared at the edges of his vision. Weakening, Arthur gasped for air, but there was none.

And then the world faded to black.

****

Gunner released his chokehold the moment he felt his prize go slack. After a quick check to make sure the man was still breathing, he hoisted the limp body over one shoulder.

Picking his way barefoot through the stinking puddles, he nodded at a puzzled-looking Willie. "Let's go," he said, not stopping.

"With 'im?" Willie said, falling in at his side. "What for?"

"Got a whiff of 'im, didn't I?" Gunner said, trying to control the driving sensation inside him. *Home, get him home, naked and in bed, and then—*

"And?"

His jaw muscles bunched, and he shifted a shoulder under his burden. "The little toff's my mate," he muttered. *And I need to make him mine.*

Chapter Two

When Arthur awoke, he was in bed. The awful scene in the alley drifted through his memory, dim now from sleep. *It was just a nightmare. Oh, thank goodness.*

He tried to turn over, and couldn't. Looking up, he saw that a length of hemp rope had been tied around his right wrist and woven with very little slack through an unfamiliar brass headboard. The other end of the rope had been attached to his left wrist, effectively pinning his arms wide.

I've been kidnapped. But why? Lifting his head as high as possible, he stared around his prison. It appeared to be a small bedroom, lit only by a coal fire in a blackened grate. A row of hooks on the far wall held various items of clothing, and an armoire hulked in the corner. A plain wooden table stood next to the bed, bare of anything except a candlestick with an unlit candle.

He flexed his feet and found that his legs were bound as well, with the same amount of slack given to his arms. To make matters worse, someone had removed his clothes before tying him to the bed and covering him with a thin blanket.

Panic set in, making his heart lurch. "Help!" he shouted. "Please, I need help!"

The door opened and his hopes were dashed as the handsome werebeast sauntered in, carrying a wash bowl and water jug. He'd taken the time to rinse the blood from his face and slick his hair back, and an old, threadbare towel hung casually over one shoulder.

"Someone's up, I see," he said in an East-End accent.

Arthur fought down his fear and gave the man his best glower. "Untie me immediately, sir!"

"Can't do that. At least, not just yet." The man approached the bed, giving him an appreciative look. Arthur belatedly remembered his nude state, and cringed under the cheap blanket that protected his modesty. "I suppose you want to know why you're here, then."

"Indeed I do," Arthur said, hoping he sounded braver than he felt. "I am a solicitor, sir, and if you do not untie me this moment, you will find yourself in grave trouble with the law."

The man shrugged. "Won't be the first time. Doubt it'll be the last." He moved to the bedside table and deposited the jug and bowl on it, then sat down on the mattress. That blue gaze trailed over him dispassionately, but there was a flicker of something else as well, something that tugged at Arthur's senses and caused his breath to come faster.

The man grabbed the edge of the blanket, dragging it down to just below Arthur's waist. The solicitor flinched as the cool air of the room hit his skin, causing it to break out in embarrassing gooseflesh.

"You're trim. I like that in a bloke," the man said conversationally. "Don't spend all of your time on your arse, do you?"

Arthur gaped at him. "I—how—that's none of your business!"

"Oh, but it is my business." His captor sounded amused about that. "Everything about you, Mr. Arthur Finter, is my business. Now that we're to be mates and all."

The bizarre comment would have made Arthur laugh in other circumstances. "If you mean we're to be friends, sir, I can assure you that I feel no such friendship with anyone who ties me to a bed and terrorizes me in such a manner!"

The man tilted his head to one side, and Arthur was forcibly reminded of his other shape. "You're tied to my bed to make sure you don't run away," he said. "I know you saw what happened in the alley, and I'll explain it in good time. As for terrorizing you, it wasn't what I had in mind for us tonight."

He reached out and touched one of the tiny nubs on Arthur's chest, tracing a circle on it. The caress caused Arthur to gasp, an indecent zing of pleasure arrowing down to his groin.

"Thought so," the man said in satisfaction. "You long for the touch of a man, Mr. Finter. I'll be that man for you tonight and ever after. We're mates, you and me."

"M—" The other, more marital meaning of the word dawned on him, the calumny he'd hoped never to hear addressed to himself. "Are you implying that I'm a, a filthy *sodomite*?"

"Implying?" His captor laughed. "I'm saying it full out. You're as queer as I am."

Arthur bristled. "That is a foul lie!"

"The bond don't make mistakes," the man said, caressing Arthur's nipple again and causing more of those horribly delicious sensations. "It chose you because you wanted a man in your bed, between your thighs, doing unholy things to you." His eyes darkened, the storm blue draining away and replaced by obsidian. "So I'll tup you tonight, my mate, and put my mark on you. I'll give you the pleasure you've craved for so long. Then you'll understand."

Beneath the blanket Arthur's organ twitched, plumping at the man's low, luring promises. "I'm not your mate. I'm not your anything," he insisted, wishing he could bring his legs together or at least raise his knees for camouflage. "You're not even human!"

His captor leaned back, desire tempered now by annoyance. "I think and reason, just the same as you. Only I can do it in two shapes. That's more than I can say for you."

"I beg your pardon?"

The man stood and picked up the jug, pouring hot water into the bowl. "I have the sense not to wander the alleyways alone like a foolish pup," he said, putting the jug down with a thump. "What were you thinking, walking by yourself like that? And not even a penknife on you for defense."

Arthur blinked at the utterly unexpected scolding. "I was simply trying to get home," he said. "It wasn't my blasted fault there was a fire on High Holborn."

The man grunted. "Well, stay out of the alleys unless I'm with you."

"You're not—why are you not listening to me? We are not mates, and I have no idea... why...."

He trailed off as his captor slung the towel onto the bed, stripping off his shirt and revealing the beautifully muscled torso Arthur had seen all too briefly in the alley. Fine silvery scars could be seen here and there, the remnants of battles past. Trousers and undergarments followed, revealing the rest of the man's body. His hips and thighs were just as muscular as his torso, and equally decorated with scars. Arthur tried to look away, but his gaze was drawn to the irresistible sight of the werebeast's beautifully formed cock, nestled in a halo of black hair.

He swallowed. "If you lay even one finger on me, I shall have you arrested," he said, appalled at the breathlessness in his tone. "Don't think I won't!"

The man glanced down at the bulging blanket over Arthur's groin and smirked. "That cockstand you're sporting says otherwise, Mr. Finter. But have it your way."

He picked up a smaller flannel that had been hidden within the towel's folds, soaked it in the bowl of water, then proceeded to wash himself. Slowly, he ran the cloth over his chest and arms, coating his skin with a sheen of water. He kept his gaze on Arthur, as if daring him to look away.

Arthur couldn't. It had somehow become the most erotic thing he'd ever witnessed. He licked his lips unconsciously as the flannel went back to the bowl for more warm water, then resumed its trip over his captor's body.

With some shock, he realized he wanted to be the one washing the werebeast. In the safety of his own mind, beneath the outrage and ignominy of his current position, he could admit that to himself. He wanted to run the warm, wet flannel over firm muscles and pale skin, wipe away the sweat and dirt of the day, make his captor clean as a newborn.

And then…

The breath died in Arthur's throat as the werebeast's hand dropped to his groin, lazily washing the proud flesh there. The shapely cock began to rise, encouraged by the stroking cloth.

His own cock throbbed like it was on fire, and he could feel droplets of wetness dampening the head. A sudden image of the werebeast pulling down the blanket and crawling over him to mouth at his foreskin and lick at the wetness made him moan.

His captor smiled, but said nothing. He finished rinsing his legs, turning slightly to expose a beautifully curved buttock with a muscled hollow in the side, then tossed the flannel in the bowl. "That's better," he said as he sauntered to the bed, resting a bent knee on the mattress. The movement made his now rigid cock bob, as if gesturing to Arthur.

He gasped as the blanket was yanked unceremoniously from his body, revealing his own cockstand. His captor's eyes glittered as he studied it, head tilting to the side again in a decidedly canine manner.

"You're perfect," he said softly. "Absolutely perfect."

Arthur felt his cheeks flame. At no time in his life had he ever received such a compliment on his physical form, especially in its current state. "I—thank you?"

In response his captor trailed fingers along Arthur's thigh, up toward his groin, then wrapped his hand around the rigid shaft. "Nice and thick," he said in approval, stroking it.

Arthur shuddered at the pleasure that surged up from his caressed manhood. He'd taken himself in hand enough times, but it had never felt like this. "Please," he whispered.

"Please what?"

He licked dry lips. "What's your name?"

The man smiled at him. "Gunner. Gunner Jones."

And with that he leaned over and ran his tongue over the mushroom head just peeping out of Arthur's foreskin. The shock of it made Arthur yelp.

Gunner chuckled against his sensitive flesh. "You'll enjoy this, love. Just relax."

The man's firm lips formed a tight O around Arthur's shaft, and a velvet tongue began scrolling decadent designs along the underside. It was debased, immoral, absolutely sinful.

And Arthur wanted to throw his head back and shout at the joyous sensation. A fireball began to build in his bollocks, far sooner than he wanted. He needed the other man to ease off, give him more time in that hot, wet haven. "Gunner, please," he begged.

The werebeast's blue eyes rolled up to look at him mid-suck. The vision was deliciously obscene and cleaved Arthur's tongue to the roof of his mouth. The fireball exploded and he shouted as seed boiled up through his cock gushing out into Gunner's mouth.

He swallowed hungrily, going deep so that his throat muscles could milk Arthur's prick. The added sensation sent Arthur's head into a spin and he sagged back against his pillow, lost and moaning in carnal ecstasy.

After what felt like an eternity Gunner pulled off, licking his softening prick lovingly and bestowing a kiss on each bollock before crawling up to Arthur's side. "You're delicious, pet," he said, kissing Arthur on the cheek. "I could drink you every day and still want more."

The compliment was utterly debauched, and yet it made his heart glow. "That was astounding," he said, his voice hoarse from crying out.

Gunner made a low rumbling noise in approval. "And there's so much more to come," he said. "All you have to do is yield to me." This time he kissed Arthur's lips, his own mouth warm and firm. "Say it, pet. Say you yield to me."

Arthur tried to corral his skittering thoughts. Never in his days had he ever felt anything like what Gunner had evoked in him. Not only the astoundingly wonderful physical sensations, but the shocking burst of emotional connection that had followed his climax. It ran counter to every thought of propriety, but his heart now insisted that he belonged at Gunner Jones's side.

"I don't even know you," he said, making one last grasp at reason.

"And I don't know you. But we'll learn about each other," Gunner promised, laying a hand over Arthur's heart. "Every dream you've ever had about another man's body, I'll make happen. You'll have a home with me, and my love and protection. We were meant to be together, you and me. I'll make you happy, my Arthur. All you have to do is yield to me."

Arthur licked his lips, tasting a hint of his own seed. As well as being wicked and sinful, physical love between two men was illegal under Her Majesty's laws.

And oh, how he wanted more. "I yield to you," he breathed.

Gunner beamed at him, the expression setting his handsome face aglow. "And I shall guard you with my body and my life," he said. "Heart of my heart, mate of my soul."

He shifted to cover Arthur, his cock rigid and leaking. Arthur's mouth dried again, wondering if Gunner was going to do what he suspected. Before he could find out, however, a loud rap sounded at the bedroom door.

Growling, Gunner lifted his head. "What?"

"Pack business, guv," drifted through the door. "It's Lizzie Jessup. Her Maggie's in trouble."

Chapter Three

"Bloody hell," Gunner muttered. He clambered off Arthur and pulled on his discarded clothes, glaring at the door as he did so.

Arthur gathered his scrambled wits. "Who are Lizzie and Maggie?"

"Part of my pack." Fishing in his trousers, he pulled out a pocket knife. Arthur stiffened, then relaxed as Gunner cut through the ropes binding him to the bed. "You need to get dressed."

Arthur sat up, giving the room a pointed look. "My clothes?"

Gunner scowled. "You can't wear those fancy togs where we're going." He went to the armoire and rummaged through it. "Here, these should fit you."

He tossed a shirt, an old but serviceable jacket, and somewhat ragged wool trousers to Arthur, who held up the clothes. Damn his beautiful blue eyes, Gunner had judged the sizes well.

"Where are we going?" he asked, pulling on the trousers.

"Not sure yet." Gunner's scowl deepened. "I'll find out once I talk to Maggie."

****

Dressed and swiping at his hair, Arthur followed Gunner down a dusty staircase to the ground floor. They went into what turned out to be a parlor, where a woman in a worn dress stood with Willie. Thin and washed-out, her eyes were reddened and dried tear tracks could still be seen on her cheeks. A fading bruise graced one cheekbone. A young boy clung to her skirts, giving them all a fearful look.

The woman bobbed a wobbly curtsey to Gunner as soon as he walked in. "Alpha, I come here beggin' your help," she said after a gulp.

Gunner took a seat on one of the parlor chairs, waving Arthur to the other. "Is it Jimmy, then?"

The woman hesitated, giving Arthur a leery look, but nodded. "He's been drinking these last few weeks, worse than I ever seen before. And then today he comes home and tells me he... he put Maggie into service." She sobbed once, the sound harsh in the room. "Said she was old enough to earn her keep, and it would be one less mouth to feed."

Gunner's eyes narrowed. "Who's got her?"

"Mr. Day, down the goblin market." A fresh gout of tears coursed down the woman's sallow cheeks. "You know what he does with his girls, Alpha!"

Gunner's expression turned frightening. "He didn't have leave from you to do this, did he?"

Lizzie shook her head, wispy hair flying. "We may be poor as church mice, but I'd never give me own blood to Mr. Day!" she cried. "Please, Alpha, help her. I'll pay what I can, whatever you want—"

Gunner held up one large hand, cutting her off. "No one gives one of the pack to Day. I'll get your Maggie back for you," he said. "But tonight, Jimmy Hamm dies. That's the price."

Arthur's gut chilled at the pronouncement. Even he knew that a destitute woman with children and no husband in London had a dark future ahead of her. She would have to turn to begging, or more likely prostitution, to survive.

Lizzie paled but nodded, clutching her son tighter. "He deserves it, for what he's done. I never should've gone with him, Alpha. I know that now."

"Right." Gunner stood, eyeing mother and son, then pulled out some coins from his pocket. "I've got a mate, now, and I'll need someone to do for us around here," he said. "You and your lad can have the rooms at the top of the stairs, and Maggie the one next to you. Room and board, and fifteen pound a year."

The woman's eyes widened in shock, then filled with relieved tears. "Bless you, Alpha," she said, plucking the coins from his hand before grabbing it and kissing it. "I'll keep a fine house for you and your missus, I swear."

Gunner extricated his hand with some difficulty. "My mister," he said, nodding at Arthur.

Arthur stiffened at the blatant announcement of their sodomite status, but Willie didn't seem fazed. After a single surprised blink, Lizzie gave him a bobbing curtsey. "Sir."

"Er, yes," Arthur said, hoping that Gunner didn't expect him to take up the wifely role of overseeing the servants. "Lizzie, is it?"

"Yes, sir. And this is little Bert." She squeezed her son. "He's very handy about the house. Knows how to black boots already, he does, and he can stir the fire as well as any maid."

The little boy peered dubiously up from behind his mother's skirts. "I'm sure he'll do a splendid job," Arthur said diplomatically.

Gunner grunted. "We'll be back late, Lizzie. There's food in the larder—make supper for yourself and the lad, then lay something cold out for us."

The newly minted housekeeper bobbed again. "Yes, Alpha."

Arthur found himself whisked out into the foyer between Gunner and Willie. "I take it this Day is some sort of villain?" he dared to ask.

"The worst," Gunner said. "He's a ghoul. Peddles flesh to any who want it."

Arthur shuddered. "And her own father turned her over to this scoundrel?"

Willie snorted as Gunner pulled on a jacket. "Jimmy Hamm ain't Maggie's father," the grizzled man said. "Hamm's a layabout who started sniffing 'round Lizzie after her Rory died. She took him in, common law. Thought Bert needed a pa."

It was the stuff of a penny dreadful. "And the goblin market?" Arthur asked.

Gunner's mouth twisted. "You'll find out. First though, I've got to mark you."

"What—" Arthur's back thumped against the wall as Gunner pushed him into it. He sucked in a breath to complain, then held it as Gunner's mouth went to the crook of his neck, running his tongue over Arthur's skin. Frantic, Arthur looked at Willie but the other man had turned to study the faded front door.

A stabbing pain exploded in his neck, making him yelp. *Christ, he bit me!*

He tried to escape but Gunner held him still, tongue dragging over the wound to soothe it. The pain turned into a barbed sort of pleasure, and to his dismay Arthur felt his prick stir in his trousers.

The werebeast lifted his head, licking away a smear of crimson. Arthur clapped a hand to his neck, expecting to feel an oozing wound. But when he pulled his hand away it was clean.

Willie glanced over his shoulder, smirking at Arthur. "You're an Alpha's mate now. You need his mark on you to keep you safe."

He opened the front door and Gunner escorted them out before Arthur could ask *safe from what?*
****

25

The goblin's market turned out to be a nazareth, one of the unauthorized black markets that popped up around London like mushrooms and disappeared just as quickly. At the door, they were stopped by a hulking creature wrapped in a battered overcoat and swathes of scarves that seemed excessive for the October weather. A craggy dome covered with dun fuzz rose out of the scarves like a Welsh mountain, and two eyes caught in a net of deep wrinkles gleamed at them.

Leaning over, he sniffed at Gunner, Willie, and then Arthur. On the last he recoiled.

"*Hoo*man," he grunted, jerking his chin at Arthur. "What's 'e doin' 'ere?"

"He's my mate." Arthur felt a soft jerk as Gunner hooked a finger in his collar and tugged it to one side, exposing the bite mark.

The doorman studied it, then grunted. He moved to the side much like a boulder grinding away from a cave entrance, and Arthur was ushered past by the werebeasts.

This particular goblin market had formed in the shell of a burnt-out warehouse, and the stalls were crowded close to the walls in case of rain. Packs of what Arthur could only assume were people wandered through the open space, while an enterprising cook offered bowls of stew and pints of beer from behind an impromptu bar. Arthur's empty stomach gurgled at the surprisingly enticing aroma.

Gunner and Willie moved through the market with ease, intent on the far end of the structure. Arthur followed close behind, eyeing stalls that offered everything from furnishings to foodstuffs. It seemed familiar enough; it was the hawkers who were unusual. He was absolutely sure one woman selling second-hand clothing possessed a set of fox ears, and a burly man guarding a mismatched collection of china had the coloring and teeth of a badger.

"Are all of these people like you?" he muttered to Gunner.

His mate glanced around. "Some are. Others are fae, and a few have no name. Stick by me and you'll be all right."

Arthur bristled at the implication that he was some sort of damsel in distress until Gunner and Willie stopped in front of a stall draped in black velvet. The dark space gave off a sensation of desolate hopelessness, and Arthur shivered in his borrowed jacket.

Gunner stepped up to the stall and knocked on an upright. "I've got business with you, Mr. Day."

What came out of the stall made Arthur's flesh crawl. He'd thought Gunner's description of Day as a "ghoul" was hyperbole, but it turned out to be fact. Corpse-white skin was the best part of the creature that parted the velvet curtains and slouched into the light. Its sharply sloped ears ended in tufted points, and obsidian eyes glittered out of cavernous sockets.

Day smiled, revealing far too many teeth that were both pearly white and pointed as needles. "Mr. Jones," he said in unctuous tones. "I thought I might see you soon—" He broke off, sniffing the air, then stared at Arthur. "Oh. Oh, my, Mr. Jones. You're breaking the rules, you are."

Gunner shifted, positioning himself in front of Arthur. "He's my mate, Day. Marked and all. You'd be wise to remember that."

Colorless lips pulled back from that hell of teeth. "Such a pity. He's a bit old for the trade, but I'm sure I could have found an appropriate … position for him."

Arthur recoiled from the loathsome promise in that statement, while Gunner lifted his chin. "Someone sold you a member of my pack without my permission," the werebeast said. "I'm here to take her back."

Day clucked at that, lacing bony fingers together in front of a sunken belly. "A bully girl? No, I can't remember seeing one like that."

Gunner leaned closer, looming over the creature. "I know she's here, Day," he said softly. "Jimmy Hamm sold her to you. I'm taking her home, one way or the other."

Day rotated his head to the side, the gesture unpleasantly lizard-like. "Ah. Now that you mention it, I do remember a sweet little pup of a girl. But I'm afraid you're too late." He leered up at Gunner. "Her contract has already been purchased."

Both werebeasts' fists clenched at that. "Who did you sell her to?" Gunner demanded.

"That information stays between myself and my client, Mr. Jones."

"That's a foolish choice to make, Mr. Day," Gunner said in a soft voice that vibrated with menace. "Your teeth may be sharp, but I promise you, mine are much sharper."

Some of Day's oleaginous attitude drained away. "Her father signed the contract," he muttered. "It's perfectly legal. Nothing to do with me if you don't care for it."

Arthur started at that. Edging out from behind Gunner, he cleared his throat. "If you're referring to this Jimmy Hamm individual, he wasn't her father or legal guardian," he said. "Which means he had no legal right to sign a contract for a minor person."

Day glared at him, but Gunner gave him an approving wink before turning back to the ghoul. "It seems you've broken the law of the land, Mr. Day," he said. "I wonder what the magistrates would have to say about that?"

Arthur suspected Gunner didn't mean the Royal Courts of Justice. But the threat caused Day to shrink inside his suit like a cornered albino bat. "Damn you," he hissed. "Fine. It was Fred Bunton."

Gunner and Willie shared a dark look. Arthur felt Gunner's hand clamp on his upper arm and they were off, the market crowd parting like the Red Sea for the two werebeasts.

"Who's Fred Bunton?" Arthur said, a bit breathless from trying to keep up with Gunner's long strides.

"He's the bloody Alpha of the Hays, isn't he?" Gunner growled. "The ones we were fighting in the alley."

More weredogs then—from an enemy pack no less. "What does he want with Maggie?" Arthur asked, a horrible suspicion occurring to him.

It was confirmed when Gunner growled. "To get her with pup, most likely. If he mates her, I can't bring her home."

Chapter Four

Back on the streets, Gunner gave Arthur a brief history of the Haymaker Gang in regard to the Black Staffs; namely, they were both bully dog shifter packs and competitors for territory on the east end of London. For this Bunton to steal a fertile young bitch from Gunner's pack was meant as a mortal insult. If he successfully marked and mated Maggie, she would belong to the Haymaker Gang.

"So that's not going to happen," his mate said, grim. Willie looked equally determined, and Arthur wondered how two men, shifters though they were, would win out against an entire pack of their kind.

He found out when they approached a rundown pub boasting a sign naming it the Rat Hole. On the sign, a weathered bull terrier was tearing into, unsurprisingly, a rathole.

Gunner grimaced at the sign but led them into the dark, smoky interior. The background noises of men with pints died as the three of them headed to the back. A table had been set in one corner there and a blond man with a rawboned face and glittering green eyes held court with a gang of men in working-class attire. A girl, not more than thirteen to Arthur's eyes, cowered on the blond man's knee.

The man looked up at their approach. "Wondered how long it would be 'til you showed up," he said, sneering. "How many times did you have to bite the old ghoul for my name?"

Gunner gave him a flat look, then nodded at the girl. "She's part of my pack, Bunton. I want her back."

Bunton chuckled, dandling Maggie roughly. "I paid for her, Jones. And I plan on getting big, strong pups out of her, too."

Arthur watched as his mate's lips drew back from teeth that were now sharper than normal. "We can do this easy, Bunton, or we can do it hard. Jimmy Hamm didn't have the right to sell her to Day, but I'll give you her cost."

Bunton laughed raucously at that, and the other Hays chimed in. "Don't want her cost, Jones. I want her on her hands and knees while I plow her little pink quim and seed her deep. Isn't that right, petal?" He squeezed one of her tiny breasts in a plate-sized hand, smacking his lips at her. She winced, turning her head away.

"Fine," Gunner said coldly. "I'll fight you for her."

Bunton's attention swung back. "Yeah? What're the stakes?"

"If I win, I take her home. If I lose, you kill me."

Arthur stiffened at the offer, fists clenching at his side. But Bunton smiled, thick lips revealing teeth that were much yellower than Gunner's, but no less sharp.

"I got summat better," the Hays alpha said. "If you win, you take your chit home. If I win," he nodded at Arthur, "I get him, too."

Arthur's gorge rose at that. Gunner turned sharply, staring at him.

"Didn't know you liked cock, Bunton," he said, still looking at Arthur.

"Oh, I don't," Bunton said mockingly. "But I'll take pleasure in bumming your mate over and over again until he whimpers like a whipped pup. And every time I loosen his arse a little more, he'll know it's because you weren't man enough to keep him."

Rage flickered through Gunner's eyes, but there was also cunning and determination there. *Do you trust me?*

It was as if Arthur heard the words whispered in his mind. He felt his own resolve rise. Maggie couldn't be left with Bunton. If he had to put his own body up as stakes for her safety, then so be it. *I do.*

Gunner gave him the tiniest of nods, then turned back to Bunton. "Deal. Let's settle this."

With another harsh laugh, Bunton unceremoniously heaved Maggie off his lap into the arms of a waiting Hay. "Out back, then."

****

"Out back" was a cobblestoned courtyard in back of the pub that served as the delivery entrance. Tonight, Arthur assumed, it would also serve as a fighting ring for the two alphas.

Both of the men stripped to the waist. Bunton was thicker than Gunner, with heavy muscles in his shoulders and chest, as well as a pad of fat around his middle. "Hope you enjoy the show, boys," he said with a grin to the other Hays.

Gunner tossed his shirt to Arthur, stretching lean arms over his head. "What d'you say to a little extra, then, Bunton?" he asked.

The Hay alpha leered at him. "Adding your arse to the pot, are you?"

"No. We do this as men. First one to shift loses."

For a fleeting moment Arthur saw Bunton's leer falter, but then it returned. "Done. I can beat you to a bloody pulp in either form," he boasted.

"Go on, then." Gunner crouched into a fighter's pose, bunched fists up and ready.

Bunton mimicked his form. As Arthur and the others watched, the two men began to circle each other, throwing experimental jabs to test the other's defenses. Bunton was the first to land a blow, a ham-sized fist glancing off Gunner's shoulder.

Gunner didn't even wince. He darted in, throwing a flurry of bare-knuckled blows into Bunton's padded midsection. The air whoofed out of the Hay alpha and he staggered back, glaring at Gunner.

The fight quickly heated up after that, with Bunton using his height and weight to throw powerful blows at Gunner. One landed, clipping Gunner's mouth and snapping his head back. To Arthur's dismay he spat out a mouthful of blood, giving Bunton a gruesome crimson grin.

A hand squeezed his shoulder, and Arthur looked up at an intent Willie. "The guv's got this,' the Black Staff whispered. "Just watch."

Arthur did. Gunner kept his cool, constantly moving around Bunton and forcing the larger man to move as well to avoid his stinging punches. Bunton was starting to pant and turn red when he growled and lunged at Gunner. Even Arthur could see he planned on taking the dark-haired man to the yard floor and beating him against the curved cobblestones.

Gunner stayed in place until the last moment, then danced to the side and stuck out a foot. Bunton tripped and went sprawling into a knot of the Hays. Roaring with fury, he pushed off of them and came back for another charge. This time Gunner didn't move, launching a roundhouse punch that smashed directly into Bunton's oncoming nose.

Arthur grimaced in reluctant sympathy as he heard the meaty crunch. The Hay alpha's nose exploded under the impact, dark droplets spraying into the air. The bigger man staggered back and Gunner stayed right with him, throwing punch after punch into Bunton's gut, chest, jaw. Bunton managed to recover long enough to grab Gunner, squeezing him in a punishing bear hug. Gunner jerked his head back, then slammed his forehead directly into Bunton's dripping nose.

This time Bunton squealed, dropping Gunner and tumbling onto his backside. Panting, he rolled onto hands and knees and shifted, turning into a massive brindle terrier with a blood-streaked snout. Bunton lunged at Gunner, slavering jaws dripping spittle.

Gunner met the terrier mid-lunge, but didn't shift. To Arthur's shock he shoved his fisted hand deep between the dog's jaws, into Bunton's throat.

Grim, Gunner forced the alpha down to the cobblestones again, throwing an arm around Bunton's neck for better traction as he continued to choke his opponent. The Hay alpha struggled, flailing paws raking red welts into Gunner's chest as muffled cries and yelps rent the air.

Slowly, the brindle terrier weakened, jaws wedged open by Gunner's now torn and bleeding forearm. Finally it gave a shudder, then went still. Gunner pulled his arm free just before Bunton shifted back to human form, bloodied mouth open in a rictus gape.

Panting softly, Gunner got to his feet, ignoring the blood streaming from his wounds. "I beat him fair and square, aye?"

The Hays muttered amongst themselves, but no one disagreed.

Gunner nodded. "Where's your beta?"

A redheaded man with a thick spray of freckles stepped forward, staring at the body of his former leader. "That's me," he said, reluctantly bowing his head. "Alpha."

Gunner straightened. "I want my pack member back. Now."

The beta nodded, and the Hay holding Maggie let her go. She dashed over to Willie, throwing her arms around him and sobbing softly.

Gunner eyed them for a moment, then turned back to the Hay beta. "What's your name?"

The man's jaw muscles tensed. "Merring. Jack Merring."

"Right." Gunner raised his voice. "Jack Merring's your alpha now. I'm declaring this by shifter law."

The muttering died away and Merring's expression eased. "The Staffs are willing to call a truce," Gunner continued. "We stay in our territory and you stay in yours. What d'you say?"

He thrust out a spittle and blood-streaked hand. Arthur held his breath, and suspected he wasn't the only one to do so.

After a long moment, the new alpha took Gunner's hand and shook it once.

"Truce," he said.

****

Arthur followed the three Staffs through the winding London streets back to Gunner's house. Maggie clung to the alpha's arm as they spoke in quiet tones. Willie strode behind them as an outlier, constantly scanning for danger.

Once, Gunner glanced over his shoulder and gave Arthur a still-bloody smile. Before this night the solicitor would have recoiled at such a feral expression, but now it made his groin tighten.

The four of them finally arrived at Gunner's door. Unlocking it, he let Willie usher Maggie inside first, and Arthur could hear the happy cry of a relieved Lizzie reunited with her daughter.

But Gunner didn't follow. "You head inside as well," he told Arthur. "I'll be back in an hour or so."

Arthur hesitated on the step. "Where are you going?"

"I'm not finished yet. Need to take care of Jimmy Hamm."

Belatedly, he remembered the statement Gunner had made to Lizzie. "You're going to kill him, then."

Gunner nodded. "He sold a member of my pack to Day. I'd kill him for that alone. But Maggie wound up in the hands of the Hays, and I had to kill another alpha to get her back. Someone has to pay for that."

Arthur shuddered at the savage new world he had entered. Before he could say anything, however, Gunner stepped close and grasped his shoulder. "Hamm is filth, love," he said softly. "A cowardly drunkard who cares for nothing but himself. Don't waste your pity on him."

Arthur thought back to the grotesque Day and his human chattel booth, and the revolting way Bunton had manhandled Maggie. "I won't," he said quietly, wishing they weren't in public and he could give Gunner a goodbye kiss. "I'll wait up, shall I?"

Some of the grimness faded from Gunner's eyes, and the corner of his mouth curled up. "Do that," he advised. "We still have business of our own to finish."

This time, Arthur shivered with longing. "Don't be long."

"I won't."

With a parting squeeze, Gunner melted into the shadows.

Chapter Five

After accepting a tearful hug from his new housekeeper, a somewhat hesitant but equally tearful hug from Maggie, and a solemn clap on the shoulder from Willie, Arthur sat down with his new pack for a cold evening meal that was far more enjoyable than anything he'd ever received from his former landlady. After cleaning his plate, he made his excuses and left the Staffs at the dining table, heading upstairs to Gunner's bedroom.

My bedroom as well, now. He went to the washbasin and touched the water jug, surprised to find it still warm. *Lizzie must have had every confidence that Gunner would bring her daughter home.*

And now he's out there killing her common-law husband. Oddly enough, it didn't disturb Arthur as much as he thought it would. Jimmy Hamm was a heartless villain to sell a young girl like Maggie into brutal slavery. And while Gunner would undoubtedly be ruthless about his dispatch, Arthur suspected that the werebeast would also make it quick and clean.

Finish it, then, and come home to me.

Still thinking about his mate, Arthur stripped and poured some of the water into the washbasin, giving himself a quick, efficient scrub. He lingered when he reached his groin, cupping the sensitive flesh there and remembering Gunner's mouth on it. *I want to do that to him. I want to kiss him all over, lick his member, suck it, swallow his seed. I want him to bugger me and mark me from within.*

I want him. So much.

His shaft began to thicken. Entertained by his own daring fantasies, he dried himself and crawled under the covers, one hand still wrapped around his member but not allowing himself release. That would come at Gunner's touch or not at all.

He hadn't realized he'd drifted off to sleep until he woke to feel another, larger hand caressing his hip and a long, warm body stretched out behind him.

"You fell asleep," Gunner said in his ear, low and amused.

Arthur flushed. "I'm sorry. I didn't mean to—"

Gunner chuckled. "Don't be sorry, love. I'm glad you had some sleep. Means you'll be awake for this."

Something thick and hard pressed against Arthur's backside. He rubbed back against it and drew a low groan from his mate.

"Evil, you," Gunner said, pressing open-mouthed kisses to Arthur's bare shoulder. "Wicked, wicked man. And all mine."

Arthur turned in his arms. Gunner had lit a candle, and the gentle amber light transformed the bigger man's face into chiaroscuro. "All yours," he said, reaching up and touching Gunner's cheek. "Although I'm sure I'll have a number of questions as we go on." He frowned. "And I don't know what I'll do about my position. It's too far to walk to the office from here, and using the omnibus daily will be expensive, I fear."

Gunner leaned down and kissed him, a warm brush of lips that held the promise of more. "We'll work all that out tomorrow, love. Tonight, it's our time."

He pressed Arthur onto his back, kissing his way along the solicitor's jaw line before working his way back up to Arthur's lips. There he paused, eyes shadowed in the candlelight. "Arthur, the bite was for your protection," he said softly. "It's not binding. Once I claim you, though, there's no going back. You're mine for the rest of our lives."

Arthur's heart swelled with emotion at the tenderness in Gunner's tone. He slid his arms around the alpha's solid torso, pulling him closer. "Then take me, love."

Gunner lunged down, capturing his lips in a sweet, fierce kiss. The dim room disappeared into a haze of pleasure and need as Gunner proceeded to worship every inch of Arthur's body, starting at his mouth and working downward. Arthur had never known his nipples to be sensitive before, but Gunner's warm tongue and teasing bites woke them to aching life. The werebeast's mouth was everywhere, shameless and greedy; lapping at the shallow bowl of Arthur's armpit, biting a loving path across his pectorals, tracing the lines of his belly with a teasing tongue.

Arthur crammed a fist into his mouth to smother his cries as Gunner finally took in his rigid, aching flesh and sucked it with lubricious abandon. He didn't dare look down, sure that the sight of Gunner's lips stretched around his prick would cause him to spend right then and there. He wanted far more of his new mate before he reached his pinnacle.

He reached down, winding fingers into Gunner's raven hair and tugging gently. Gunner came loose with a wet sound. "What?" he said roughly, clearing his throat. "Did I hurt you?"

"No." Arthur licked his lips. "It's just ... I want my turn."

A long exhalation, and then Gunner crawled back up to his side. "Christ, what you do to me," his mate said, craving in his voice. "I want that, too. Learn me, love."

Arthur did, mapping Gunner's skin and the firm ridges of bone and muscle beneath. His mate's body was a wonder, worthy of being carved in marble and displayed in the British Museum. But no one would see it, Arthur thought fiercely, stroking the soft skin of Gunner's inner thighs. *He's mine, just as much as I'm his.*

When he took Gunner's cock in his mouth, it was a revelation of salt, musk, a faint tang, and something that he could only call male. He slid his tongue under the foreskin and licked along the tiny slit, tasting his mate's essence there. He learned that he loved the feel of the silky flesh on his tongue and the granite hardness underneath, tracing the dark lacework of veins with his tongue.

After a deep breath, he took in as much as he could and closed his lips around the shaft in a seal, suckling. Above him Gunner gave a lost, broken moan that set Arthur's blood on fire. He redoubled his efforts, worshipping Gunner's manhood with lips and tongue.

"Christ, Arthur, stop," Gunner begged. "'S too good."

Arthur pulled off with an obscene little pop, enjoying the desperation in his mate's voice. He licked his lips. "Are you close?"

"Too close." Gunner urged Arthur back up the bed, leaning over him to rummage in the bedside table. "I'll spend in your mouth another night. Tonight, I'm claiming that sweet, tight arse of yours."

With some trepidation Arthur had assumed that the shifter would put him on all fours like a dog, but Gunner surprised him yet again by arranging him on his side, facing the wall. "It'll be easier for you," he said, uncapping the pot he'd pulled from the table.

It turned out to be Vaseline. Arthur felt Gunner's wet fingers slide into the crease of his backside, teasing the forbidden flesh. One finger brushed against his entrance, then pressed again with more enthusiasm, rubbing circles into the tight muscle.

Arthur gasped when the first finger penetrated. Gunner kissed his shoulder, whispering sweetly filthy encouragement as he worked the muscle. Slowly, Arthur felt himself opened on Gunner's long fingers, biting his lips as the burn of the stretch turned into a dark, aching need for more. One finger rubbed against a spot deep inside him and he gasped again as fiery pleasure licked upwards through his belly.

After a delicious time, Gunner pulled his fingers free, shifting and pressing the large, blunt head of his cock against Arthur's hole. "Ready, love?"

Eagerness combined with a pang of fear, but Arthur nodded. He took a deep breath and held it as the pressure increased, cutting through the fog of pleasure. And then he was breached, Gunner's cock pushing past his internal muscles and making itself known.

The man himself gave a choked sigh. "So tight," Gunner murmured into his ear. "Breathe, love."

Arthur grunted incoherently, overwhelmed by the sensation in his backside. Lord, it burned like blazes, but there was a luring undertone to the pain that hinted at pleasure if he could just hold on a bit longer.

After a minute his muscles did begin to accept the intruder. Gunner pushed deeper in tiny increments, whispering encouragement to Arthur, reminders to breathe, to relax. Finally the alpha was fully seated inside him.

"You have no idea how you feel, love," Gunner said in that rough velvet tone. "Gripping me like that. Sweet Lord, you were made for me."

"Yes," Arthur said breathlessly. And then again, more loudly as Gunner's hand came over his hip and closed around his cock. Its hardness had subsided during the initial penetration but Gunner soon remedied that, slick fingers stroking him back to rigid life.

He started rocking inside Arthur at the same time, each thrust shifting minutely until the head of his cock rubbed over that strange, hungry space deep within Arthur and set off another round of internal fireworks. The alpha was apparently determined to drive him out of his mind with pure pleasure.

"Can you feel me, love?" Gunner said hoarsely, thrusting faster now. "I'm taking you, making you mine. You'll never want for another, never want for anything, I swear. You're mine."

"Yes," Arthur moaned, pushing back against the welcome invasion, each slide and retreat stoking the rising flame in his bollocks higher and higher. "I'm yours, love. All yours."

He clutched Gunner's hand tighter around his own cock, speeding up the slick slide of palm and fingers. The increased friction was too much, too delicious to resist. But before he could spend, Gunner went rigid behind him, roaring as he thrust into Arthur one final time.

The unstoppable invasion triggered Arthur's own climax. He keened as electricity exploded along his nerves, setting body and soul on fire. His throbbing cock stiffened impossibly in Gunner's hand, and thick, scalding spurts of white bubbled over their conjoined fists.

It seemed an eternity until Arthur regained his breath and wits. When he did, he felt Gunner's forehead resting against the back of his shoulder like a warm, smooth stone. His mate was whispering something too soft to hear, but Arthur thought they were vows linking the two of them together as surely as standing before a minister in church.

He sagged into the mattress, sore in spots that he never thought to experience, and happier than he ever had been in his life. He would have to resign his position at Burcham and Stowe; not only was the office too far away for commuting to be fiscally reasonable, but Stowe continuing to push Eleanora on him as a potential wife would make his guts curdle.

The thought of abandoning what he had worked so long for didn't pain him nearly as much as he thought it would. *Do shifters need solicitors?* Perhaps there was an established firm that catered to this hidden class of Londoners—

Gunner's chuckle pulled him out of his reverie. "You're thinking, love. I can hear the gears churning."

Arthur squeezed his hand, gasping at the pressure on his own sensitive flesh. "My apologies. You've taken a mate who thinks a great deal, I'm afraid."

Gunner nipped his earlobe. "Hm. Well, I'll just have to find ways to distract you from that great brain of yours, won't I?"

There was so much promise in those words, a lifetime of it. Grinning, Arthur turned his head and claimed a kiss from his mate. "Challenge accepted."

The End

www.nicolacameronwrites.com

7 AUTHOR ANTHOLOGY

THE ALPHA'S ASSASSIN

Copyright © 2015

Doris O'Connor

Chapter One

Zayden rolled his massive shoulders and assessed his opponent. The young cub exuded confidence, and showed off to the assembled crowd by prancing around the cage like a fucking pussy. The leopard shifter might have youth and speed on his side, but Zayden had the experience. He'd lost count of how many of these overconfident types he'd crushed in the thirty nine years since his father had sunk his dick in his mother, and then left the young human to fend for herself.

A grim smile kicked up Zayden's lips, like it always did when he thought of his first kill. He'd tracked his sperm donor down to a rundown bar, and taken the asshole out in front of a bunch of terrified humans. Not the cleverest of things to do, and it had earned him his first—and only—spell in prison, but you could say that had been the making of him.

Folks paid highly for a man willing to take care of their *problems.* And there was nothing like a prison stretch to put you in touch with the right people. Zayden shrugged out of his shirt slowly, and the youngster danced up to him and poked him in the chest.

"Nice tats, man, but I'll so own your ass tonight."

Zayden didn't bother to dignify that with an answer. He simply dropped his gaze to where the youngster poked his finger right into the eye socket of the skull tattoo on his chest. He had to smirk. Just like his ink depicted a bear's head crushing a skull, this impudent cub would soon be history. Shame, really, as he was rather cute, and in another place, Zayden would have had fun shoving his cock down this boy's throat before he reamed his ass.

For now, his bear's warning growl made the leopard swallow before he danced away, giving a show to his audience while he stripped out of his clothes. Zayden toed his boots off and was in the process of shedding his jeans when the streak of dotted fur shot toward him. Teeth sunk into his bicep and his bear roared his fury, the animal bursting from his skin, shredding the remains of his clothes.

So, that's why this young one had won the last few fights. He was a fucking cheat. Zayden shook the leopard off easily enough. A chunk of his flesh had sailed through the air in the process, but high on adrenaline, Zayden had hardly felt it. The crowd went wild when his huge grizzly stood on two legs and swiped the leopard away with one massive paw. Mid leap as the cub had been, he sailed through the air and bounced off the cage. With the inherent grace of his species, he twisted to land on all fours and immediately advanced again. It was almost too easy—the speed in which this idiot was trying to get himself killed.

Zayden dropped back on all fours with enough force to shake the cage, and turning, simply rammed the leopard off his feet. Claws sliced through Zayden's fur, and blood dripped into his eyes, forcing him to shake his head to clear his vision. The other shifter hissed and snarled and Zayden stepped back, narrowly avoiding the leopard's lunge as he tried to go for Zayden's throat. His jaw and teeth snapped together in thin air instead, and Zayden swiped his paw underneath the shifter's soft underbelly. Blood sprayed onto the ground as his claws sliced through fur and tendons and the leopard whined and collapsed.

It was tempting to end this now, but Zayden had been paid a lot of money to make this youngster die slowly and to give the audience a show. So that's what they were going to get. These fights didn't normally end in the death of the opponent, but this one would. Served the leopard right for not keeping his dick in his trousers. Sleeping with your crime boss' mistress… that was never gonna end well.

The *lady* in question had already been fed to the dogs—literally—and no doubt this boy's remains would end up in the kennels too. Zayden smirked as he circled his prey slowly. They had thought themselves *in love*. Zayden shook his head in disgust. Love was for fools.

Tender feelings had no place in his life. He had buried whatever tenderness there had remained in him the day he'd stood over his mother's grave.

He parried another feeble attempt of attack from his weakening opponent, and opened up a new piece of the large cat's body with a well-placed swipe of his paw. The shifter howled in agony, and someone in the audience was sick when the cat's guts spilled on the bloodied ground.

Time to end this. With a growl strong enough to shake the foundations of the cage, Zayden turned the boy over and stomped on his chest. The ribcage gave way with a satisfying crunch and the light dimmed in the cat's eyes. Zayden looked across to the man who paid him, and when the silver-haired human put his thumb down,

Zayden tore the leopard's throat out, and ended the shifter's misery.

His inner beast roared his victory, and after taking in a deep breath to gain control, Zayden shifted back.

Covered in blood as he was, he knew he made a gruesome sight. He fed off the waves of fear that came from the audience. A path opened to him when he left the cage and stalked over to where he'd placed fresh clothes. Upending the ice-cold bucket of water over his head, he got rid of the worst of the stench and pulled on a new pair of jeans.

"That was impressive."

The feminine drawl behind him made him spin around. The skimpily dressed blonde smiled seductively at him, and Zayden grinned back at her. She was too skinny for his liking, but she was pretty enough. When he did take some pussy, he preferred to have some flesh to hold on to. This one looked as though a man could give himself friction burn thrusting into her ass.

"That was nothing, darling," he drawled. "Is there something I can do for you?"

Her green eyes lit up with lust as she stepped closer and ran her hands over his chest. He had yet to put a shirt on, and something about the way she trailed her fingers over his ink set his teeth on edge. He sniffed and detected the scent of wolf all over her.

"It's more what I can do for you," she said and ran her hands along his beard-covered jaw and up into his hairline while she pressed her tits into his chest.

Zayden's bear growled a warning, and she blanched when he grasped her wrists and pushed her away with a shake of his head.

"Don't touch what you can't afford, darling. Tell whoever sent you I don't talk to the monkey. If he wants me to do a job, then he needs to tell me himself."

Fire flashed in her eyes before she masked it. Pushing her tits out, she tried again.

"Don't you want me?" she asked and Zayden laughed and shrugged into his shirt.

"No offense, darling, but no. Right now I want to get pissed, kick back, and not think—"

"Would twenty grand change your mind?"

Zayden couldn't see the owner of that deep growl. It was a wolf, he sensed that much, but the actual features of this shifter were hidden underneath a cloak.

He grinned and nodded.

"Who do I kill?"

A week later, Zayden shut off his Harley outside the biker bar in one of the less salacious parts of London and sniffed the air.

The stench of humans and a wild array of shifters was everywhere, and he wrinkled his nose in disgust. According to the intel he was given, the Alpha of this particular pack was a wolf, and given to allow any old stray shifter to join. Something that was going to get him taken out. Well, that and his *unnatural tendencies.*

Zayden had had a hard time keeping a straight face when the old wolf shifter had parted with that titbit of information. It seemed there were those in Quinton Thorn's pack who didn't think a gay Alpha should be allowed to live. Zayden reached in the back pocket of his jeans to study the picture he had been given of this Quinton, and his bear rumbled.

Mine.

Crushing the picture up in his hand, Zayden scowled at the door of the bar as two rabbit shifters came out. The inebriated girls giggled when they caught sight of him, and clutching onto each other, disappeared down the path.

Zayden shook his head and ignored his beast's strange mood. He was here to kill the man, not fuck him, regardless of how much this wolf seemed to appeal to his bear. Besides, appearances could be deceiving, and he sensed that taking this Alpha out wouldn't be as easy as he first thought.

Quinton Thorn might only be in his mid-twenties and have the angelic look of a choir boy with his shoulder-length blond curls and baby-blue eyes, but he was also deadly in his own way. So far, every attempt at challenging him had been thwarted by the Alpha. He was known for his kindness, but since he couldn't kill folks with that, he had no qualms ripping their throats out. That's where Zayden came in. It seemed he was the pack's last hope of usurping Quin.

Sure enough, when Zayden pushed through the door into the gloomy interior of the bar, all conversation stopped briefly, and he could sense the waves of suspicion in the air aimed toward him. Ignoring the assembled crowd, he strolled over to the bar, and got the barmaid's attention.

"What can I get you?" the middle-aged woman asked while wiping the bar top down with a washcloth.

"A beer, and some information," Zayden said. She narrowed her eyes, and shook her head.

"Beer I can do, but information will cost you."

Zayden flashed her a grin, and the woman's cheeks pinked up nicely.

"I'll make it worth your while," he drawled, and she stopped mid draw of pulling him a beer. The front door opened and the gust of air that swept in brought with it the most intoxicating scent. His bear grumbled low in his throat, and it took all of Zayden's willpower to not turn around and see who had just walked in.

"Sorry, can't help you." The woman slammed his beer in front of him and smiled at whoever had just walked in.

"The usual, boss?" she asked, and everything inside Zayden tightened when a muscly, denim-clad thigh slid on the stool next to him.

"Thanks, Tilly."

The deep voice held the distinct growl of a wolf, and Zayden forced his gaze away from the way this male's jeans hugged the impressive bulge in his groin. He trailed his eyes up the man's sculpted abdomen, clearly visible through the tight t-shirt he was wearing.

Zayden took in the bulging biceps that flexed in a manner that made him want to run his tongue along the swirls of this man's ink, and watched as the wolf shifter ran a hand through his blond hair.

His gaze arrested at the far-too-enticing sight of the way the shifter's Adam's apple bopped as he swallowed. A hard jaw covered in stubble, his cheeks showing dimples as he smiled at the bartender, a sinful mouth, and blue eyes the color of a summer's sky.

"That your Harley out there, stranger? Nice bike."

Quinton Thorn raised his glass in a silent salute, and Zayden's world tilted when he looked into the eyes of his prey.

Chapter Two

Quinton took a long swallow of the ice-cold beer Tilly had placed in front of him, grateful that the action hid his trembling fingers. He had no idea who this bear shifter was, but his wolf didn't care. The beast had salivated from the first whiff of this man's scent that had clung to his Harley, and had urged him to walk into the bar and see who the owner of that musk was.

His gaze had zeroed in on the broad back of the male who seemed to have reduced good old Tilly to a blushing school girl, and after giving curt nods to those of his pack in attendance, he had slid on the chair next to the bear shifter. The front of this bloke was as impressive as his back had been. Even sat down, this man exuded confidence, power, and leashed aggression—everything that made Quin's wolf want to roll over and submit, which was an odd sensation to say the least. As the Alpha of his pack, Quinton was used to being in charge in all things, but he couldn't shake the feeling that he would gladly yield to this man—in a sexual sense at least.

The stranger was huge, with not an ounce of fat on him, and Quin estimated him to be several inches taller than his own height of six foot two. Close-cropped brown hair framed a harsh face set in granite. A scar ran from one side of his cheek and disappeared into several days' worth of stubble grazing a prominent jaw. The stranger stared at him, and had it not been for the flare of lust and recognition in the bear shifter's amber gaze, for the way his eyes bled to the golden yellow of his inner animal's, Quinton would have thought his salivating wolf's reaction had been completely one sided. There was no mistaking the quiet grumble of the man's bear that joined his own beast's excited yips. Over the ringing in his ears, Quinton could hear only one word, *mate.*

Only problem was, that if this man *was* his mate—and the longer Quin sat and drank in the mere presence of the bear shifter, the more convinced he became that he was—the hunk didn't look pleased about this realization.

After what seemed like an eternity, during which the mountain-of-a-man leaned closer and inhaled sharply, he finally gave a tight nod.

"Yes, she's mine. Fancy getting out of here and taking her for a spin?"

Quin's wolf chased his own tail in his excitement at the thought and he grinned and nodded.

"Sure, if you don't mind giving me a ride." He inwardly grimaced at that inane innuendo, and the other man grinned. It lit up his rugged features and made him look years younger. Quin's fingers itched to run them through the strands of silver just about visible in the bear shifter's brown hair. He curled his digits around the edge of the bar instead, mindful of the expectancy in the air.

His pack was watching his interaction with this stranger, and he couldn't be that obvious in front of them. While most of them had come to accept that their Alpha's sexual preferences ran against the norm, he knew full well that there were those who would pounce on his showing any open affection to another man as a sign of weakness.

Quinton would rather spend his time fucking in private than having to squash another rebellion. The last one had still left a bitter taste in his mouth. He had had to kill the cousin of his beta, and while Orgon seemed to have accepted that Quinton had done nothing but defend his position, he couldn't help but feel uneasy around the older man now.

Orgon had been Quinton's father's beta, and as such, a trusted member of his pack. He had been charged with looking out for Quinton, which seemed to mean that he had taken it upon himself to make sure Quin chose a young eligible female shifter to father little wolf cubs.

"It's about time you thought of settling down, Alpha. It's what your father would have wanted."

Quin had put him off, by way of saying he would settle for nothing less than his own true mate. It's what his father had wanted for him after a lifetime of denying his own feelings in favor of the pack. Quinton senior had made the ultimate sacrifice and married Quin's mother. While the two of them had been as happy as they could have been, something had always been lacking. His mother had known it, and so had Quin once he was old enough to understand why he felt nothing when the other pack youngsters talked of their female conquests.

It had been his father's dying words that had set him free.

"Follow your heart, son, and the pack will follow you regardless. Times have changed, and while the path you need will not be easy for you, it will be worth it in the end."

The short laugh coming from the huge chest he was admiring shook him out of his maudlin thoughts, and his dick shot to attention at lightning speed when the other man spoke.

"Oh sure, boy. I'll give you the ride of your life."

Quin knew he ought to protest at that title, but delivered as it was in that deep, sexy whisper—and for his ears only—he wanted to roll over in submission, just like his wolf did, but he couldn't do so here.

Instead he raised an eyebrow, and stared the other man down.

"The name is Quinton Thorn, Alpha of this pack, and you'd do well to remember that."

The stranger laughed, took one last long draught of his beer, and stood up.

"Oh, I'm well aware of who you are, wolf boy." He tempered the harsh words with a smile that didn't quite reach his eyes, and after a moment's hesitation, stuck out his hand. Quin's wolf whined at the jolt of electricity that shot up his arm when he took the other man's hand, and the bear shifter's eyes widened in recognition. His scent grew stronger, pulling Quin further under the spell of the mating bond, and the rest of the crowded bar faded away as they stared at each other, assessing, wondering.

"Zayden Reid, beholden to no one, Alpha of no pack and...." He leaned in closer and inhaled sharply. "I want you, *boy*."

Sexual tension pulsed between them for the few seconds it took before Quin managed to let go of Zayden's hand and push him away. The other man nodded, mumbled something under his breath, and stalked from the bar.

Quin made to follow him, when Orgon stepped in his way.

"Don't. You go with him and you'll regret it."

Quin's wolf snarled at his beta in his agitation. The other man's wolf showed briefly in his eyes before his beta bowed his head and stepped out of his way.

"Only looking out for my Alpha, that's all," Orgon said, but something in the tone of his voice made Quinton's hair stand on end, and he gave the older man a hard stare.

"I appreciate your concern, but there's no need, unless you know something about him I don't."

Orgon spread his hands out in a defensive gesture, and shook his head.

"You'll find out soon enough, Alpha. My debt is paid. I warned you." With that, Orgon walked off. Quinton would have gone after him to demand an explanation, but the throaty sound of a motorbike starting up meant he walked out of the bar instead. He had a mate to get to know, and he would find out whatever was eating Orgon, once he had claimed his mate. To let him go was out of the question.

****

Zayden revved the engine again, ignoring his bear's incessant growl. Every fiber in his being urged him to walk back in there and drag his mate out. Quinton Thorn *was* his fucking mate. The universe was having a great big laugh at his fucking expense. He'd come here to kill his *mate.* His bear roared at the mere thought, and Zayden shook his head. He could no more kill the man than he could have killed his own mother. He wasn't a complete fucking animal, but the new tender feelings that had coursed through him when he'd shaken Quinton's hand meant he felt like a fish out of water. He knew how to kill and fuck, but he had no idea what to do about these *emotions.*

Already he felt as though he was missing a limb. It had caused a physical ache in his gut to walk away from Quinton. His dick was so hard he could pound fucking *concrete* with it, and there was no chance of getting relief any time soon. The wolf shifter wasn't coming. It was Zayden's damn luck that he had to fall hard for a man who didn't seem to return his feelings, despite the connection that had pulsed between them in the bar.

Regardless of that, he would stick around and watch over his mate. Whoever wanted him dead was a member of his pack, and Zayden would make damn sure that fucker wouldn't get a chance to charge someone else with the job of killing the Alpha.

His heart stopped, and then turned into a jack hammer when the door to the bar opened and Quinton approached him. He didn't look happy at first, but his face broke into a wide grin when he spotted Zayden waiting for him.

"For a minute there, I thought you changed your mind." The hint of uncertainty in the younger man's voice soothed Zayden's agitated beast, and he shook his head and passed him his spare helmet.

"Hop on," he said, and took a deep breath when Quinton joined him on his Harley. The heat of the other man's torso branded his back, yet it calmed his volatile bear to have his mate this close to him. He opened up the throttle and simply gave himself over to the sheer delight of the ride, his mate safely ensconced behind him.

After riding around and showing off his bike as best he could, he switched on the intercom connecting the helmets, and instantly wished he hadn't. Every harsh breath Quinton expelled in reaction to Zayden taking the corners too fast, shot straight to Zayden's balls. He had to clear his throat several times to get his voice to work.

"Ready to be taken for a proper ride now, boy?" he asked, and closed his eyes briefly when he heard Quinton's reply.

"Fuck, yes. As much as I'm enjoying your bike, I need us to fuck."

Zayden grinned and automatically turned in the direction of Quin's house before he caught himself and took a wrong turn. This whole mate thing was messing with his head. He shouldn't know where the other man lived.

"Where to?" he asked, and following Quinton's directions in his earpiece, they reached the other man's modest home mere minutes later.

A heavy silence fell between them after Zayden parked his bike and shadowed Quinton up the path to his house, his gaze snaring on the way Quinton's ass cheeks clenched and released as he walked. Stepping into the hallway felt like signing his doom, yet he couldn't *not* follow the other man. The wolf shifter's scent was everywhere, driving his bear insane. His jaw ached with the need to claim what was his.

"Welcome to—" The rest of whatever Quin was going to add was left unsaid as Zayden lost the tenuous control he had on himself.

Spinning the other man around, he pinned him against the wall. He slammed his lips over Quinton's and at the other man's sharp exhale, slipped his tongue past the firm lips. His mate's flavor exploded on his taste buds. Groaning, he took the kiss deeper, pleased to note that Quin seemed to be as much in thrall of this thing between them as he was.

The growl of Quinton's wolf joined the incessant rumble of his bear, and he grunted when Quin's hands grasped his ass cheeks and pushed their groins together. Even with the rough denim between them, Zayden could feel the heat and length of his mate's cock. He drank in the needy little moans Quin made as Zayden's dick grew bigger still.

With a loud growl, he wrenched his lips off Quinton's, and pulled the man's hands off his ass. Quinton groaned and tried to close the distance between them, but Zayden grasped his wrists and pinned his hands high above his head. He glared at him and growled.

"No."

Quinton's eyes widened and bled to the softly glowing yellow of his wolf as he snarled at Zayden.

It was the vulnerability Zayden sensed in him though that stopped his bear from reacting. Instead he let him go and stepped away with a muttered, "Fuck, I need another drink."

Quinton's humorless laugh made his chest feel tight. He closed his eyes and fisted his hands when the other man grasped his dick in a firm hold.

"We should have stayed at the bar for that. There's only one thing I want to do, and that's taste my big... bad... bear."

Zayden's cock jumped at the heated words delivered into his neck, and awareness of the other man seeped through his veins like molten lava. Quinton suckled on his skin, then bit down slightly before he dropped to his knees. With a wicked grin up at him, he nuzzled into Zayden's groin.

Seeing his mate kneeling on the floor, making short work of releasing Zayden's cock from his jeans, made all coherent thought flee his brain. He hissed through his teeth as Quinton freed his dick, wrapped his fist around the base of his shaft, then ran his thumb through the drop of pre-cum already escaping his slit. He then wrapped his lips around the tip and sucked hard.

Pleasure erupted along his sensitive skin, and with his fists by his side, Zayden shut his eyes, let his head fall back, and simply gave himself over to the skilled tongue of his lover. In no time at all he felt his release building, and he yanked Quin off his dick with a hoarse shout. The other man's teeth scraped along his shaft as he let go and the sharp pain dulled his arousal somewhat, only to flare anew when he pulled Quinton up and kissed him.

He could taste his own saltiness on the other man's lips, and it drove his bear wild. Marching him backward until Quinton's back hit the wall, he took the kiss deeper, then ran his nose along the rapidly beating pulse point in Quin's beard-roughened neck. He inhaled deeply, drinking in the scent of his man.

"You're mine, wolf boy."

He growled the words into his mate's collar bone as he continued his journey south. Quinton grunted and swore under his breath as Zayden used his claws to tear the other man's shirt off.

But it was his own turn to groan when he caught sight of his mate's nipple rings.

Bending lower, he tucked at first one and then the other with his teeth, and Quin's claws ran out and dug into his scalp as he pulled Zayden in closer.

"Fuck, yes."

Zayden grinned as he pushed his hand under the waistband of Quinton's jeans. His mate wasn't wearing any underwear, and Zayden groaned anew when he encountered the piercing adorning his mate's cock. He ran his thumb over the weeping slit, tugged on the ring attached to Quin's hood, and caught the other man's lustful groan in his mouth as he scooted back up to kiss him.

Heat scorched his fingers as the cock in his hand lengthened and thickened further under his none-too-gentle ministrations. They were both gasping for air, their respective animals' growls filling the space between them. Zayden wasn't at all surprised to see the other man's canines appear. His own stung his lips, and he licked the resulting drop of blood away.

"You're pierced." He ground the words out through gritted teeth as he struggled with the intense need to sink his teeth into the beefy shoulder in front of him and cement this bond between them.

"It's a sign of the Alpha in my pack." Quin's grunted reply should have cooled Zayden's ardor. Quin was the Alpha, and marking him as his would cause him no end of trouble, but his bear wasn't listening. This man was his, and no one and nothing was going to take him away from him. Fuck the consequences. He would deal with the inevitable fallout later. If he had any decency left in him at all he would put a stop to this before they were both too far gone. But Zayden was consumed with the need for this man, and instead of pulling away, he tightened his hold on the other man's shaft.

Perspiration broke out on Quinton's forehead and he howled when Zayden pulled on his piercing again. He then ran his canines along the other man's neck—not hard enough to break the skin, just to leave a red trail and to warn Quin of his intentions.

"Yes, fuck yes, bite me already. I want to be yours."

Quinton's claws dug into Zayden's shoulders, as he pulled him closer still and his heavy breaths raised goosebumps of need across Zayden's exposed skin. With almost super-human effort, he pulled back and studied Quinton.

"I will, but not in the fucking hallway…. Where…?"

He didn't get to finish his question since Quin pushed his body away, grasped hold of his hand, and pulled him up the stairs. They tore at each other's clothes as they went, and when they finally tumbled through a door and Zayden saw the bed, he picked the slighter man up and threw him halfway across the room and onto the mattress. He followed him in one massive leap and after pinning Quinton down under him, sank his teeth into his mate's shoulder with a growled, "Mine."

Chapter Three

The force of the mating orgasm took Quin's breath away. His cock jerked and ejected thick spurts of his cum all over his abs and he lay gasping for air under Zayden's big body. Utterly pinned by him, he couldn't move as the bear shifter let go of his shoulder, licked his bite, and roared. The force of it shook the bed. It roused his wolf, and using the animal's strength, he flipped the heavier man over until he could straddle him. Zayden's magnificent cock stood up like a come-get-me beacon out of the thick thatch of hair on top of his groin. Quinton's mouth watered.

The bear's dick was huge and heavily veined, and Quin's stomach hollowed out in anticipation of taking that monster up his ass. But first things first. Letting his claws spring free, he ran circles around the bear shifter's nipples, admiring the art work that graced his left pectoral. He grinned at the way Zayden's flat buds firmed and stood to attention. The shifter growled and buried his hands in Quinton's hair, tugging him closer with a groan.

"Quit messing around and fuck me already, wolf boy. It's the only chance you're gonna get."

Quinton grinned to himself as he licked and bit his way down the magnificent muscles in front of him until he reached the other man's cock.

"Bossy, aren't you, teddy bear?" He smirked at the affronted growl of his mate, but it was the affection that shone out of the other man's amber gaze that meant he had to hurry this along. Zayden's hips shot off the bed when Quinton licked his finger and pushed one of his digits through the tight ring of muscle guarding the man's ass. He swallowed Zayden's cock whole at the same time, and was rewarded by his mate's salty pre-cum. It slid down his throat in ever-increasing amounts, and

Quinton grew hard as nails again, hearing his mate pant and curse.

While fondling the bear shifter's hairy sac, he thrust his finger in and out of the tight clasp of Zayden's body. He could tell how close the other man was to his own release, and when Zayden's balls drew up tight, ready to shoot their load, he pulled off his lover's dick and squeezed the shaft tightly.

Zayden swore, but it had the desired effect of staving off the man's impending orgasm long enough for Quinton to reach across and find the lube he kept in the nightstand. He smothered his cock in a generous amount and then squeezed a whole lot down his mate's ass cheeks. He worked two fingers into Zayden, and eventually a third.

"Fuck, you're so tight. Not normally at the receiving end?" He looked up to find Zayden watching him. Half shifted, his bear looked terrifying and sexy as fuck. Quin lost himself in the intensity of his gaze.

"Not usually, wolf boy. Get on with it already and fuck me."

It was all the encouragement Quinton needed, and after yanking the other man's legs over his shoulders, he lined up his cock with the clenching hole in front of him and pushed in slowly. Heat engulfed him, and sweat dripped into his eyes as he made steady progress. By the time he finally bottomed out, Quinton's wolf was foaming at the mouth.

With the last coherent thought he had, he guided Zayden's hands to the man's swollen cock and grunted. "Fist yourself for me, I want you to explode."

When Zayden complied with a muffled growl, Quinton gave his wolf full reign and started thrusting into the other man's ass. Pleasure built, so intense that nothing mattered but the connection that arced between them.

Faster, stronger, with more and more violent moves he sought his release, and when he sank his teeth into Zayden's shoulder, they climaxed together in a cacophony of noise and sensation that meant Quinton lost touch with reality.

He collapsed on top of his mate, barely able to draw breath into his lungs as their scents and souls mingled, their animals' joined grumbles filling the air around him. Eventually, his softened cock slipped from the tight clasp of Zayden's ass, and he frowned at the other man's wince.

Pushing himself off the bear shifter, he studied his expression, renewed anxiety churning a hole in his gut. Zayden didn't look hurt, but he didn't look happy either—and sure enough, the minute Quinton rolled off him, Zayden shot off the bed. He glanced at Quinton, looking as though he was about to say something, before he turned on his heel and disappeared through the door into Quinton's adjacent bathroom.

He heard the toilet flush and then the shower come on briefly before his mate reappeared. With nothing but a towel flung round his slim hips, and drops of moisture still clinging to his hair-roughened abs, Zayden looked good enough to eat. He also looked pissed off and dangerous.

Quinton's wolf's hackles rose in response to the danger the animal suddenly sensed. It was almost as though Zayden meant to harm him. But that was impossible. He was his mate. They had in fact mated, and mates could not harm each other. Ever.

At least that was what Quinton had always been told. He found though, despite the situation—or maybe because of it—his cock started to harden again.

A grim smile kicked up his lover's harsh features when he noticed, and he gestured to the bathroom.

"You ought to freshen up."

Quinton grinned and swung his legs off the bed, fisting his now fully erect cock slowly.

"Why? By the looks of you, you're ready to go again too, so why waste water? Let's fuck, then we can shower together." He smiled up at the other man, who was indeed tenting the fabric wrapped around him. Quinton ran his hand up the huge thigh and under the towel, but Zayden pushed it away with a low growl and shook his head.

"No, we should have had this conversation before we...." He let his words trail off, and his gaze settled on the bite mark on Quinton's shoulder. The area throbbed and heated as though Zayden had been running his tongue all over it, making the air thicken between them.

"Fuck this, are you regretting biting me?" Quinton had to force the words out. Fuck, even asking the question hurt as though a million razors were slicing his skin open to tear out his heart. He hardly knew this man, yet he loved him with an intensity that bordered on obsession. Maybe they should have taken their time to get to know each other, to see if they meshed in other areas of their lives, but it had felt so right, so natural. This connection they shared, that even now pulsed between them like a living entity... that couldn't be wrong, could it?

His wolf growled at the direction his thoughts were taking, and an ice-cold fist wrapped itself around his heart. If he had made the wrong choice, then his whole pack could be in danger.

The way Zayden's head shot up and he frowned soothed Quinton's agitation somewhat, and he forced a smile on his lips.

"No, I could never regret what we shared." The conviction beneath those words, delivered as they were in that deep growl of Zayden's beast, made Quinton's wolf settle back down again. This time, his smile came easily.

"You're my fucking mate, and I'll rip anyone to shreds who is intent on harming you, but...." Zayden started to pace the floor. Quinton could almost see his bear prowling underneath the man's skin, and he wouldn't have been surprised had his mate shifted right there and then. He barely seemed to have a hold on his animal, and while the thought of having a huge grizzly wreck his bedroom didn't exactly appeal, Quinton found himself longing to see his man in his animal form. He would be beautiful and deadly, no doubt.

One day soon, when they had sorted whatever was worrying his teddy bear, after he'd announced to his pack that he had indeed taken a mate, they would have to make a trip to the forest so they could run and hunt together. His wolf yipped his excitement at this plan, and as though Zayden's bear could read his thoughts, the animal answered.

Maybe their inner animals could indeed communicate. They *were* mates after all, acting on instinct. Their beasts weren't dictated to by the restraints and expectations of society on the whole, and the pack in particular.

Zayden stopped his incessant pacing and sat down heavily next to Quinton on the bed.

"You might not want me once you know who I truly am and why I was at the bar."

Quinton nudged the other man's shoulder with his and laughed.

"I highly doubt that. Stop looking so serious, teddy bear. It's not as though you're a serial killer, now is it?"

The words hung in the air between them, and when Zayden didn't respond other than to run a weary hand over his face, Quinton's gut churned in sudden fear.

"What if I am?" His mate's pained reply made Quinton shoot off the bed, and his mouth fell open at Zayden's next words. "And what if the sole reason I was in that bar was to kill you?"

****

Zayden had never felt so unsure of himself as he sat on the bed watching the myriad of emotions flit over Quinton's face. Shock, disbelief, hurt, betrayal, and finally anger. Red-hot fury blasted him, and he shut his eyes, half expecting Quin to shift and tear him limb from limb. He would let him, too. There was no way he could harm his mate.

Instead of an attack, however, Zayden felt Quinton step closer, and when he opened his eyes he got a full frontal view of his mate's cock. Half erect as it now was, it still made a mouthwatering sight. His piercing twinkled in the glare of a passing car's headlights that stole in through the gap in the curtains, and it took all of Zayden's will power not to lean in closer and taste his mate anew.

He smelled like him. The scent of sweat mingled with their combined cum that had dried on Quin's washboard abs made his bear roar in delight. This man was his, and always would be. Sharp claws digging into his chin forced his head up until Zayden looked into the eyes of Quinton's wolf. The animal was furious and clearly baying for blood, but he also read love in that gaze, and without thinking about it he blurted out what was in his heart.

"I love you."

The pressure on his chin increased until he could smell the coppery scent of his own blood in the air, but he held the wolf shifter's gaze.

After what seemed like an eternity, Quinton nodded, released the hold on Zayden's chin, and sat back down next to him.

"That why you didn't kill me?" he asked, and there was a world of hurt in those few words.

Zayden's bear growled. He buried his hands in the other man's golden locks, pulling him closer until their foreheads touched and their breaths mingled and became one. Their heartbeats synchronized and Zayden pulled his mate's scent deep into his lungs.

"Yes," he said simply, and he felt the other man relax.

"I'm glad, because I don't think I would have won against you. You're fucking huge, man, and I bet your bear is massive."

A slight smile kicked up Quinton's lips as he spoke, and when he pushed against Zayden's chest, he reluctantly let him go.

"I'm sure you would have held your own," Zayden said. "For a while anyway, but yes, eventually I'd have ripped your throat out, and I wouldn't have felt any remorse over it either." He paused at Quinton's sharp intake of breath, and his stone-cold heart squeezed painfully in his chest. He didn't want his mate to think less of him, but he still couldn't change who he was.

"Have you killed many?" Quinton finally asked, and Zayden nodded.

"Yes."

"Why?"

Zayden shrugged noncommittally, and Quinton frowned.

"A man's got to make a living, and besides, killing is all I know."

Quinton shook his head and took Zayden's hand in his. The move was oddly comforting, as were his mate's next words.

"I refuse to believe that the man I fell in love with so hopelessly at first sight, is nothing but a killer. Besides—" an impish smile curved Quinton's lips and he traced the gruesome tattoo on Zayden's chest with one long finger. "—You're good at fucking, at least."

Zayden threw his head back and laughed. He grasped the other man's head and kissed him. Unlike the other kisses they had shared, this one was tender. Zayden poured all of his emotions into the kiss, and Quinton returned them tenfold. By the time they broke apart, they were both breathing heavily and Zayden was pleased to see Quinton's cock was as hard as his own.

"We should do something about that," he murmured, and smiled when he took Quinton's cock in his hand, making the other man groan. "Perhaps I'll fuck you in the shower. I think my little wolf boy would like that."

Quinton hissed a *fuck yes* through his teeth and Zayden's chest swelled with love for his mate. They had a lot to sort out—least of which to find the fucker who wanted Quinton dead—but it would have to wait for now.

Zayden followed his mate into the shower and admired the tat of a prowling wolf that filled one half of his lover's back. It was a damn sight nicer than his own rather gruesome one, but he could never regret having it done. It had marked his first kill, that scumbag of a father. If ever someone deserved to die, then it had been the man who had left Zayden's gentle mother to fend for herself with a volatile bear-shifter cub.

He blinked back unexpected tears, grateful for the stream of the hot water that hid the evidence of his unexpected breakdown, but Quinton noticed anyway. He stopped mid-lathering of Zayden's chest and frowned up at him.

"What's wrong, teddy bear?" he asked and Zayden's mood instantly lifted. If anyone else were to dare call him that, he'd rip their fucking throat out, but hearing it from his mate's lips just made him want to fuck him. One day he would tell him all about his sordid youth, but not now.

"Nothing that sinking balls-deep into my little wolf boy's ass won't cure," he said, and taking the other man by the shoulders, spun him around.

He grabbed the waterproof lube Quinton kept next to the shower gel, and squirted a generous amount into his lover's butt crack, gently working it into Quinton's anus. His little wolf boy groaned and pushed his ass back on Zayden's questing fingers while Quinton fisted his own cock. It was damn hot to witness.

Having lathered his dick in lube, Zayden lined up with the tight rosette he wanted to claim. A deep-throated grunt escaped him as he pushed in, his lover's ass opening up for him beautifully. With one hand in Quinton's hair for anchorage, he started to thrust. Reaching around, he grasped hold of his lover's cock, simultaneously jacking off his mate.

Arousal surged through his veins, obliterating all else bar their harsh breaths. The water cascaded down on them in their intimate, steamy cocoon, and he caught Quinton's scream of completion in a kiss.

Zayden followed moments later, shooting his load into his man's ass before they both collapsed onto the shower floor. Somehow they managed to struggle upright, wash off, and fall back into bed.

Tomorrow he would find and kill the fucker who wanted Quinton dead, but for now, he allowed the oblivion of sleep to claim him.

Chapter Four

The bar was full of people that night despite being closed to the public, and Quinton took in the sea of faces that was his pack. Stood on the small stage reserved for the entertainment they held on Friday and Saturday nights, his mate's low growls joined his wolf's own. Zayden was furious with Quinton's plan to announce their mating before he had the chance to kill the piece of scum who had employed him to kill Quinton.

"Why the fuck would you put yourself at risk like that, wolf boy? I didn't see the fucker's face, but I'll track him down by his scent. Let me do that and dispose of him, then you can make all the fucking announcements you want—but only once I know you're safe."

Quinton had shaken his head at his outraged teddy bear.

"No, I'm the Alpha of this pack, and I will not hide away behind my mate while this challenge exists. This is my mess, and I'll deal with it my way."

"And what makes you think he'll play fair? He hasn't so far—and I can't risk you. I won't. If I have to keep you tied and gagged to our bed then that's what I'll fucking do."

Zayden's fury had been an almost palpable force, but Quinton had refused to be drawn into his mate's dominance. As much as he appreciated it and submitted gladly in the bedroom, it had no place in any decisions regarding his pack. They'd had an almighty argument over it, and his house would need redecorating. The make-up sex however, had been the best he'd ever had, and the agreement they'd reached had cemented the basis of their relationship.

In the end Zayden had reluctantly agreed to what he called Quin's *hare-brained, crazy-ass, suicide mission,* which had led to them standing at the bar after Quinton had called a special pack meeting.

Scanning the crowded room, his heart sank when he realized that his beta wasn't there. From the little description Zayden had been able to give, Quinton suspected the traitor in his pack to be Orgon. He hadn't wanted to believe it, but what other explanation was there for his beta to not be in attendance at this special meeting?

It made his wolf want to kill something. The bitter taste of betrayal sat heavily in his stomach, but he had to hold it together now for the sake of the pack.

Spotting Tilly moving through the crowd with refreshments, he called her over.

"Any word from Orgon?" he asked.

"No, boss, none. I have no idea why he's not here, but this lot are getting restless, so...."

She blanched when Zayden stepped up behind him and growled at her. He smiled.

"I know, Tilly, thank you. Don't mind him." He glanced over his shoulder at a furious-looking Zayden, and smirked. "He doesn't get out much around civilized folk."

Zayden flipped him the finger and Quinton laughed. A few of his pack close enough to hear their exchange stared at him with astonished expressions, and Quinton knew he had to explain who Zayden was to him. For anyone to get away with showing him this much disrespect in front of his pack was unheard of, and a ripple of anticipation went through his people as he stepped up to the microphone and tapped it.

Everyone winced when a loud screech hurt their ears, and Stan, the wolf in charge of acoustics, held up an apologetic hand and then nodded at Quinton.

"Sorry about that, folks," he said as he spoke into the microphone. "It seems Stan has already had one-too-many to drink, which reminds me—the drinks are very much on me tonight."

"Hell yeah!" One of the youngsters, a pup they had taken in only recently—who was barely even legal enough to drink—punched the air in triumph, and a ripple of laughter went through the crowd.

"I'm sure you're all wondering what this is about, and why Zayden is here on stage with me." Quinton paused and searched the crowd. He sensed a certain amount of hostility from the back of the room where Orgon's family was huddled together. There was still no sign of the man himself, and Quinton swallowed his wolf's growl.

"So tell us already, and we can get this party started. We are celebrating, right?" The same young pup smirked, and promptly winced when one of his friends swatted him upside the head.

"Shut up and let the Alpha speak. Show some respect, dude."

Another ripple of laughter went through the room, and even Zayden cracked a smile. His mate was still on full alert, his amber gaze scanning the room, muscles coiled for a fight, and Quinton drank in the sight of the man he loved.

"Yes, this is a celebration. I'm here to introduce you to my mate, Zayden." He gestured toward the bear shifter, who stepped forward while still searching the crowd.

A stunned silence had fallen on the assembled pack, and Quinton firmed his voice as the back door opened and Orgon stepped through. From the way Zayden tensed and his head whipped in the elderly wolf's direction, nostrils flaring, Quinton knew his worst suspicions were about to be confirmed.

He put a hand on Zayden's tense arm to stop him from charging forward and stepped in front of him, all too aware of the hostile glare from his beta. The venom in his eyes made his gut churn. He'd trusted that man, as his father had done before him, and he swallowed down the bile collecting at the back of his throat.

"I realize this may come as a shock to some of you, and if you cannot condone your Alpha mated to a man, then now is the time to say so. I'll bear no ill will to anyone who wishes to leave the pack. All I ask is that you do so now. If you stay, I'll expect you to swear allegiance to myself and Zayden."

Orgon murmured something under his breath, and a handful of people made to leave, but the vast majority stayed. Some of them cheered, others wore big grins, while others still looked thoughtful as the occasion demanded.

Quinton looked around the room again, breaking eye contact with Orgon for a second, and smiled.

"I'm glad you decided to—"

His beta's snarls filled the air, and cut him off.

"Over my dead body, you perverted piece of shit."

Before anyone had a chance to react, Orgon drew out a gun and pulled the trigger. All hell broke loose as Zayden shoved Quinton off the stage, and Quinton watched in horror as the bullet meant for him lodged itself in Zayden's chest instead. The bear shifter staggered forward for a few steps, a stunned expression on his face, before he fell face down to the ground, and Orgon started shooting indiscriminately.

With a roar of grief, Quinton shifted into his wolf mid leap and advanced on his former beta. A shot glanced off his leg, but he barely felt the pain. His nostrils filled with the acrid smoke of gun powder, and he tore the other man's hand clean off. It fell to the floor still clutching the gun that had killed his mate, and Quinton sank his teeth into Orgon's throat.

Blood spurted in a wide arch, and the bastard's fluid-filled gurgles sounded too loud in his ears as his former beta lay on the floor in a pool of blood, taking his last few breaths. His wolf wanted to tear him limb from limb, but his mate's faint heartbeat called to him.

Shifting back into his human form, Quinton shouted for the doc. Tears clouded his vision when he reached the stage and turned Zayden over. A deeply unconscious Zayden was bleeding out badly, his face ashen and his heartbeat getting slower and slower. Quinton was dimly aware of the pack's doc working on him as he sat cradling his mate's head, just whispering the same words over and over.

"Don't you fucking die on me, teddy bear."

****

Zayden struggled to open his eyes, and when he did manage it, he wished he hadn't. The lights were too bright, there was an annoying beep in his ear, and the place reeked of disinfectant. An iron band of pain seemed to have wrapped itself around his chest, and he frowned when he raised his head and saw the bandages covering his upper torso. Something or someone had him restrained, because he couldn't move his right side at all. When he tried, a soft grunt brought with it the scent of home, and Zayden smiled as he realized why he couldn't move.

Of course, he'd been shot by that fucker Orgon, and he was in some sort of hospital? No, that wasn't right. He was lying on a hospital bed but he recognized the wallpaper. They were in Quinton's spare room and his mate had one leg draped over his.

Perched on the side of the bed, his mate was fast asleep, clutching Zayden's unencumbered hand. His other arm had some sort of drip attached to it.

Zayden grimaced at the contraption, and then settled for watching his mate sleep. Quinton looked like shit. Dark purple smudges under his eyes spoke of how much he must have needed this rest. His beautiful blond locks were a tangled mess, his clothing torn and blood spattered, and he didn't smell too nice.... But it was unbelievably good to see him alive. His bear grumbled his approval and Quinton's wolf answered.

It woke up his mate with a start, and tears sprang into his eyes when his anxious gaze connected with Zayden's.

"Oh, thank god, you're awake. You've been out for days. I thought.... Fuck, don't you ever scare me like that again, do you hear? As your Alpha, I forbid it."

Zayden laughed and promptly winced as pain shot through his chest and made breathing difficult.

Quinton made a strangled sound at the back of his throat, and framed Zayden's face with his hands. When Zayden could breathe normally again, he brushed his lips over the other man's and drew back with a grin when Zayden tried to deepen the kiss.

"Oh, no you don't. You need rest right now. You almost died taking that fuckin bullet. What were you thinking?"

Zayden grasped Quinton's hand and squeezed.

"Just protecting what's mine, that's all." Zayden paused briefly. Orgon?" he asked and Quinton's blue eyes turned to ice.

"Won't bother anyone anymore. I ripped that fucker's throat out, and his family has left the pack. There is no room for their bigoted way of thinking. Not in the future I envisage for the pack and us."

Zayden nodded and warmth spread through his veins at the love that shone from of his mate's eyes.

"Us, huh?" he asked and Quinton growled at him.

"You bet, teddy bear, and for once you're going to do as you're told and rest. Follow the doctor's orders and your Alpha's command."

Zayden raised his eyebrows at that, but all that talking had exhausted him, and he shut his eyes.

"If you say so, wolf boy. Don't think you can boss me around when I'm back to full strength, mind you."

Quinton's soft laughter was music to his ears and he allowed himself to sink back into the sleep he needed to heal.

Maybe love wasn't for fools after all. Not that he would ever admit that out loud to anyone but his wolf boy.

www.dorisoconnor.com

DISCARDED PUP

Copyright © 2015

Angelique Voisen

Chapter One

Beyond the grime-stained floors, in the tiny concrete boxes where men paced, cursed, raged and occasionally went crazy, a clock ticked.

One second. Two. Three.

Years ago, Cole Reyes would have gripped the bars, pushed his face through the space, and let a howl spill from his throat. He'd scream in frustration, let off steam on some poor random mortal, and get a taste of batons and tasers. Be shoved into solitary confinement. Rinse and repeat.

Once or twice, Cole's wolf almost got free, but he remembered to pull the beast back.

Not anymore. Cole grunted, lowered his body to kiss the ugly floor and rose up again.

"Seventy," he managed. Sweat coated his face and body, but he had a couple more sets to go.

A steel cage is no place for a wolf. Cole learned early he had two options. He could lose control, let his beast take over, and end up rampaging through the halls until the prison guards put him down. Cole's death would tell the human world the supernatural existed, something he'd rather avoid.

His other option was to wait. Bide his time. Let rage purify him. Watch his wounds fester. Fantasize about the deeds he'd do to the bastards who put him in his cage once he got out.

Other men thought about the good things, the people they left behind to pass away the time, but Cole had no one. An orphan, bitten and picked up by the previous alpha of the Redstone Hill pack, Cole grew up and saw the other wolves as family. Jonah, the beta who had betrayed him, was the old alpha's only son and had once been like his own blood brother.

Blind to Jonah's jealousy and ambition, Cole had trusted Jonah to have his back. When Cole chanced upon Jonah raping a woman from the town they had sworn to protect, he went berserk. Cole recalled the events in his cell. The bloody fight to the death, falling unconscious, and waking up handcuffed to a police cruiser while an officer read him his rights.

No pack member spoke up against Jonah. They watched with the entire town as Cole was taken away for rape. Jonah had played him well. Cole couldn't just fight his way past the local authorities without revealing what he and the others were.

Cole had only one thing on his mind planned for when he would finally taste the sweet air of freedom. *Vengeance.*

"Eighty," Cole hissed through his teeth.

Through the tiny bars of his window, Cole caught the first glimpse of orange and yellow. Sunrise. His sensitive ears caught the sound of other men groaning, complaining, waking up from sleep, ready to repeat the same old motions. Not him though.

"You're up early as usual man," called Bear from the opposite cell.

"Special day," Cole replied, panting.

"Yeah? Good for you, Cole. Don't forget your friends when you're outside. Fuck a pretty whore for me, won't you?"

Cole managed to flash a smile. "I don't forget easy and it's not a woman I'll be taking first."

From the reports his outside sources provided, Cole visualized what River Daniels looked like in his mind—wide and innocent clear blue eyes, dark blond hair and a lean body girls would gush about. *Twenty-five.*

River—Jonah's current favorite toy and Cole's golden ticket. Cole wondered if the pup had any idea how often he masturbated to his image at night when it was lights off. He no longer gave a fuck about clearing his name when the world stood convinced of his crime. The past couldn't be changed, but the future could still be shaped. Cole only lived for vengeance. Once he achieved his goals, who knew?

Bear raised both his hands up in mock defeat. "No judgment here, friend."

Cole hadn't thought he'd make any friends during his time here, but he did. To ground himself, he kept his human half busy. He talked to the other men. Hit the gym during his break time, and continued shaping his body back in his cell. Cole pushed his body to its limits to prevent insanity from taking over.

Tick tock. Cole rose after hitting a hundred then took hold of the bolted bar affixed to his cell and began his pull-ups. In all his years here, the bar had been the only thing he'd asked for. Once he'd assured the warden he wouldn't be cutting off pieces of his bed sheets in an attempt to hang himself, the bar was approved.

Before doing time, Cole had already been one big bastard, but these days, he hardly recognized the face staring back at him in the communal showers. Hair shaved close to his skull, rough stubble coated a hard face, and a body to match. Cole covered every inch of sinew, muscle and scar with black ink, but it was his eyes that made other men leave him alone. Black, like his soul, lacking mercy and any other soft emotion.

A shattered man came in, unable to believe those he trusted with his life would betray him, and a broken man would come out—tempered by fury, fueled by revenge.

A guard appeared by Cole's cell just as he began wiping himself off with a towel. "Reyes, it's time."

Cole's meager belongings had been stuffed into a battered knapsack last night. He picked up the bag before walking up to the guard. Cole knew most of the inmates and guards by now. He offered his wrists as Preston put on his cuffs.

"You think I can take one last shower before I leave, Preston?"

"Don't think it would be a problem. Need to have a few words with the Warden first."

"Works for me." Cole walked those hallways one last time, and nodded at the hard men he learned to know on a first-name basis. Fail or succeed, Cole swore he'd never come back here. He might pride himself as one tough son of a bitch, but if someone shoved him into a cage again, he wouldn't be able to control himself.

By the time Cole finished with the necessary procedures and was let out of the prison's doors, the sun had risen up high above his head. He wore the clothes he had come in with, but they felt tight around his new steel-hard frame. Cole raised his hand against the sun and closed his eyes for a while. He breathed in and out, savoring the taste of freedom, before opening them again to see the wide road before him.

"No bars and walls. No mother fucking rules to chain me down."

"Hey, Reyes. You need me to call you a cab or something?" one guard called.

"No. I think I'd like a run." Cole walked, marveling at the feel of the gravel crunching against the new shoes that were on loan from the warden because his sneakers had rotted away a long time ago. A good distance away from the prison, Cole stopped following the road to civilization and entered the thick cluster of trees on the side. He kicked off his shoes, pulled off his tight shirt and jeans until he stood, nude as the day he was born.

His wolf breathed against his skin, filled with longing, eager to reconnect with nature. Cole almost thought he'd forgotten how to shift, but it came to him easily. Fur covered human skin. Cole dropped to all fours. Claws and paws replaced limbs. Power raged inside him, mingling with all the hate he'd been hoarding. The great weight building inside him for years pushed— threatened to be unleashed, and Cole didn't hold back.

Cole opened his great jaws and let the howl tear through the woods.

Chapter Two

On his way home from work, River Daniels shivered for some unexplainable reason. He heard a howl, but that was ridiculous. Not a howl, but a pure, terrifying song of rage. Lightning flashed across the jet-black starless sky, making River jump. He glimpsed dancing and twisting shadows, and thought he saw a pair of savage amber eyes peering at him in the distance.

River's pack was the law around Redstone Hill. The top of the food chain. Very few members of the town's supernatural community messed with them. No reason for him to be afraid. River rubbed at his eyes and strained his ears. Nothing

"Must be all the extra shifts I'm pulling at the club," he mumbled to himself. A rumble of thunder made his entire body tense up. *Rain's going to fall soon, better get to the car.*

By instinct, River nervously glanced around the darkened streets and pulled his jacket tighter around his skinny frame. He debated if he should walk back down the alley. The neon lights of D'asses, the gay strip club where he worked, would still be blinking. It was still open for business with the late-night crowd hanging around, along with the shifter bouncers the owner hired. River might have had his fill of men pawing at him for the evening, but at least he would be safe there.

Jesus, I'm going insane. Cowering because of my imagination running wild, or finally facing Jonah? No contest. River hastened his footsteps and headed straight for his beat-up Chevy. Parking at the tiny lot behind the club was always a headache, even for employees, so River always left his ride in the lot two blocks away.

Besides, Jonah had been smug and in a strangely good mood all week long over some deal he had made with a visiting pack. It was the perfect time for River to bring up his brother's debt.

The street lamps flickered weakly as he passed. Silence. River kicked at the garbage he came across— torn condom wrappers, beer cans and cigarette butts. D'asses wasn't located in the best part of town, but in all the three years River had worked there, he'd never been this spooked.

By the time he reached the Chevy, rain began falling in fat droplets, blurring his surroundings. River reached for his car keys in his jeans pocket, nearly dropping them when the sound came again. A gut-wrenching howl, slightly warped from the rain, but it was the same.

Through the curtain of water, River caught the sharp flash of yellow, razor-sharp teeth, and the rough outline of the largest fucking wolf River had ever seen. The wolf's coat was the pure color of night—no wonder River couldn't see him at first.

This unknown powerful wolf didn't need to throw power around to establish his dominance. River knew the stranger would tear him to shreds even before he could start to shift.

By werewolf standards, River existed at the bottom of the barrel. Weak and submissive, the only way he knew how to survive was to cling to the protection of another wolf, to stoop so low that he allowed a bastard like Jonah to turn him into his toy.

God, and tonight had been the night River had sworn he'd put his foot down and stand up to Jonah.

His fingers froze. River barely heard the sound of his keys clattering on wet cement.

The beast's angry golden gaze locked with his. The wrath was unlike Jonah's sudden flare of temper, which often ended with River tasting blood in his mouth and his head reeling from pain—but a different kind of anger. The worse sort, cold and tempered with steel. The monster didn't need to make his threats known through claws and teeth. One look at those eyes told River the torment he promised would certainly end in his death. But not the swift kind.

"What did I ever do to you?" River whispered.

Rain pounded on the lot, soaked through his hair and clothes, but all River heard was the click-clack of paws. *Move your ass.* River swiped his keys from the ground and it took three times for him to press the button. Hearing the mechanism unlock, River let out a sound of relief.

A quick look showed him the gigantic bastard taking his time. He didn't lunge, didn't break into a run even as River slammed his foot on the ignition. His tires squealed. River nearly let go of the wheel, but he managed to get the beat-up machine under his control. He nearly ran into the wolf, but the beast gracefully danced out of the way.

River nervously checked his rear mirror several times, but the black monster didn't follow him. Clamping hard on the wheel, River's knuckles turned sheet-white from fear. He had a hard time focusing on the road. After his near brush with death, River wondered if he could still face Jonah.

Questions raced through his head. Why did that wolf want him so badly? A guy like him, who didn't pull rank in the pack, didn't have many enemies.

"Jonah must have pissed him off. It's happened before," he said to himself. Hearing the sound of his voice made thinking easier. "But shit, Jonah. Why take on someone that powerful?"

All River needed was one look. Jonah needed to exercise his power, flaunt his dominance through the pack bonds to remind everyone he was in charge. But the older pack members had never forgotten he did not earn his position, but stole it.

Alphas were biologically different from the common stock. Any wolf could rise through the ranks through power and skill, but only an alpha could create new wolves. Jonah wasn't born an alpha. He couldn't create new wolves, so he took members from other packs or paid other alphas to make new wolves, like River and his twin, Ron.

"I never wanted this shit," he whispered to no one.

Twenty-five and jaded, River took off his clothes for a living to pay off Ron's gambling debts.

River could still remember Ron breaking down in front of him six years ago. Growing up, he and Ron were inseparable, but they had drifted apart once they hit high school. River had packed all his belongings in the Chevy, his parents' last gift to him before they died, ready to move into his new college. But then Ron had appeared in the driveway, bruised, battered and bleeding. River had managed to squeeze his story out.

How Ron had wasted the trust money their parents had left them on gambling.

That same night they drove to Redstone Hills to meet the man Ron owed the money to. Jonah Myers. River used up his own trust, the money he was going to use to pay for college, but it hadn't been enough. He never arrived on the front steps of his dorm and he let a stranger bite him and take his humanity.

"Humans are fragile. You and your brother won't survive as my toys otherwise," Jonah had said, and took both of them to a lone wolf, an alpha in a nearby town to change them. There was a fifty-fifty chance of surviving the bite.

Ron didn't make it, leaving River to clean up his mess.

"I didn't work my ass off doing overtime so I could remain Jonah's whore. I'll tell him about the black bastard looking for him, then discuss our arrangement." River's stomach coiled at the thought, but he was done with cowering. With putting up with another's man abuse.

River wanted to go back to the life he had lost. The reality that had crumbled the moment he saw Ron stumbling toward him, his mind halfway broken. River didn't know if he could go back to where he started, but he had to find out.

Chapter Three

River drove like a madman. This late at night in a town with a population of ten thousand, the roads were deserted. He didn't stop by his favorite burger joint to get a bite like he had initially planned, although his last meal had been hours ago. River's nerves twisted into knots when he spotted the lights on Jonah's front porch and the bikes and cars lined on the sidewalk.

River knew those cars. He scented the familiar smell of musk from his fellow pack members the moment he steered his beat-up Chevy to a vacant spot. What little courage he summoned during the drive withered and died.

An emergency pack he didn't know about? River fished out his phone after killing off the engine. His hands shook. He swallowed at the two unopened messages and a missed call from Dan, Jonah's second.

"Shit." River's plan to be on Jonah's good graces while he gave his little speech was as good as gone. He watched the droplets of rain slide down his window, feeling all hollowed out and numb inside. Knowing Jonah's mercurial temper too well, Jonah didn't relish heading inside to become his master's punching bag.

Fuck. He had a double shift tomorrow evening too. Forget earning double if Jonah decided to pretty him up with shiners. His phone vibrated. River jumped in his seat. Dan again. Taking deep breaths, River cradled the phone to his ear and answered.

"Where the fuck are you, River? You're the only member in the pack not accounted for. Jonah's pissed."

You're just looking for your favorite scapegoat. "I'm parking my car. Give me a fucking break, Dan. I had to escape a nasty black monster."

There was silence on Dan's end. River got out of the car, raised his head to the night, and let the drizzle drench his face and neck. The calm before the storm.

"A large black wolf? An outsider?" Dan asked carefully.

"Yeah. Some lone alpha."

"You hurt?"

"No. I managed to get into the car before he reached me. Who the hell is he, Dan? Some asshole Jonah pissed off?"

"Did you lose him, or did he follow you here?" Dan asked sharply, ignoring his other questions.

"I'm not an idiot, of course he didn't follow me."

How predictable. Dan only cared about his own hide. As beta of the Redstone Hill pack, the welfare of the pack members fell to him, but Dan couldn't care less about others. River knew he obtained his position because he was Jonah's long-time drinking buddy and friend. No one dared challenge him for fear of Jonah.

"Get inside the house." Dan cut the line. River couldn't keep delaying the inevitable. He headed inside and walked passed the men and women in the hallway, feeling like a condemned prisoner headed for the executioner's block. Most of them avoided his eyes. One or two gave him brief nods of acknowledgement.

River didn't hate them, not exactly. Not when negative emotions weighed heavily in the air; gloom and despair, fear and worry, mingling and seeping into their fragile pack bonds like poison. It didn't used to be like this, some of the older wolves whispered behind Jonah's back, but this was all River had known.

Why do I continue putting up with this? Because I don't want to die—because I owe Jonah a debt I will continue to pay until I die?

The truth sunk in the closer River came to Jonah's hulking and fuming frame in the living room. He'd known for a while. Deep down, he knew no matter how many extra hours he took at the club, numbers became irrelevant the moment Jonah made River his toy. Perhaps he'd clung to the hope of freedom so desperately because without that illusion he wouldn't be able to wake up each morning and tackle the present.

"Where were you, you useless son of a bitch?" Jonah thundered.

He punctuated each word with his fist. All the air in River's lungs whooshed out. Jonah slammed his fist into his gut, making him double over. Another sharp uppercut to his face sent his head reeling, his body hitting the hard floor. River groaned in pain, arms protectively covering his front, but Jonah's foot easily caught him the ribs.

"Who the fuck do you think you are, you piece of shit?"

Matthias, one of the older wolves interrupted, "Alpha, we have important matters to discuss. The black wolf who came after River—"

"Unless you want to take my bitch's place, shut up."

No one interrupted Jonah after that.

Fire spread through his body. River gritted his teeth against the pain.

He didn't bother getting up. Experience taught him that would enrage Jonah, so he stayed down. Told himself to take the blows until Jonah had his fill. Then he would present his belly and throat in submission. Jonah would then drag him up the stairs and fuck him raw in the bedroom. Typical cycle.

River saw stars. Jonah didn't stop and he didn't look like he *would be* stopping anytime soon. Pleas spilled out of River's mouth. *God*. Shame filled him, but fuck pride. River had little to begin with.

"Should have torn out your damn throat long ago."

Was tonight the night Jonah finally got careless? River desperately sought for anyone to come to his aid. But why would they? When had anyone dared stand up to Jonah?

Jesus, he was pathetic. Jonah dragged his battered body up by his shirt, his eyes narrowed to wolf-amber, his teeth lengthened to canines. Memories flashed through River's head. River licked his lips, tasted copper and his own despair. His defeat. He had never been a fighter, but River was sick of being the victim.

Something inside River splintered. Broke into two. He stopped taking his blows like a good submissive pup. River screeched and clawed. He fought and kicked, fingers sinking into Jonah's skin as his beast surged to the surface of his skin. Jonah snarled, easily tossing him against the wall. Pain streaked up his spine, but River forced himself unsteadily back to his feet.

"Looks like my bitch grew a spine." Jonah flashed River a toothy grin. "You're going to regret this, boy. At the end of this, you're going to roll over and offer me your throat and belly, and beg for the mercy I'm not going to fucking give you."

River spat out blood and placed a hand against the wall to avoid falling on his face. Forget shifting. River had zero chances of winning anyway. He was too weak, too inexperienced in a fight. By the time he finished shifting, Jonah would have torn out his throat.

"You want to let everyone in the pack know what's gotten you in such a mood, Jonah?" River asked, wiping the blood off his lips. "I know why. You rule us through fear, because you're not powerful enough.

You're nothing but a fucking bully, and when a real monster finally comes along, you're scared shitless."

"That's it. You've crossed the line, boy. You die tonight."

Before River could move a muscle, Jonah shoved him against the wall. Powerful and partially shifted claws dug against his neck. Jonah dragged him up until his legs uselessly kicked and dangled in the air. River gasped desperately for air as Jonah closed his hands over his windpipe. His vision began to blur.

Somewhere nearby, glass shattered. A bone-chilling howl sounded. *Why did that sound seem so familiar?*

From the corner of his eye River saw half-shifted bodies flying, moaning and twisting on the carpeted floor. A black blur cut through the pack like a battering ram.

One scrawny wolf with mottled gray fur ran at him with canines bared, but the outsider met him mid-leap, and tackled him to the ground. The gray wolf whimpered in submission, just as another sand-colored pack member came at the outsider from behind, clamping his teeth over the outsider's back. Snarling, the black wolf twisted like a well-oiled machine.

Jonah dropped River, whirling. River slumped against the wall, breathing hard.

The sandy wolf moaned in defeat a few paces away, paws twitching. The large bastard padded toward Jonah like it had all the time in the world. He could afford to. After asserting his dominance, the Redstone Hills wolves admitted defeat. River saw why the pack didn't have a chance. Old scars marred one side of the black wolf's muzzle and left flank, telling River he had seen his fair share of battles. Had lived in a world where he fought tooth and nail to survive.

A white wolf, Dan, lunged recklessly at him from the side. The outsider flattened his ears, turning in time to avoid Dan's rake across his throat. Relentless, Dan clamped his powerful jaws on his neck, refusing to let go. River thought it was an even fight, but the outsider shook Dan off with force then came upon him like a cat upon a fleeing mouse. Without hesitation, he tore out Dan's throat in one jerk. The other wolves remained where they were, reluctant to throw away their lives for Jonah.

By the time the outsider finished off Dan, Jonah finished shifting.

"Look out!" River rasped. Jonah let out a howl. He pounced on the black wolf, going all out for the kill. Claws extended, teeth snapping, Jonah aimed for the outsider's throat, barely missing by inches as the black beast danced away.

Jonah never had a chance, River realized. The outsider might outweigh Jonah by a couple of pounds, but he moved with an unexpected speed, like a beast fueled with a singular purpose.

On his back now, Jonah bared his throat and belly, sought mercy, but River knew it was all an act. He'd seen Jonah make the same plea to more powerful wolves before. Once the challenger had dropped his guard, Jonah took him out. The black wolf didn't make the same mistake.

He sunk his canines deep into Jonah's throat. The outsider fastened his teeth there even as his prey fought for every inch of his life, as if he wanted Jonah to feel the inevitability of his death before tearing out his throat. Blood spurted out in jets, spraying the stranger's muzzle and coat.

The black wolf spat out the wad of flesh, and let out a triumphant, earth-shattering howl. The other wolves cowered against the corners, making pathetic mewling noises as the pack bonds connecting them to Jonah were severed. River though, he threw back his head and laughed. Then kept on giggling hysterically. He didn't see the champion looming over him until it was too late.

"Holy shit." River looked up, expecting fangs and fur. His turn next, he knew, but malice remained absent.

All he saw was miles of sweat-soaked muscles and ink. The scent of fresh kill and blood hit his nose, but underneath the smell of fresh violence, lurked the alpha's signature scent. Pine mixed with cigarette smoke, leather and motor oil. Wolf musk. The scent of a powerful male.

"Something funny, little pup?"

Fingers curled into his hair and jerked him up. River mentally took inventory—cropped dark hair, hard denim-blue eyes set in a face lined with sharp angles. River's heart thumped painfully against his chest. Why did it hurt so much to breathe? It felt wrong, to feel emotions other than raw fear.

"Don't call me that. I have a damn name, you know." God. How could he still be talking? Worse still, the alpha didn't cuff him the way Jonah did when River mouthed off.

He leaned in close, severing what little distance was left between their bodies.

"Do you now, pup?"

Nothing about the alpha was soft, River realized. Every inch of him was hard, unrelenting, and cruel like steel. Speaking of hard, River became aware of the alpha's erection, pressing firmly against his belly. The way those frightening dead eyes stared right at him, as if he were intent on unearthing his soul. River's deepest secrets. His shame. Whatever thoughts crossed the man's mind, none of them were pleasant or safe.

The blatant truth was there too, whispering through the heat ignited between their bodies. The way the alpha's bare flesh collided against the thin material of River's shirt.

The man's lips curved into a smile. There was nothing nice about that smile either. River whimpered. His imagination ran on overdrive. River imagined a man like this—a man who saw what he wanted and took what he wanted, no questions asked—wouldn't be capable of sweet kisses or lovemaking. He would consume and devour. Take and leave him wanting and panting, without ever giving River an inch.

Jesus, what was this man doing to him?

"River Daniels, you have no fucking idea how long I've waited for this moment." The man's breath felt warm against his neck. River felt something wet—the alpha's tongue!—flicking and licking at his jumping pulse. "To meet you. Finally take you and make your sweet body mine."

River managed to find his wits. "How do you know my name?"

His brain might not be able to function, but his hands had other ideas. River didn't know what possessed him to touch, to explore. He palmed his way up the stranger, his unexpected savior's defined abs, the swirl of black ink up his ribs, his pectorals. River wanted to do more than touch. He needed to cross the line that divided flirting from fucking.

"I know a lot of things about you, River." He shrugged. "This wasn't in the fucking plan, but the end result is the same."

"What wasn't part of the plan, killing Jonah?"

"No, that was the objective. He just died far too fucking fast for my liking. I wanted—no, needed—to make the bastard pay."

River swallowed. Jesus. *Died too fast?*

The man standing in front of him might be a killer. Definitely dangerous. But some part of River knew, although he couldn't comprehend why, that the alpha wouldn't hurt him. Not when he had a raging hard-on and not when his body language conveyed what he wanted. Which was *River.*

Why? River wanted to ask. Why him, when he could have anyone? Worse—the way his body reacted, River wouldn't bother resisting the alpha's charms.

The alpha caught his wandering hands. River let out a gasp when he tightened his grip. That devilish grin widened when both of them realized the sound that came from River's lips wasn't one of refusal, but one of needy admission.

He didn't care if this was wrong, or if he wanted this dangerous stranger for all the wrong reasons. If it was because he saved River and River wanted to repay the favor, or because no other man had ever looked at River the way this man did—with desire hot enough to burn, to singe and leave lasting marks on his skin.

"Cole Reyes, you've made your point. Let the boy go. He's done you no harm," someone interrupted. Matthias stood cradling one broken arm with a determined expression on his face.

Cole. Finally, River had a name. Cole loosened his grip. River stayed where he was, hungry to know more about his savior and new captor. Could he still call Cole his captor, if he were willing?

A couple of the other wolves began to groan and return to consciousness. Did Cole purposely spare their lives? Some of them warily looked for possible escape routes, but a warning growl from Cole kept them from moving an inch.

"I'm surprised you're still alive, old man." Cole kept River cornered, but he shifted his body slightly to keep an eye on Matthias and the other wolves. *He was a careful man.* "But no, I don't fucking think so. This pup is mine, and I intend to keep him."

"Even without his consent? Where is the honor is that, Cole?" Matthias asked.

Cole's face darkened and took on a feral edge. "Don't fucking talk to me about honor, Matthias. Every last one of you betrayed me. I spent the last ten years rotting behind bars. Don't make me change my mind. It won't cost me a thing to reduce this place to a fucking slaughterhouse."

Matthias paled. Fear crawled down River's spine at those words. When he joined the pack, Jonah had already been the pack alpha, but he had heard awful rumors of the previous one. Supposedly, he was exiled and put behind bars for killing and raping a mortal woman.

"We did you wrong," Matthias admitted, sounding guilty. "We regret our actions to this day. We had no choice—"

Cole let out a disgusted snort. "Don't fucking give me excuses. I didn't come here for a reunion. I came here for Jonah's head."

"You don't want our apology? Fine, but leave the boy alone. He isn't some trophy you can keep. Just because he used to be Jonah's toy doesn't mean he had anything to do with Jonah or his deeds."

"Are you going to get in the way of what I want, Matthias? Go ahead. Try. I fucking dare you." Cole cracked both his knuckles. Looked Matthias in the eye. *God.* The undiluted rage emanating from Cole stunned River. Thick and heavy, unrelenting, and completely without mercy. How could anyone let so much anger consume him?

Matthias' silence was as good as any answer.

Cole turned his attention back to River. "Your master's dead, pup. I know what he was to you. You want to stay here, with the pack that turned a blind eye on your torment, or you want to come with me?"

"You're giving me a choice?" River couldn't help but ask. He shivered when Cole gave him a knowing look.

"We both know you're my toy now, but I want to hear the words from your own lips."

Possessive bastard. But River couldn't deny the truth. He had wanted to get the hell out of Redstone Hills for a long time, even though he knew he couldn't simply go back to his old way of life. Jonah had killed River's old self the day he let a lone wolf give Ron and River the bite. It pained him, but River knew that though he couldn't go back to the past, he could move forward. Even if that meant taking uncertain paths.

When Matthias and the others looked at Cole, all they saw was a killer who wanted vengeance. River hardly knew a single thing about Cole, but he knew enough. Saw through the tiny details the others couldn't, like the way Cole didn't injure the other wolves badly. River had a sneaking suspicion Cole hadn't planned on recklessly attacking Jonah in his home, but he wasn't naïve enough to think Cole did it for his sake.

"I don't have all night, pup," Cole warned.

Cole mentioned how he intended to take River away from Jonah for the sake of petty vengeance. He wasn't a decent man, certainly not River's prince in shining armor. He didn't come here to save River. Cole might have been wrongly imprisoned, but time behind bars could change a man. Warp him into something he wasn't.

Cole came here to claim him because he used to belong to his enemy. To take him as a prize. But was there anything wrong with wanting to be taken?

Nothing kept River in Redstone Hill. Jonah isolated him from everything else the moment he made River his toy. Ron, his only family was dead. Reconnecting with the people in his old life had never been an option, because *that* River Daniels—mortal and foolish with a bloated head full of dreams, had died a long time ago.

River held his gaze. "I want to come with you."

Cole showed him his teeth. "Good answer, pup."

Chapter Four

The steady purr of his bike, the powerful motor between his legs, and River's warmth behind him, made for one heady concoction. Triumph still sung in his veins, but Cole was far from sated. He still couldn't wrap his head around what had happened. How his blood had boiled and his vision had tinted red when he smelled River's fear from outside the house. Cole hadn't meant to linger. He came by to see if Jonah managed to get wind of his return.

The Redstone Hills pack didn't even sense his presence. 'Weak' and 'prey' were the two words that immediately came to his mind. The pack bonds hadn't felt that way when the old alpha used to rule, but with Jonah at the head, he had reduced the pack to whimpering dogs.

"Cole?" River hesitantly asked behind him, breath tickling against the nape of his neck. Cole expected River to be trembling by now, but the skinny arms around his frame tightened. He nearly lost it when River leaned his head against his back and held onto him like a safety net, when the first thing he should be doing was running as fast as he could.

River made a request to make a quick stop by his apartment. Cole obliged, expecting him to take his time, but River stuffed a few clothes, his wallet, and a shoebox containing some cash into a backpack, and announced he was ready. Also implying that he'd been ready to leave at a moment's notice.

Fuck. Explained a whole lot concerning what kind of damage that sick fucktard Jonah inflicted on him. Cole didn't need to know anything else. Even before Jonah started pummeling him, Cole smelled all of River's old hurts.

"What?" Cole asked, voice hoarse, thick with need.

Jesus. He needed to get off the road. Find some sleazy motel soon, or risk stopping by the road and fucking River in the open. Cole needed to sate the needs of his beast. Repressed for so long, it needed an outlet for release, and why not, when River proved to be a willing accomplice and not a captive?

"Thank you, for saving me."

Cole's cock twitched in his jeans at the sound of River's soft voice.

"I didn't come back to Redstone Hill to save you." Cole dispensed with lies and dragged the truth out in the open to avoid misunderstandings. "I took you because I could. Because you were Jonah's discarded toy."

"I know you think you're not a good man—"

Cole cut River off. "You don't know shit about me, pup. Don't start getting delusions either, because you're in for one hell of a disappointment."

The dim lights of Redstone Hill faded away behind them. Cole steered his bike to the open highway. He grinned when he caught sight of the sign of a seedy motel in the distance.

Cole got off the gravel road and entered the dirt path leading to the motel's empty lot. He killed the engine, got off and felt River following. "I'm going to have you now, whether you like it or not. Discard you when I'm done. You understand, pup?"

River bit his lip. He aimed huge, wounded brown eyes at Cole. Cole glimpsed the momentary vulnerability there, before River replaced it with anger. River crossed his arms, every line in his gorgeous body screamed stubborn defiance, doing little for Cole's cock.

Fuck, just when Cole thought Jonah had beaten most of the fight in him.

River muttered something under his breath.

"What?" Cole asked. "Speak the fuck louder."

"After you have me, what then?"

"You're not going to fight me?" Cole asked, amused.

"You seem to have the mistaken impression I didn't come with you out of my free will. Why would I miss the chance to ride a big bad alpha like you?"

River's breathing pitched when Cole gripped his wrist. Cole pressed River's hand to his mouth, and lashed his tongue at River's pulse. A soundless cry escaped River's lips. *Such a needy pup.*

"Make no fucking mistake, pup. If there's any riding to be done, it would be done by me. After I'm done with you? You can do whatever the hell you want. I'm not your fucking captor and you aren't my prisoner."

"I don't know what to say," River admitted.

Cole released his hand. Reached over to squeeze the back of River's neck and gently pushed him toward the motel. "I do. Let's get this party started."

He hardly remembered pulling out cash, taking the keys to their room, or what the dingy space looked like. All Cole saw was River.

Cole turned the lights on. The light bulb flickered like a dying flame, but both of them hardly cared. Cole slammed the door against the night wind and prying eyes, then pushed River against the wood, annoyed when River began to tug at his shirt.

Cole growled and pinned River's hands above his head. "I lead the dance here. We clear, pup?"

Cole traced the tip of his nose up the side of River's neck. River let out a throaty moan and pressed his body against Cole's.

"Clothes off. Please, I want to feel your skin against mine," River murmured.

To shut him up, Cole plundered his lips. This time River didn't simply lie back. Their tongues and teeth tangled until River conceded, letting Cole's prodding tongue in, then sucking down hard. The sweet taste of River flooded down his throat, eliminating any logical thought left in Cole's mind except for one.

Not enough.

Cole wanted more. No. He *needed* to taste more. To feel the slap of River's skin, his body pliant and eager against his own scarred and hard flesh. Releasing River's mouth and arms, he tore River's shirt, the ripping sound disturbing the silence. Cole began to yank down his jeans, but River caught his hand.

"I want to see you too," River insisted. Growling, Cole let him until no fabric got in the way of their mating.

"Happy?"

"Far from it. We've barely even started." River licked his lips, and then groaned when Cole dug his fingers into his hips. Apparently his pup liked a little bite to his pleasure. Mouthy too, but Cole rather liked River's sassy attitude. Fuck, it turned him on. To wipe away the cock-confidence on River's face, Cole knelt.

"Cole, what are you— "

Cole wrapped his fingers around River's base, and then tongued the pre-cum gathered at his tip. River groaned loudly above him. Cole paused. "What, never had a blow job, pup?"

"Not in a long time. Jonah…. Well…." River didn't need to say the rest.

Cole knew Jonah well enough. A man like Jonah would take, but never give back. Cole continued working River's base, applying just the right amount of pressure to his balls. He licked River, tip to balls, savoring the taste of him. Kept on teasing until River clasped the back of his neck and uttered the words Cole had always wanted to hear.

"Please, Cole. I won't be able to last."

Feeling generous, for now at least, Cole conceded. He took River's shaft between his lips. He gagged at first, but quickly got used to River's size. Cole didn't move his gaze from River's face as he applied suction with every inch he covered. He devoured every little moan and reaction he wrangled out of River's lips. *Such a responsive pup.* Cole doubted he wanted to part with River anytime soon. Maybe they could work something out if River wanted to stay.

"Cole, I'm going—" River whispered. A loud moan spilled out of him. His entire body shuddered as Cole swiftly withdrew from River's shaft. River's load coated his chest. Knowing he was capable of rendering River like this, face blissful and relaxed, made Cole's balls draw tight against his body, his cock rock hard and aching. Cole managed to find clean hand towels in the bathroom. After cleaning both of them, he found River's hand on his member.

"Time I return the favor," River said suggestively. Cole lifted River's hand and pressed a kiss on it. River looked unsettled by the tender gesture. Exposed to abuse and cruelty for so long, Cole knew it would take time and patience for his pup's wounds to heal. *What the fuck?* Since when did he start calling River his?

"Lie on the bed on your back." River looked relieved by the command.

"I would expect a man like you to want me on all fours the first time." River commented idly. His lean and slender body looked like sinful temptation against the flowery comforter. River swallowed when Cole crawled between his legs and grabbed his ankle.

"Who said anything about fucking you once? I'll fuck you in a hundred different positions all night long. Make sure you wouldn't be able to walk straight come morning." Cole palmed his way up River's knee, his inner thigh, then began to pump River's cock back to life with slow and steady movements. River moaned under his ministrations.

"Jesus Christ, Cole. You confuse the hell out of me. One moment you're rough, the next you're unexpectedly tender."

Cole growled, but River continued, despite his panting breaths as he worked his shaft. "Don't get me wrong. I know you're a hard man. You scare the shit out of me, but you're the only man who's ever helped me and looked at me that way."

"Like how?" Fuck. Why did River want to have the girly talk now of all times?

"Greedily, like you want everything, and not just my body."

Cole growled. "My patience is standing on thin ice. Spit out whatever the fuck you want to say, River. You want this, or you having second thoughts?"

"I want this," River said firmly. "But I'm terrified. Scared shitless, because I know this would be mind blowing, but you'll only leave me in the morning."

River looked panicked when Cole rolled off the bed. "Wait, Cole."

Cole only took out the lube from his back pocket. Werewolves didn't catch anything and he liked fucking bareback. River looked relieved to see him return.

"Who said anything about letting you go?" Cole asked. River seemed to understand the words he couldn't grit out. *You can come with me, for now.*

"Okay, good," River breathed. Smiled up at Cole like a happy puppy as Cole lifted River's legs up Cole's shoulders. Shit. Cole hated that lethal look. It made him all soft. Fallible.

He drizzled a generous amount of lube over River's crack, then over his own fingers. River squirmed when Cole teased the puckered ring, groaned when he finally slid one slick finger in, then a second.

"Please, Cole."

"I haven't even started and you're already begging me, pup?" Cole asked, amused.

River pouted. "You're such a damn tease."

Cole smirked, then scissored his fingers to prepare River. He nudged his tip into River's asshole. Sensing the change in River's breathing, he said, "Breathe easy, baby. I'm going to go slow, make sure you get used to me before I start riding you hard, you understand?"

"Yeah."

River relaxed his muscles and Cole pushed his way in. He groaned as River's tight heat enveloped him. River let out a sigh once he pushed passed the tight ring of muscle. "God, Cole. You're huge, but you feel so good."

Cole grinned, sunk his way hilt-deep. "Nicest compliment anyone paid me. Ready for me to move, baby?"

"Ride me hard. Please."

Cole complied. Sinking his hands into the flesh of River's hips, he began to move, fast and faster, deep and deeper until the bed creaked with the force of his thrusts. River moaned, clawed at the sheets, and still urged him to go faster. Growling, Cole continued the collision and merging of their bodies.

Jolts of electricity crawled up his chest and core, pushing him closer to the tipping point. Cole pulled out, shifted his angle, and plunged into River yet again. River gasped, screaming out his name as Cole aimed repeatedly for his prostate. Cole reached out for River's steel-hard cock and began to pump him in tune with his strokes.

"Come all over my hand." His words triggered River's climax. River screamed out his name again, spilling strings of his warm cum over his chest and hand.

It wasn't long before Cole's orgasm took hold of him. The pressure building inside him exploded. Gripping River's thighs hard, Cole emptied his load, and then blanketed River's body with his.

River smiled shyly at him, and then offered his throat. Cole pulled him close, thumbed the sweat-soaked and silky expense of skin.

"Do it, Cole. Please, make me yours."

"Do you understand what you're begging me for?" Cole had to ask.

"I'm certain. Actually, I knew the moment you came tearing into Jonah's house to get to me."

Cole licked at the skin thoughtfully. His blood hammered in his ears and throat, and his beast itched against his skin, surging, wanting to tie itself to River's wolf. Cole saw it clearly now. Knew his wolf had been called to River's hurt beast when Jonah decided to teach River a lesson. *Mate.* One simple word that could tie them to each other metaphysically until death.

But both of them knew nothing came easy. Cole had learned that the hard way. Happy endings and fairy tales didn't exist. Men like him needed to forge their own path. Fight their way to get what they want.

Cole unsheathed his canines, felt River's fingers gently nudging the back of his head in encouragement. It was enough. Maybe River had come with him out of need and desperation. Maybe those two emotions triggered this, whatever this was, but if Cole looked passed the primal savage, he glimpsed something else. Not permanence or security, but a promise of a future.

Cole sunk his canines home, and made River his.

After making his mark, Cole leaned against River's chest for a moment. Letting the adrenaline singing in his veins die down. River stroked his hair, not saying a word. Through their fresh bonds, Cole sensed his emotions. Contentment. Peace. Tenderness. Affection Cole had yet to earn.

River threw him a questioning look when Cole got off him. "Going to find a first aid kit, the motel ought to have one."

"Don't forget to put on clothes," River reminded him.

"Do I detect a note of jealously?" Cole chuckled when River crossed his arms and glared at him. "I'll be right back, baby."

River snuggled happily into the sheets. "Don't take long."

****

River woke up to the sunlight streaming through the dusty blinds of the room. Bed empty, save for him. River jolted up, desperately searching for Cole. Nothing. Not even the clothes Cole wore the night before.

"Don't panic," River whispered to himself. Still, he drew his knees painfully to his chest. Kept rubbing at the bandage on his neck, and told himself furiously not to cry. God. The bandage was fresh. Cole bothered to change it before he left.

"Fucking bastard." River knew he only had himself to blame. After all, didn't Cole tell him what he intended to do after he fucked River? The chill in the room made River shiver. "What the hell was I thinking? Who would fucking want me?"

River's hand crept to the bandage on his neck. Cole asked didn't he? Did Cole bite him without caring about the consequences? Alphas were different from other wolves after all. Maybe emotions rode Cole, or… River didn't want to think about the other reason. That maybe Cole changed his mind.

In the dark, it was easy to lose to base emotion. To let desire decide for them. But in daylight, maybe Cole finally saw what River was. A discarded pup.

A key sliding into the lock made River jump. He crawled back to the edge of the bed. The door swung open. *Oh god. Was it one of the Redstone Hill pack coming back for revenge?*

"Pup, you awake?"

River didn't know why he started crying, hearing the sound of Cole's voice. Cole put down bags of fast food on the table, and then frowned at him. He snarled softly and quickly came by the side of the bed. "What happened?" Cole asked, voice cold, pissed, protective.

River sniffed, looked at Cole through red-rimmed eyes. "I thought you decided you didn't want me. I thought you left without telling me."

Cole let out a breath, and then sat beside him. "Then why the fuck would I put my mating mark on you, pup? That bite on your neck tells the world you're mine. You think I'm going to just let you go?"

River glared at him. "You don't have to be such an arrogant asshole about it."

"Why shouldn't I? I like telling the world you're mine." River had a couple of smart remarks to that, but the words died when Cole began rubbing circles on his back. He let Cole pull his head to his lap. River closed his eyes and nuzzled his head against Cole's thigh, sighing.

"Like that, don't you, pup?"

At the start, River got pissed whenever Cole called him that, but now he found he liked it. Cole wasn't going to leave him alone. River let out a breath he hadn't realized he was holding. Cole continued sending warm, soothing energy through their mate bond.

"I got us breakfast from the nearby diner. Didn't know what you'd want, so I got one of each."

"You're going to make me fat." River rubbed at Cole's knee. He realized they might be practically strangers at this point, who didn't know the basics like each other's wants and dislikes.

Cole tugged one of his ears. "Thinking much?"

"Nah." River rose, planted a kiss on the side of Cole's jaw. "Just thinking I don't know a lot about you, but that's okay."

"Yeah?"

River watched Cole pick up a few of the bags, and returned to the bed, chewing on a piece of waffle. "We have all the time in the world to find out."

"Damn right."

The End

www.angelvoisen.blogspot.com

7 AUTHOR ANTHOLOGY

YELLOW EYES

Copyright © 2015

Gale Stanley

Chapter One

Wyat stepped out of the shower and snagged an old towel, pulling the rusty hook and a piece of plaster along with it. He made a mental note on his to-do list, then he tossed the hook and rubbed himself down. The friction of stiff, scratchy fabric on flesh set off sparks that made him throw back his head and howl.

The sun hadn't even set, but already he felt the tug of a full moon. A shifter could no more deny the lunar pull than he could stop breathing. Once every month, Wyat's lupine pheromones took over and all he could think about was getting his rocks off. In a few hours, he'd be ready to stick his dick into anything that moved. Well, maybe not anything. Wyat didn't do pussy.

Funny how things turn out. The pack never envisioned a gay man as their alpha, but fate had other plans. Leadership passed from father to son and there was no doubt royal blood pulsed in Wyat's veins. So did the desire to suck cock—but for a long time Wyat had kept that part of his genetic endowment hidden. Wolf-shifters were manly men, and they expected their leader to fight harder, *fuck* harder, and produce lots of pups.

Acting the part of a domineering prick came easy to Wyat. He already had the packaging. His six-foot-five, two hundred and forty pound body was a lean, sculpted canvas for some intimidating ink. A half sleeve on his left arm contained tribal tats representing loyalty, honor, wisdom, and strength. On his right bicep, he wore the sign of the shifter, a man's face and a wolf, forming a circle as if they were two halves of a whole. Wyat's back bore his family tree, a masterpiece that took two sittings to complete. The pack tattoo artist added Wyat's favorite quote beneath it. *A haven in a heartless world.* A wolf was nothing without his pack. It pained Wyat that so many on that tree had been lost in the war, his father among them.

Ironically, the alpha hadn't died in battle. The war had already ended, but Wyat considered it a casualty just the same. In the aftermath, everyone worked to rebuild what had been destroyed. The old man was repairing a roof when he lost his balance and fell thirty feet to the ground. He died instantly.

Ready or not, Wyat had been thrust into the role of alpha. The Separatists had welcomed him with open arms. They'd always been at odds with Wyat's father, a pacifist who believed in an ideal society, where shifters and humans intermingled and worked together. Equality, peace, and prosperity for all. A pipedream, in Wyat's opinion. Humans were two-faced. Their treaties worthless. Any wolf who put his trust in humanity would end up on a leash.

There was no honeymoon period for Wyat when he came into power. Shortly after he buried his father the elders approached him with a list of eligible females. As alpha, he was expected to produce heirs and populate the pack. Wyat begged to differ. He intended to remain a bachelor. The more they pushed, the more Wyat dug in his heels and refused. The elders wouldn't let it go, they threatened to depose him, and Wyat had finally blurted out his secret. 'I'm gay. I'm never getting married. Deal with it.'

Determined to live life on his own terms, Wyat had moved into an abandoned dump in the gay ghetto, and cultivated a group of loyal followers. Long months of backstabbing and brawls almost tore the pack apart, but Wyat never backed down from a fight. No one was going to take away the honor that rightfully belonged to him.

It was largely due to his beta's wisdom and diplomacy that the rest of the pack was finally won over. That, and Wyat's promise to initiate free elections in the future.

It's a new world. Wyat pulled a clean white t-shirt over his head, and then slicked back his damp hair. He didn't do deodorant or cologne. A wolf didn't cover up his god-given scent. Natural pheromones were more than enough to turn on another shifter. And on a full-moon night, anything goes. Sweaty, funky, musky. It was all good.

Struggling with the zipper on his jeans, he was sorely tempted to go out buck-naked. *Why not?* He'd be taking his clothes off sooner rather than later. *We claim we're not like them, but we dress up and play human all the same. Why are we still trying to prove we're civilized?* Frustrated, Wyat pulled at the zipper—

"Fuck!" And caught a tuft of pubic hair in the process.

"What's up?"

Wyat's head jerked up, and he glared at his beta. "Did you forget how to knock?"

Jack shrugged. "Lock your door if you don't want company." His gaze dropped to Wyat's crotch, and he grinned. "Need a hand?"

Accepting help meant admitting he couldn't do something, a sign of weakness that Wyat's pride wouldn't allow. "No."

"You sure? That's gonna hurt like a motherfucker."

Wyat snarled. "Piss off."

Jack put his hands up in surrender and stepped back.

Wyat clenched his teeth, gripped the tab and gave it a strong tug. The zipper came down, taking the hair with it. He muffled a yelp and clapped a hand to his junk.

Jack burst out laughing. "Ah. Poor baby. Want me to kiss it and make it better?"

"Fuck you," Wyat spat out. He hobbled to the kitchen for an ice pack, Jack on his heels.

Wyat sat on a rickety chair, stretched out his legs, and dropped the towel-covered ice on his lap. "Don't know why I bother with jeans. I'll just be taking them off when I get to the bar."

"Keeps us civilized," Jack said. "Speaking of which, maybe you should do some hedging down there, or stop going commando."

Wyat smiled benignly. Only Jack could push his buttons and get away with it. "Why bother? We're not like them. We can dress up and play human all we want, but they're never gonna accept us."

"We have to try. We need their help to rebuild, especially with implementing new technology."

"Fuck technology! Information overload started the war in the first place. They were spying on us for years."

Jack shook his head. "Maybe we didn't have fancy surveillance equipment and drones, but we did our fair share of spying."

"Don't go there," Wyat warned. "You sound more like my father every day."

Jack kept talking as if he hadn't heard. "And the militant Separatists among us stirred things up—"

"With good reason. In case you've forgotten, it was the humans who claimed there were too many of us."

"They only wanted a few sanctions and restrictions on immigration."

Wyat snorted. "Sanctions? Hah! You mean mass murder. Separation of species is the only answer. Humans are incapable of getting along with each other, let alone a different species." Wyat carefully zipped up his fly. "We don't need their help."

"With all due respect, Alpha, I don't agree. Fangs and fur don't cut it in today's world. It's all about technology, and if we don't make sure our kids are prepared, they'll end up serving human masters."

Wyat pushed his chair back violently. The ice pack fell to the floor as he stood. "There'll be another war before that happens."

"That's what I'm afraid of," Jack said softly.

"That's why you're not the alpha," Wyat stated. Jack was one hell of a wingman, but way too careful about avoiding risk and confrontation. *He's a worrier not a warrior.* "I'm not afraid of anything."

Chapter Two

Quitting time. Camden laid his sledge on the ground and wiped sweat from his brow. He'd put in a good eight hours with this road crew, but it was almost dusk, and he was anxious to go home and take care of his mother. Anxious to get his hands on that pay envelope, too. They needed the money bad.

A lean six-footer with smooth hands and a shy manner, Camden didn't look like a construction worker. And he had yellow eyes. At first, the foreman didn't want to hire him, but after he saw how Camden could swing a sledgehammer he changed his mind. Repairing roads was tough, physical work. Even harder without electricity or jackhammers. Sold on Camden's superior strength, the man reluctantly offered him one day's work.

Camden thought he'd be bored breaking up concrete all day, but swinging a sledgehammer wound up being the perfect job for a half-breed wolf who had a bone to pick. Every time that hammer pounded the concrete, Camden imagined it crushing his father's skull. A hell of a lot of concrete had been pulverized today. His boss would be pleased.

The foreman appeared to be a stand-up guy. Camden was counting on strength and enthusiasm to win the man over and earn him a permanent place on the crew. Spotting the foreman talking with a small group, Camden walked over to collect his pay.

"Everything okay?" The foreman asked.

"Yeah. It's almost dusk, and I'm done."

"Nope. We're not nearly done. If that full moon comes out, we can work all night. Right boys?" The others nodded.

"I'm sorry, I can't stay."

"Not acceptable. I expect you to put in the same hours as everybody else."

Camden bristled at the unfairness. Everybody else took numerous breaks, while he kept working. "I gotta get home to my mother."

"Hear that, boys. He has to get home to mommy. That's a new one."

Camden's face heated, and he averted his eyes. "It's the truth. She's sick, and—"

One of the guys grinned, showing off a set of discolored, rotten teeth. "Sick, my ass. He doesn't want us to see him turn into a werewolf when the full moon comes up."

Everybody laughed. Camden forced a smile. "That's just an old myth."

"But you do turn into a horndog," the foreman said. "I hear your kind will fuck anything that moves when a full moon rises. You can't help yourself."

"Shit," snaggletooth blurted out. "Let him go home, boss. I don't wanna be looking over my shoulder all night."

I wouldn't touch you with my sledgehammer. Unless I was smashing it over your head. Rattled, Camden worked hard to keep his cool. These men were ignorant human trash who couldn't tell fact from fiction. Camden didn't get horny, not even under a full moon. Maybe it was the weird mix of genes that made up his biology. Maybe he just had too many other things to worry about.

Just as well. Not many humans wanted him, only werewolf groupies looking for a thrill. Sometimes he gave it to them. When he needed the money bad enough. "I'm not like that," Camden said.

"Yeah, right." The foreman sneered. "I never should have hired you. A man who thinks with his dick is no good to me. Go on. Get out of here."

Camden snarled. His fists clenched at his sides. "Pay me first. I worked all day—"

Snaggletooth picked up a pry bar. Another man grabbed a hammer. They closed in on Camden.

"Hold on, boys. One of you gets hurt, we can't finish this job on time." The foreman reached in his pocket and pulled out some bills. He shoved them at Camden. "Take this before I change my mind. And don't come back."

Inside, Camden's guts were churning, but he was outnumbered, and his instincts shouted flight, not fight. He'd never even shifted—didn't even know if he could, but these men thought he was an animal who only lived to fight and fuck. They would never believe otherwise, and they wouldn't think twice about killing him.

Camden grabbed the money and took off. He didn't stop until he put a mile between him and the crew. Then he sank to the ground and counted the bills. *Fucker!* It was only one third of what he expected. Bile rose in his throat, but he calmed himself. Things could have turned out worse. If he got killed, who would take care of Lila?

He felt like crying. *Man up.* Life was hard. He should be used to it by now, but every injustice brought buried emotions to the surface. Some wounds would never heal. Especially when they concerned his mother. He knew Lila was exhausted, her world torn and battered. She felt she had nothing left to live for. Nothing except her son. Her need kept Camden going, gave him a reason to look for work every day and stay out of fights. Camden walked a little faster. He was a long way from the dump they called home. One room and one meal a day. And they wouldn't have that much longer if Camden didn't get back and give the landlord some money. *Fucking war!*

By the time Camden was old enough to fight, the war had ended, and thank goodness for that, because he didn't identify with either side. He'd heard the stories often enough, though. Lila wanted him to know his human roots. She talked about her family all the time, but when Camden asked about his father, all she could offer was a horror story. Camden was a child of rape.

The pack of shifters that killed Lila's family in an ambush twenty years ago, raped her and left her for dead. But Lila survived. Injured and in shock, she wandered through the smoking ruins of her home until someone found her and brought her to a homeless shelter. Months passed before she realized she was pregnant. There was no one Lila could turn to for help. Wartime rape was considered a crime against humanity. Forced abortions were common, and live births were tossed off Suicide Bridge like garbage. *"But, I already loved you,"* Lila would assure Camden. *"I lost my family. I didn't want to lose you, too."*

When her growing belly grew too big to hide, Lila had left the shelter. An abandoned building provided a roof over her head, but no electricity or running water. That's where she gave birth to the son she named Camden, after a city that no longer existed. With another mouth to feed, Lila was forced to trade sex for money or food.

One night an enterprising John offered Lila a job in his roadhouse. *"Just keep the yellow-eyed brat out of sight,"* he had told her. *"Don't let him near my customers."* Grateful for a roof over their heads, and food in their bellies, Lila took the offer.

Eventually, the active war ended. A peace treaty was in effect, but reality was anything but peaceful. When Lila took Camden out, people pointed and whispered. *"Look, it's one of those yellow-eyed dogs,"* They would say. Worried for his safety, Lila kept Camden isolated in their room at the roadhouse. Camden accepted his life. What choice did he have? He and Lila were better off than most. At least they had each other.

Lila brought him old books and taught him to read. Taught him other things, too, history and math. Camden studied while his mother took her clothes off downstairs in the bar. If the men liked what they saw, they paid for a blowjob or a fuck. When they came upstairs, Camden hid in the closet.

Camden hated the men, but they needed the money. When he got older, he begged the landlord to give him a job instead. The man laughed at him. "Nobody wants to fuck a yellow-eyes." Camden hated the wolf eyes he'd inherited from his father. Sometimes he wished he'd never been born, but he understood why his mother chose to keep him. He was her only family, and she loved him.

Then consumption attacked her lungs. There were no antibiotics, and Lila got sicker and sicker. Few men wanted to pay for sex with a woman who coughed up blood and looked like a skeleton. The proprietor made it clear: Lila and her half-breed would have to start paying rent if they wanted to keep the room. Once again, Camden offered to work, serving, mixing drinks, cleaning toilets... he'd do anything. But just like always, the proprietor refused. *"No way! My customers would freak out if they saw a yellow-eyes behind the bar or handling their food."* The running battle over unpaid rent escalated and Camden traveled farther and farther to look for work.

Camden had such high hopes for this job. He wasn't coming home with good news, but at least he had money for cough medicine. The apothecary shop was just closing, but Camden pounded on the door. An annoyed chemist let him in, and for an extra fee, he mixed the elixir.

Camden practically ran the rest of the way, anxious to get the medicine to his mother. He rounded the back of the roadhouse and tried the door. Locked. He banged on it with his fists, but nobody came to let him in. Well, fuck it. He'd just have to use the front door tonight.

The landlord was busy behind the bar, and he didn't see Camden come in. Camden scanned the room, but there was no sign of his mother. Sick as she was, she spent most of her time in bed. Camden headed for the stairs that led up to their room, but a heavy hand landed on his shoulder stopping him.

"Where the fuck you going, boy?"

Camden turned, but he looked down at his boots. "Up to my room."

"It ain't your room anymore. I warned you—"

"I have money." Camden pulled the bills out of his pocket. "This should take care of our rent."

"You're too late. I gave the room to someone else." The landlord pointed to a bag in the corner. "There's your stuff."

Camden's heart missed a beat. "Where's my mother?"

"How the hell should I know?"

Camden wanted to punch the smug expression off the man's face. Taunts from the customers fueled his anger. Like a cornered animal, ready to confront its attackers, Camden drew his lips back, and tilted his head forward. His hands curled into fists. Then, from the corner of his eye, he saw a man smash a liquor bottle and come toward him. Others followed.

No way did Camden want to waste precious time fighting when he should be looking for his mother. He turned and ran, grabbing the bag on his way.

Chapter Three

Camden checked a few places where his mother might be waiting for him. An all-night diner that made good, strong coffee. Her favorite bench in the little overgrown city park. The old church.... Each stop took him further into a blighted area that looked like a ghost town.

Frantic, Camden hurried along the cracked sidewalks, crushing beer cans, broken glass, and cigarette butts under his boots. It was hard to believe this used to be a thriving neighborhood. There was a scattering of occupied houses, but mostly abandoned buildings and vacant lots. All the traffic lights were dead. Every corner had a stop sign, but drivers who could afford cars and the gas to run them rarely obeyed signs. Camden always checked for oncoming traffic before he stepped into the street.

An old car stopped at the crosswalk just as Camden reached the curb. The driver honked, and waved at him to go. Camden waved back, and started to cross. As soon as he stepped in front of the car, the driver hit the gas. It scared the piss out of Camden, and he dropped his bag as he ran for safety. Panting, he stood on the curb, watching the taillights get smaller. Then he took a deep breath and walked out to collect his stuff. He bent to retrieve a book, and the screech of tires jerked him upright.

Oh my god. The son of a bitch is turning back. Playing games? Or out to kill me?

Camden didn't wait to find out. He ran. He didn't stop until he was sure the car wasn't following him. Shaking uncontrollably, he sank to the ground, and leaned back against a broken hydrant. *Why do they hate me so much?* But he already knew the answer. To the humans, he was still the enemy, a yellow-eyed dog. Camden couldn't blame them. He hated the shifters as much as they did. Hated himself, too.

I wish I'd never been born.

He looked down at the book he was still clutching in his hands. His mother's bible. A note was sticking out from the well-worn pages.

Goodbye, my sweet boy. I wish to spare us both from my slow and horrible decline, and this is the only way. Prevail and the future is yours. Please don't be sad. You'll always be in my heart, and someday we'll be reunited.

Your loving mother.

Camden's heart twisted and he started crying. He knew exactly where she'd gone. Blinded by tears, he leaped to his feet and ran to Suicide Bridge. It was chilly and quiet, except for the lapping of waves. Camden lifted himself over the rail, and stared down at the murky water. There was nothing to see, but he knew in his heart that she'd jumped. Once she made up her mind, there was no going back.

Lila had been the one constant in his life. No matter what misery he had to endure in this fucked up world, she'd been there to back him up. Now, he had no one.

I can't make it on my own.

"Why did you leave me behind?" Camden screamed.

You don't have to stay behind. A voice in his head told him to jump. Camden was prepared to die, but suddenly, another voice spoke to him.

Is this what you really want? A coward's death? Avenge your mother first. An eye for an eye.

Camden made his decision. He could die any time. Why not get revenge first? He had no hope of finding his father, but he'd settle for another yellow-eyed monster. They were all the same.

Camden climbed down, and followed the pedestrian walkway until he left the bridge behind. The clouds drifted off, and a full moon appeared to light his way. He'd never been on this side of the bridge, and curiosity overwhelmed him.

Camden knew very little about *that* side of himself. Living among humans, Camden did his best to fit in. Trying to hide his shifter traits had become second nature. As a kid, he wore sunglasses to hide his eyes, but it only attracted more attention, so he gave it up. Humans were a suspicious bunch, and Camden learned not to let anyone get too close. But blending in only went so far for a man with yellow eyes.

The west looked a lot like the east. A road littered with the residue of war, ruined buildings, rusted vehicles, broken glass… They were all familiar reminders of the carnage. Eventually signs of life started to appear. Houses and shops, some boarded up, others clearly inhabited. Camden kept to the shadows. He had no clear idea of where he was headed. He would let fate lead him.

Suddenly, a door opened, and the sound of male laughter and drunken voices drifted out. Camden's heart pounded in his ears, and he ducked into an alley to hide. Entering enemy territory without a plan had been stupid. Suicide by wolf. What did it matter? He had nothing left to live for. As long as he took one of them with him, he'd die happy.

****

The lights of The Rusty Trombone drew Wyat as surely as the light of the moon, and the scent of sex drifted on the breeze. But Wyat couldn't wait. A slave to his pheromones, he spun, leaped, and pinned Jack to the ground.

Fuck! Wyat stared down at his beta.

Jack's eyes glittered, his nostrils flared. "Do it."

Mutual need aside, the top dog did not fuck his beta. Wyat sprung to his feet before he could change his mind and took off in a sprint. He reached The Rusty Trombone a few seconds before Jack.

When the pack rebuilt, they couldn't decide what to call their bar. Then, one full-moon night, a drunken shifter gave every man in the pack a rusty trombone, and everyone agreed the bar should be named for the sex act, a simultaneous rim-job, hand-job.

Jack opened the door and let Wyat enter first. The smell of sweat, sex, and testosterone hit Wyat hard. The bar was a dump, but it had the necessities. Beer, loud music, and a pack of horny wolves. Upstairs, there were rooms with mattresses on the floor, but not many wolves opted for privacy. Grady, one of Jack's frequent fuck buddies, was already on the dance floor, and that's where Jack headed.

Nobody tended bar on full-moon nights so Wyat grabbed a beer from a cooler on the floor. He leaned back against the empty bar, took a long swallow, and then held the can to his face to cool off.

His gaze settled on a tall, dark shifter who danced alone. The boy's white t-shirt was dark with sweat. Somehow, he pulled it off, and flung it away without missing a beat. Well-worn jeans hugged his slim hips, enhancing every shake of his ass. Wyat wiped saliva from his mouth. The moon was rising, and it pulled at every nerve ending. Hot blood surged through Wyat's veins, filling his cock and making him eager to fuck.

The dancer caught Wyat staring. He stared back, popped a button on his fly and let his jeans ride lower, trying to entice Wyat with a glimpse of his bush.

Tease! Another buzz of arousal shot to Wyat's groin. *I want a piece of that.*

Wyat took a step toward the boy, but someone beat him to it. *Mine!* Wyat's temper flared, then waned. An alpha could take what he wanted, but animal instinct told Wyat to wait. He settled back to watch the show.

Big Red swiveled his hips behind the dancer. The boy bent his knees, and rubbed his ass against Red's groin. Red let out a howl, and they settled into a hardcore grind. Lyle, the pack tattoo artist, strutted across the dance floor with an arrogant swagger. Picking up their rhythm, Lyle moved in close, gripped the kid by the neck, and yanked him forward for a kiss. From behind, Red nipped the boy's neck and pinched his nipples. Lyle started working on the kid's zipper.

One, two, three, he and Red had their partner's pants off. The boy wasn't complaining. His rock hard dick begged for attention, and the two older, more assertive wolves appeared ready to gobble it up. Lyle sank to his knees and swallowed the boy's prick, sucking like a vacuum hose. It didn't take sixty seconds for the kid to shoot. He must have scored some kind of record. Big Red was already spreading the boy's cheeks, ready to shove his cock up that tight ass right there on the dance floor. *Full-moon lust.* Wyat almost came in his pants.

Wyat was ready to choose a partner, but first he needed to take a piss. He headed for the back door that led to the alley.

****

Camden burrowed under a pile of old newspapers, cardboard and rotting garbage. Lost in his thoughts, he didn't realize he wasn't alone until the shifter was almost on top of him. The hairs on the back of his neck stood straight up. Holding his breath, Camden stayed as still as possible while the shifter unzipped and took a piss not two feet away. The man's impressive anatomy was so distracting that Camden let out a breath. Silently cursing himself, he clapped his hand over his mouth.

"I know you're there. I smelled you as soon as I walked outside."

Shit! Camden thought the garbage covering him would also cover his scent. Not so. Suddenly, he was learning more than he wanted to know about his other side. They had huge genitalia and heightened senses. Obviously, Camden was no match for a full-blooded shifter.

The big man gave himself a squeeze and a shake, but didn't bother to tuck himself in. A few steps brought him uncomfortably close to Camden's hiding spot.

Camden's gaze slid up a pair of powerful thighs encased in denim, and got no further than the shifter's perfect cock. Curving up from its dark nest, it swelled with arousal and demanded attention. The man fisted the root and tugged, milking a bit of precum from the slit.

A robust, musky scent filled Camden's nostrils, and imprinted on his brain. Suddenly, he had to have that big, warm cock in his mouth. It wouldn't take much to close the distance between them, and lap up those glistening beads of fluid. God, he wanted to.

"Get out here, and let me take a look at you."

The demanding voice brought Camden back to his senses. He tensed his muscles, willing himself not to move, but arousal burned between his thighs. *What's wrong with me?* He was no virgin, but the humans who paid him for sex never made him feel like this. This man hadn't even touched him, yet Camden's entire body hummed with an urgent need to get close to him.

"Don't make me drag you out." The shifter chuckled. "On second thought, it might be fun."

A bolt of excitement shot right to Camden's groin. His head jerked up, knocking off some of his covering, and Camden locked gazes with the best looking man he'd ever seen. Not human pretty, but a god with shaggy dark hair that framed an angular face and a stubbled jaw. *And those eyes!* My god, those eyes were beautiful, hypnotic. Camden had judged his own eyes by human standards, and thought them ugly. He'd been wrong.

"Well now, what do we have here?" Full lips curved in a predatory smile that bared perfect white teeth. "Do you know where you are, half-breed?" The shifter paused for a few seconds. "I bet you do. I bet your human lovers don't satisfy you, and you're here to get your tip wet with one of your own kind."

That hit home. "I'm nothing like you."

A low growl rumbled from the shifter. "You're fooling yourself, boy. But you don't fool me. Come out of there and I'll give you what you want. I'll hurt you so good, you'll never want to go back east."

Kill me, is what you really mean. But, it's all good, 'cause I'm taking you with me. Camden felt around the ground for anything he could use as a weapon. His hand closed on a large shard of glass. He only had one move, but it was a move the shifter would least expect. Camden leaped out of his hiding place and ran straight toward the man. Ran and dived, head first, hard as he could. But it was Camden who went down. *Not supposed to work this way.* Stunned, Camden sat on his ass. A split second later, the shifter hauled him up by his shirt, and slammed him against the wall. Camden brought his hands up to punch his assailant, but the shifter evaded him easily.

"A tough guy, huh? Good. I hate playing with a chickenshit."

"I'm not playing," Camden spat out.

"Well, you're lucky I am, or you'd be dead by now. Tell me—"

Camden drove a knee into the shifter's balls. The big man clenched his teeth, but he managed to unleash a punch to Camden's jaw that made his head snap back against the wall. Stars floated in front of his eyes. When Camden shook them off, everything went dark.

Chapter Four

Wyat stood in the alley looking down at the unconscious half-breed. *He's playing possum.* "Get up you crazy fucker."

The boy didn't move.

"Come on. I didn't you hit that hard."

A moonbeam reached into the alley, reminding Wyat that everybody was fucking except him.

"Okay, you stubborn shit, stay there. I'm leaving."

Wyat stomped to the mouth of the alley, stopped and listened. Nothing. *Damn it.* He turned and went back. The boy was lying there, exactly as he'd left him.

This isn't right. The half-breed scum attacked *him.* There was no reason for Wyat to feel guilty. But he did. Wolves communicated by smell. Sometimes a man's scent told a truer story than his mouth. Wyat took a good sniff and he didn't smell a rat. Just a sad, frightened young man who put on a good show of bravado.

Now what? The more Wyat stared at the boy, the more appealing he became. His human biology softened his feral side, making him way too pretty. Why should Wyat leave him here for some other wolf to enjoy? *Mine!* Scooping him up, Wyat tossed the boy over his shoulder and carried him home.

Wyat could travel quickly when he wanted to. He arrived at his front door in record time, kicked it open, and carried his prize inside. Heading straight to the bedroom, he dumped the still unconscious young man on his bed. Wyat pulled off the boy's boots. His feet were well-formed, with just a sprinkling of hair, and his toenails were trimmed. *So pretty.* Wyat wanted a look at the rest.

The half-breed's face was turned to the window, as if he were seeking help from the moon, but his eyes remained closed while Wyat removed his shirt and admired his chest. A sexy smattering of golden-brown hair divided his pecs. Not as hairy as a wolf, but not totally smooth either.

Wyat pulled at the kid's jeans, and an uncut, hard cock sprang out. *Very nice.* Nice enough to get Wyat drooling. Only a wolf could be out cold and still sport a boner like that. Wyat was pleased. With his boyish looks, lean muscled physique, and moderate body hair, the half-breed was an exotic treat. And lucky to be here. The pack would eat him alive.

Of course, he might not think so when he wakes up. Wyat could easily imagine his captive trying to sneak out of the house. That would be dangerous. Strangers wandering around under a full moon were prey. He could be hurt before Wyat chased him down. Precautions had to be taken for his own good.

Wyat went to the closet, retrieved a few lengths of rope, and tied the boy to the bed. Every touch made him want to claim the boy now, but he didn't relish an unconscious partner. Impatience prodded him. Wolves were hardheaded. The kid should be awake already. Still, the boy did have a fragile side. Maybe an ice pack? Wyat made a quick trip to the kitchen. When he returned, the vision before him made him stop and stare.

In his wildest dreams, he wouldn't have imagined this. A human... well, half human, and a beautiful one at that, restrained in his bed, and already hard. Wyat's prick leaked. His mouth watered. He didn't know how much longer he could wait.

****

Consciousness pulled at Camden. He tried to roll over, but he couldn't move. Panic sent adrenaline pumping through his body, and his eyes flew open. *Where the fuck am I?* Moonlight illuminated an unfamiliar room, and Camden realized he was in big trouble. Naked, he lay flat on his back, limbs spread wide and tied to the four corners of someone's bed. Like a wild animal, Camden struggled to get free of the ropes.

"Ah... the rest of you is finally awake."

Camden's head jerked up. The shifter from the alley stood at the foot of the bed staring at him.

"Like what you see?" Camden spat.

"Very much." The low drawl held a touch of amusement.

Crossing his arms over his chest, the shifter studied Camden's body, head to toe. His stance exuded authority, but his eyes glittered with lust. Dread wrapped an icy hand around Camden's spine, but he refused to show his fear to this man. He pulled at his restraints. "Let me go."

"I don't think I will, tough guy. You were out cold for a long time." The shifter held up a towel. "I have some ice for that knot on your head."

"Don't need it. Untie me."

"No can do. Look at it this way. I'm doing you a favor. You're a hell of a lot safer with me than out there." The shifter nodded toward the open window. A howl sounded in the distance.

Camden shivered, but he put on a brave face. "I can take care of myself."

"Really? I haven't seen any evidence of that."

"What do you care, anyway?"

"Oh, I care." A slow smile creased the shifter's face. "I have plans for you." He reached out and trailed his fingers along a calf.

Heat curled in Camden's groin, and his dick got harder. He couldn't help it. Part of him still looked at his captor as a dangerous enemy, but another part just saw a man he wanted.

The dark head bent and a long rough tongue licked Camden's sole, then sucked on a toe.

Oh, fuck! Natural lust coursed through Camden's body, making him shudder in his restraints. Steeling his muscles, he tried to hide the effect this man had on him, but it was too late for that. His stiff prick made it perfectly clear that they both wanted the same thing.

The shifter straightened, and without a trace of embarrassment, pulled the t-shirt over his head and tossed it on the floor. His jeans followed. He moved toward the bed like a sleek animal stalking his prey. The mattress sank under his weight.

Camden screamed. "Help! Somebody, help."

"Do you really want a pack of randy wolves coming to your rescue?" The shifter grinned. "Maybe you do. Maybe a gangbang is exactly what you want."

Camden clamped his mouth shut, and turned his head away.

"Good. Keep your head right there." Fingers sifted through Camden's hair.

At first, the gentle massage felt good, and Camden instinctively tilted his head back. "Ouch!"

"That's the spot. Hold still." An ice pack pressed against the back of Camden's head. "What's your name?"

"Who wants to know?"

"Wyat. And watch your manners when you talk to an alpha."

"Or what?" Camden muttered. "You'll kill me? Go ahead. You'll be doing me a favor."

Wyat chuckled. "If I wanted to kill you, you'd be lying dead in the alley. I have something better in mind. Looks like you have the same idea." The ice pack disappeared and a big, warm hand gripped Camden's stiff prick and gave it a few strokes. "Feels good, doesn't it?"

"No!" Camden silently cursed his traitorous penis. Why did it have to come to life tonight?

"Don't you know you can't lie to another wolf? I smell arousal all over you." Wyat cut off any reply by squeezing Camden's balls. "It's a full-moon night, and I should be playing with the pack, but instead I'm playing nursemaid to you. The least you can do is be honest." Wyat released Camden's dick.

Camden couldn't hold back a needy whimper. *Damn black-haired dog. He knows exactly how to play me.*

"So, nameless half-breed, it appears you do like my touch." Wyat ran a hand over Camden's chest and pinched a nipple. "Tell me why you're so anxious to die?"

Camden shivered. "That's my business."

"Okay, have it your way. I should have known better. There's no talking to a human. You're all psycho."

"I'm not human."

"And you refuse to acknowledge your shifter genes. So what are you exactly?"

What am I meant to be? Camden had been struggling with that question for years. "I'm not anything. I'm just Camden."

Wyat's lips curved in a smile that didn't quite reach his yellow eyes. "So, Just-Camden, did you hatch from an egg, or did the stork bring you?"

Camden's nostrils flared. "I have a mother." A tear slid down his cheek. "I used to have a mother. She jumped off Suicide Bridge. Today." The words came out before Camden could stop them.

"Oh, fuck. That's rough."

"Like you give a damn. It was your kind that raped her and killed her family."

"My kind? Listen to me, you little prick. You're not the only one who lost family because of the war. I was eighteen when my father died. Just a smartass kid who wasn't ready to lead a pack. No way. No how. But I didn't have time to grieve, or feel sorry for myself, because *my* kind were depending on me."

"Yeah? Well at least you have a kind. I only had my mother. Now I have no one."

Wyat gripped Camden's jaw and forced him to turn his head. His eyes seemed to look right into Camden's soul. "You see these eyes? *You* are my kind."

****

Wyat went rigid with shock. *What am I saying?* All his life he hated the humans. Now he was claiming one as his own. Well, only half-human, still... Wyat gazed out the window, and suddenly everything was clear in the light of the full moon.

Camden whimpered and Wyat let him go.

"I shouldn't have come here," Camden said.

"You were right to come. You're here because you felt the pull of the moon. Tarqiup Inua called you."

"Who?"

"The master of the moon." Wyat shook his head. "You've been on the wrong side too long. You have a lot to learn."

"No one called me."

"You let the humans crush your soul, but the wild spirit of the wolf still lives inside you. Open your mind. Accept it."

"Two halves don't make a whole. I'm not human, and I'm not a wolf. I'm just a freak."

You're so wrong. Wyat couldn't help himself. He leaned in to smother the half-breed's frown with a kiss.

Camden whimpered and opened his lips to admit Wyat's thrusting tongue. There was passion in the half-breed's surrender, anger, too, as if he didn't understand his own feelings. Wyat was surprised by his own sudden insight, but if Tarqiup Inua accepted the half-breed as one of his own, then Wyat would too. A wolf-shifter didn't argue with his god.

The lust he shared with Camden could be the beginning of a deeper connection. One that would help Camden accept a place in the pack. Wyat's moon lust was tempered by a sense of responsibility. No rough sex. The moon God meant this to be a loving experience.

Wyat gentled his kisses, then his mouth left Camden's and traveled to the boy's ear. He licked the rim, and then sucked on the tender lobe. Camden tensed, but after a few minutes of gentle nips and soothing licks, he relaxed.

Wyat moved on, bending his head to capture a tempting nipple. Encouraged by Camden's whimpers and moans, Wyat sucked harder, and used his fingers to rub and pinch the other nub. If only he could feel Camden's arms around him, but he needed to hear the right words from the boy's mouth before he released his bonds.

Wyat slid down Camden's body, blazing a wet trail along the line of hair from belly to pubes. The boy twisted and bucked, helpless in his restraints, but he said nothing. His struggles made Wyat hotter, but he tamped down his urges, and settled himself between Camden's legs. Wrapping his fingers around the stiff cock in front of him, Wyat stroked, sliding the foreskin up and over the rim of the head. Camden moaned piteously, but not in protest. He clearly enjoyed this attention. A few minutes of teasing, and Wyat could stand no more. He wanted to have the boy's cock in his mouth, but he needed permission. He reached for the half-breed's balls, and squeezed.

Camden yelped. Wyat released him and reared up on his haunches, grinning. "Almost forgot I had a fragile human in my bed."

The half-breed lifted his head. His eyes glittered in the moonlight. "Fragile human, my ass, don't you fucking stop now!"

Said like a true wolf. Wyat laughed. "Oh, I'll get to your ass soon enough."

Wyat ducked down and gripped Camden's shaft. Pulling back the foreskin, he swirled his tongue over the slit. The taste of pre-cum exploded in his mouth. Familiar, yet exotic. Indescribable. Wyat let the head slip between his lips, and swallowed.

"Suck me. I need—"

Camden's plea cut off when Wyat did as he asked. Tightening his grip on Camden's balls, Wyat sucked hard. The boy's incoherent sounds got louder. His body tensed, his cock swelled in Wyat's mouth, and he shuddered as he came. Savoring each swallow of salty-sweet cum, Wyat sucked until Camden's orgasm subsided.

****

Camden had planned to lay rigid and unresponsive under Wyat's attention, but clearly that became impossible. He didn't regret his submission. Wyat's hands and mouth set him on fire. He'd never felt more alive.

Wyat settled on top of him. A glimpse of yellow eyes, then Wyat captured his mouth and gave him a taste of his own seed. Such an intimate act deserved a response. Camden felt a desire to wrap his limbs around the wolf. His hands jerked at the ropes, and he moaned against Wyat's lips. Wyat pulled back and looked at him.

"Untie me," Camden whispered.

Wyat said nothing.

"Please. I want to touch you."

Wyat rewarded him with a radiant smile, and released his limbs. Once free, Camden reached out eagerly for the wolf, and Wyat allowed himself to be pulled into an embrace. Camden met Wyat's gaze. The intensity in the shifter's beautiful eyes rekindled a fire inside him.

"I want to fuck you," Wyat said.

Is he asking my permission? "You could have left me tied up, and done whatever you want."

"Yes, I could have. But I've never raped anyone in my life, and I don't plan to start tonight. So you tell me what you want."

Camden couldn't lie to himself any longer. The desire he felt for Wyat was undeniable. And mutual. At least during the full moon. Camden was so tired of feeling bad about himself, why not enjoy this a little longer? He pulled his knees back, and planted his feet flat on the mattress. "I want you to fuck me."

Wyat kissed him, and slid down his body. He spread Camden's cheeks and dragged his tongue over the crease, then licked at his hole. Camden cried out when Wyat's tongue finally pushed inside. His hips arched, and he pressed back, trying to impale himself. It felt so good, but he wanted something bigger filling him. He wanted Wyat's cock.

As if he'd read Camden's mind, Wyat sat up. "Roll over," he ordered.

Camden's eyes went wide, but he complied immediately. He settled on his hands and knees, anxious for what came next. A fingertip rubbed his opening, then pushed inside. His ass clenched around the digit. Wyat pressed deep, then added another finger, scissoring them to stretch Camden's channel. He crooked his fingers, rubbing over a spot that made Camden see stars. It was half pain, and half pleasure, and he wanted more. But the fingers withdrew, leaving him empty and wanting.

Wyat fondled his ass, and then leaned over Camden's back, covering him. His warm breath tickled Camden's ear. "You ready?

Camden rolled his hips in response. Wyat adjusted his position, and gripped Camden's hips, pulling them closer. He could feel Wyat's hairy thighs rubbing against his. Then a broad cockhead at his hole. Wyat buried his length in one fierce, animalistic thrust.

Camden screamed, but the burn quickly turned into a fiery glow that spread pleasure through his body. Wyat stayed motionless for a minute, then he reached around, anchored Camden with a hand on his belly, and started a steady in-and-out rhythm. The primal position made Camden feel dominated and woke a torrid passion inside him. He moved his hips back, meeting Wyat thrust for thrust. The shifter growled out his pleasure at each stroke. Wyat had a way of twisting his hips that created an exquisite friction. It made Camden's hunger spiral higher. A wet spot formed on the mattress and spread as Camden's prick filled and dripped. The wild, musky scent of their sex grew stronger.

Wyat's cock rubbed over that sweet spot and sparks skittered along Camden's nerve endings. The hand on his belly now grasped his dick, and Wyat jacked him in time to his thrusts.

Camden urged him on. "More, Harder. Faster. Is that all you got?" He could hardly believe he was uttering those words, but he just said what he felt.

Wyat growled. Pumped harder. Stroked faster.

Camden knew Wyat was close, and he pushed back with a force that sent the shifter over the edge. Wyat let out a howl and filled Camden with his hot seed. The shifter's orgasm set off Camden's, and he shot his load on the mattress. Afterwards, he couldn't stop shaking, the pleasure had been that intense.

Wyat collapsed on Camden's back, pinning him to the mattress. A minute later, he rolled them to their sides, and held Camden close, spooning him. Wyat kissed his neck, and nipped his shoulder.

This is what I've been missing in my life. The need to touch and be touched. Camden had never experienced this degree of intimacy with another person before. It felt special, and he wondered if Wyat felt the same. He was too embarrassed to ask, and it was too late anyway, because Wyat was already asleep, his snores a comforting rumble in Camden's ear. The sound made him feel less lonely. He didn't want any of this to end. He'd stay here forever, if he could. But he didn't fit in. *I'm an outsider.* The humans had never accepted him, there was no reason to think the shifters would either. Everything looked rosy under a full moon, but it would be morning soon, and time to leave town.

Chapter Five

Wyat slept on his stomach, seemingly oblivious to the rising sun. Camden studied the shifter's back, amazed at the number of ancestors on his family tree. They were roots, anchoring Wyat to his place in the world, while Camden drifted like the wind.

Now it was time to move on. But where? Going east would take him back over the bridge, but he had no roots there. Not anymore. He thought he might continue westward and see where the road took him.

Camden left Wyat's bed, quiet as he could be. He retrieved his clothes from the floor and carried them. Tiptoeing to the door, he glanced over his shoulder for one last look at Wyat. That was a mistake. Now he wanted to jump back into the bed and cuddle up next to Wyat's big, warm body. This wasn't supposed to happen. Maybe last night was just full-moon sex to Wyat, but Camden couldn't separate the physical from the emotional. He never should have let his guard down.

In the living room, Camden started dressing. It amazed him that Wyat owned all this. He'd never had so many possessions to worry about. A small photo in a gold frame caught his eye. He walked over to the table and picked it up. One of the men was Wyat, the older man must be his father. They looked alike. Camden rubbed his thumb over the faces. If only he had a picture of his mother. He'd never forget her face, or Wyat's either, but a photo was something solid a man could hold in his hand.

Camden knew he should put it back, but he couldn't let go. On the lonely nights ahead, he could look at it and remember that once someone in this fucked up world had wanted him. Surely Wyat wouldn't mind. After all, his father face was inked on his back.

Camden slipped the photo in his pocket, shut the door behind him, and started walking. The streets were deserted. Most likely, the shifters were still sleeping off last night's revelry. *I could still be in Wyat's bed....* He almost turned around to go back. Almost. When Wyat's scent faded from his body, he'd still have his memories, and a good memory was better than a bad morning after.

The landscape became more barren the further he walked. Here, the buildings had been leveled, and only mountains of rubble remained. The sun rose in the sky. Thirsty and hungry, Camden wondered if he'd find water and shelter. He had to keep moving.

The wolves appeared out of nowhere. A big gray beast on his left, and a bigger black one on his right. Camden went rigid. Two pairs of yellow eyes fixed on him. There was no mistaking Wyat's scent. *He's here for the photo.*

Camden turned to his right, and put his hands up in surrender. "I shouldn't have taken it. It was wrong, no matter the reason." Camden pulled the photo from his pocket and threw it on the ground in front of the black wolf.

The animal spared it a glance, and closed in on Camden. Its yellow eyes darkened with an intensity that frightened Camden. *I was right to leave. Under the light of the full moon, I was an easy fuck. In the cold light of day, I'm the enemy.* These wolves weren't here for explanations. They wanted blood. Yesterday Camden was ready to die. Today he wanted to survive.

The gray wolf sprawled on the ground and licked a paw. Camden saw an opening, and he took it. He feigned a move to the right, but veered sharply to the left, and took off running. Adrenaline fueled his flight, but he knew he couldn't outrun these swift beasts, so he zigzagged around piles of debris, hoping to give them the slip. But the sounds of their hot pursuit became louder. They were gaining on him.

Camden moved faster, so fast, he didn't see the slit trench until he was almost on top of it. He sprang back, crouched, then leaped and soared high. Landing safely on the other side, he lifted his head and howled.

Suddenly confused, Camden looked down at his paws. *Paws?* Light brown, like his hair. He licked one. It was definitely his. *How the fuck did this happen? And how do I make it unhappen?*

Suddenly, a furry black body slammed into him and knocked him over. Camden snarled and showed his teeth, but the other wolf ignored the warning. He nudged Camden with his snout, and then licked him. Their eyes met, and Camden knew Wyat meant him no harm. Bathed by the soothing warmth of Wyat's tongue, Camden no longer felt scared and alone. He lay still and let Wyat groom him.

A few more licks, and Wyat sat back on his haunches. The air around him shimmered, distorting his body. Black fur receded, his shape realigned, and a last low growl escaped from his retracting muzzle as wolf merged into man. Only the yellow eyes were the same.

"Your turn," Wyat said, calmly.

I don't know how. Camden let out a mournful cry.

"Focus. Picture your human body."

Camden concentrated on an image of his body, and the sound of Wyat's voice. His heart rate sped up, his bones twisted. He watched his fur disappear, and he stretched his naked limbs.

Camden looked around. "My clothes?"

Wyat chuckled. "Probably at the bottom of the trench. We usually take them off before we shift."

"Oh, no. The photo. I lost it."

"It's not important. I have more."

"Then why are you here?"

"I'm here for you. You ran out on me."

Camden chewed on his lip. "I thought it would be better—"

"Better for whom? If my beta hadn't come looking for me, I might have slept for hours, and given you a huge head start."

"What's a beta?"

Wyat sighed. "Like I said, you have a lot to learn. A beta is the second in command. More than that, Jack is my trusted friend and advisor. He came to find out what happened last night when I disappeared from the bar." Wyat let out a little growl. "I was pissed when I realized you left. Jack offered to help me track you."

"Where is he?"

"I sent him home, and I'd like to get home myself. I haven't had breakfast yet. Let's go."

Camden remained sitting. "I don't have a home."

"I thought you figured things out by now. Ever hear the saying, birds of a feather flock together?"

"Yeah, and I'm a bird with two different feathers. I don't fit anywhere."

"I don't know about that. You fit me pretty good last night."

Camden's face burned. "You got horny under the full moon.... Okay, *we* got horny, but I knew it wouldn't last. I figured you wouldn't want me around in the morning."

"You think too damn much." Wyat let out a low primal growl and pounced. Camden landed on his back, with Wyat's big body pinning him to the ground. Wyat's hips rolled over his and started a fire down below.

Camden moaned. "Oh, fuck."

"Hold that thought," Wyat murmured in his ear. His hand reached between them and tightened on Camden's dick. He squeezed and stroked, slow and easy. And all the while, he nuzzled Camden's neck, licking and sucking. The fire inside Camden burned hotter. Pressure built in his balls—

Wyat rolled off, and left him hanging.

Camden reached for him, but Wyat evaded his grasp. "Uh-uh. Tell me how you feel right now.

Camden forced a nervous laugh. "Oh, you know."

"Spit it out."

"Hot and horny," Camden blurted.

"Okay, now we're getting somewhere." Wyat propped himself on an elbow and studied Camden. "You see a moon anywhere?"

"No." Camden sighed. There was no full moon, but the electricity between him and Wyat still sizzled. His need for the other man was just as urgent. "I don't understand."

"Here's the story in a nutshell. The moon heightens our senses and increases our sex drive, and it's all good. But sometimes it's more than good. It's great. And when the sun comes up, and it still feels great, that means it turned into something more."

Something more? With a shifter, a man whose people destroyed his mother's life? But Camden couldn't deny the attraction. He was drawn to Wyat. And Wyat to him.

****

Wyat had a feeling this half-breed might be the one. The man who could turn him into a monogamous mate. And if Camden could do that, he could do a lot more. Wyat looked at Camden and saw a man who could bridge two worlds and maybe bring them together. *One step at a time.* First he had to make Camden understand, and accept his place in the pack.

"My father always believed humans and shifters should make nice and live together. I disagreed. My beta tried to change my mind, but I wouldn't listen. I believe that Tarqiup Inua stepped in to show me the way. He put something in my path that I could not ignore. A sexy young stud who pushes all my buttons, even though he's half-human. If two different sets of genes can live in one person, then two different people should be able to live side by side."

He looked into Camden's eyes, hoping he was getting the message. "You made me see that, and I'll be a better leader for it. I think big changes are coming, and I need a man like you at my side."

****

Wyat was offering him everything he'd ever wanted, a home, acceptance, maybe even love someday. But, could Camden put aside his own hatred and prejudice? God knows, he wanted to. Wyat had turned his world around, and shown him things about himself that made him special. Wanted. Camden was beginning to believe that the full moon wasn't just about lust. It was about new beginnings and rebirth.

Camden looked into Wyat's yellow eyes, and knew he didn't want to live without him. He reached out for Wyat's hand. "If an old dog can learn a new trick, maybe I can too."

Wyat cuffed his head. "Call me old again, and you'll find yourself tied to my bed."

Camden grinned. "Let's go home, *old* man."

The End

www.galestanley.net

7 AUTHOR ANTHOLOGY

DESTINED

Copyright © 2015

L.D. Blakeley

Caleb Stokes knew he'd had too many shots of Fireball—way too many. He also knew that he didn't care. Who had time to be concerned with sobriety when they've just witnessed their boyfriend of the past six weeks bent over the DJ console being shagged to within an inch of his life? Caleb sure as hell didn't.

What Caleb Stokes didn't know was that his night was about to get worse—a whole lot fucking worse.

Dry ice, strobe lights, and sweat blurred Caleb's vision as he jostled his way through the throngs of shirtless, gyrating men who were oblivious to anything that wasn't a cocktail or a source of friction. The heavy thump of bass and rhythmic stabs of synthesizer reverberated in Caleb's head like a swarm of angry bees as he forced his way through the crowd toward the men's room.

Never in a million years would the bathroom at The Garrison be his first choice as a source of refuge, but right now anything was better than the middle of the overcrowded club. At least there was a slight chance a stall might be empty to provide a temporary respite from the din. And luck, it would appear, was at least partially on Caleb's side.

Normally teeming with drunk, horny, indiscriminate men and untold varieties of STIs, the bathroom was currently all but empty, save the couple

Caleb could hear in the last stall. Ignoring their grunts and moans, he splashed cold water on his face and dragged shaking fingers through his hair in an attempt to salvage his sweat-drenched coif.

Fuck Anthony. And fuck that slut of a DJ.

Caleb squared his shoulders and decided that some hard-core flirting and maybe a quick and dirty hand job were exactly what he needed to turn this shitty night around. For 29, he could still hold his own: cute face, decent body, still not a gray hair in sight. Besides, this close to closing, he was pretty much guaranteed to pick up. It wasn't exactly the most cheerful of thoughts, Caleb knew. But, then, it hadn't exactly been the most cheerful of nights.

Fuck it.

Caleb took one last look in the mirror, adjusted himself and turned back toward the writhing mass of men on the dance floor. For the most part, one man looked much the same as the next, and Caleb couldn't see a single one who stood out enough to pique his interest. Tall, short, bearded, clean-shaven, skinny, ripped—not one of them seemed more interesting than the next.

A drink was definitely in order. With a flick of his hips, Caleb turned away from the dance floor and headed in search of more cinnamon-flavoured whiskey to further numb his already muddled senses. A not-so-subtle grope from an interested bystander forced a not-so-interested Caleb to jerk away from the man and head in the opposite direction.

In retrospect, Caleb should have thanked the handsy onlooker. If it hadn't been for his forcing Caleb to zag, rather than zig, he might not ever have seen the vision of sex personified currently standing between him and his much-needed libation.

Jesus. Fucking. Christ.

Caleb had never seen anyone like the man who now had his undivided attention. Taller than pretty much every other man in the bar, with shoulders as broad as you would expect at that height, this dark haired vision stood nursing a beer and aimlessly watching the crowd. Dark, tousled hair and a full well-groomed beard framed a face that was equal parts stunning and terrifying. The guy had a fierce expression that Caleb was sure could freeze time. And the tight jeans and t-shirt he wore barely concealed what looked to be one powerhouse of a body. Caleb was transfixed. And suddenly his night wasn't looking quite so bleak.

With far more attitude than he would have dared were he sober, Caleb approached the man unnoticed and deftly snatched his beer in a move he hoped would come off as sexy or, at the very least, cute and charming. The intense expression he was greeted with, however, was not that of a man on the prowl.

Time to turn up the charm.

Caleb upended the bottle and took a long draw on the amber brew. As he slowly lowered the bottle, he made sure his lips kept contact with the bottle while he looked up at the stoic mountain of a man.

"Buy me my own and you can have this one back, Daddy," Caleb cooed and flashed a flirty wink in a move that had yet to fail him.

Until now.

"Not your fucking father. And I'm pretty sure you're a bit past that twink shit, so why don't you fuck off back to wherever you came from."

Caleb winced at the growled words and watched as the surly stranger turned his back and headed toward the bar. As the man effortlessly made his way through the crowd, he paused to look back and, for a brief moment, Caleb thought perhaps he had changed his mind.

"And keep the goddamn beer," he snarled.

If Caleb could have harnessed any mystical or magical power at that very moment, he'd have chosen the gift of invisibility. Because, at least then he would be the only one privy to just how spectacularly he'd failed at closing time.

Clearly his night was not going to improve, so he decided to cut his losses and head home.

Alone.

With no small effort to avoid stumbling, Caleb headed toward the exit and out into the night. The club's dimly lit parking lot wasn't Caleb's favourite place on earth at the best of times. Two rows of cars and a minefield of broken bottles and assorted debris might have provided an adventurous place for sleazy blow jobs and dirty fucks. But it wasn't the best place to be wandering through alone this late at night.

Local kids and bashers had been known to lie in wait just hoping for some poor drunken sod to stumble out alone and unprotected. Cutting through it was also the most direct route to Caleb's apartment. He'd made the trek plenty of times before but never quite this drunk. Not while alone, anyway. So he kept his eyes peeled and pricked up his ears as he speed-walked through the half-empty lot toward the well-worn path that would lead him directly to his street.

And that's when he spotted Anthony and the damn DJ walking a few paces ahead of him, hands everywhere and each practically in the other's pocket. Caleb ducked behind a pickup truck to avoid being seen because there was no chance in hell that small talk with either of them was going to be on his To Do list anytime soon.

Bastards didn't get enough back in the DJ booth?

Gravity could be a harsh mistress at the best of times, but with more alcohol in his system than a cheerleader on prom night, Caleb wasn't exactly at his most graceful. His balance shifted, through no fault of his own—surely—and he teetered forward, narrowly avoiding a side-view mirror to the forehead. Certain he was fine to make his way back toward his intended route, Caleb righted himself and peered out from behind the truck.

Nothing. They were gone.

Thank fuck.

He was barely a half dozen paces from his hiding spot, when a bloodcurdling scream rent the night air. Caleb froze as icy tendrils of fear climbed up the length of his spine. He knew that voice.

"Anthony?"

When no answer came, he nervously stepped farther into the parking lot. A gasping choking noise followed by the snarl and snap of a wild animal ratcheted Caleb's heart up into his throat. He crept slowly forward, trying desperately to muffle his footsteps on the gravel beneath him. And when he reached the far wall that backed onto the tree line, Caleb halted and stood stock still as a scream of terror strangled and stuck in his throat.

There, barely three feet from where Caleb stood, a wild beast tore viciously at something on the ground. He couldn't see if it was Anthony. The animal had whomever it was by the throat, its great, gnashing teeth savagely tearing at the prone, limp body. Bodies? Caleb couldn't tell. The vision of gore was more than he could process. *What the fuck was that?* Wolves had been known to creep into town from time to time, but this creature was easily three times the size of any timber wolf he'd ever seen.

Without another thought, Caleb turned and ran back toward the big, black truck. The sounds of ripping flesh and carnage were all he could hear as he ducked down and crawled beneath the truck, hoping it would provide some kind of shelter.

Jesus Christ! When he'd bitterly wished ill on Anthony and his new boy toy, this sure as fuck wasn't what he'd had in mind.

Terror and the night air had double-teamed Caleb with a ghastly chill and he couldn't quell the uncontrollable shiver that now wracked his body. He hadn't been to church in years, but Caleb was seriously contemplating prayer. Surely someone would come out and find him. He wriggled around enough to grab his cell phone from his pocket to check the time. *1 am. Dammit.* Another hour until last call. What the hell was he going to do? Call 911? *Yes!* Call 911. Cops carried guns. Guns could shoot whatever the hell that thing was and Caleb could go the fuck home.

As he swiped the phone to wake it up and dial, Caleb heard a high-pitched feral yelp followed by... nothing. The hellish noises had stopped. Was the creature gone? Could he—*oh fuck!* Caleb held his breath as he saw the sturdy gait of the animal as it crept toward the truck. He could only see its legs and its dark, dangerous claws, but he didn't need to see more to know this wasn't going to end well. A loud thump drummed overhead and the truck's heavy shocks groaned. *Jesus Christ! Was that a body?*

Caleb screwed his eyes shut and started that prayer.

"You can get out from under my truck, now."

Caleb didn't dare move.

"Fine." The voice paused. "I'll just run over you."

"What about the...." The what? What the hell had he seen? And what could he call it that wouldn't make him sound like a drunken lunatic?

What about the giant, nightmare-inducing beastie that was gnawing on my boyfriend's—ex-boyfriend's—limbs? Caleb shuddered and felt bile rise to his throat. No amount of alcohol was going to erase that image from his head. Ever.

"It's safe. You can come out."

The bearish tone in the stranger's voice wasn't really doing much to make Caleb feel any safer in his current situation. Of course, with the way his night had shaped up, it would be just Caleb's luck that this was precisely the deranged psychopath he was trying to hide from. But he figured accepting a hand from someone, anyone, was better than taking his chances alone and risk being torn limb from limb. So, with great trepidation—and no small amount of gravel digging and gouging at body parts far too delicate to endure such abuse—he crawled out to meet his so-called champion.

With his heart still at a gallop and his breath coming in shallow rapid gasps, Caleb brushed the dirt from his pants and stood to meet his....

Oh, come on! Seriously?

"Oh, for the love of—" Caleb nearly laughed. Instead it came out as some insane high-pitched squeak. Because Caleb's shit night wasn't already measuring off the charts, he now got to bear the indignity of being saved by... "Who the hell are you, anyway?"

"Thought I was your daddy."

Great. Sarcasm while the world is going to hell.

"What happened to the... oh, god, Anthony." Not that Caleb was about to award the man in question any Boyfriend of the Year awards, but he sure as hell didn't deserve to die.

"You knew him?"

"He was my boy—ex-boyfriend." Caleb was trying desperately to calm down, and with a dissolving adrenaline spike, he couldn't seem to stop shaking. "Is he... he's dead, isn't he?"

"Yep."

"Is he...." Caleb wrapped his arms around himself and tried not to stutter while the sheer horror of the situation left him chilled to the bone. "Did you just put him in your truck?"

"Yep."

"What the *fuck*?" Caleb knew he needed to run. For some reason though, his legs felt cemented to the ground and he simply swayed where he stood. A huge hand reached out to steady him and instead of flinching away, like his brain was telling him to do, he felt himself melt into the touch, practically purring like a damn cat in heat.

A gentle nudge turned Caleb toward the truck and the door was quickly opened.

"Get in."

With no idea what the hell was happening, and the synapses in his brain firing and landing haphazardly, Caleb did as he was told and climbed up into the cab of the pickup.

"What the fuck are you doing with Anthony? Where are you taking him? And why aren't we calling the cops?" It occurred to Caleb, the instant he asked, that there was a very good reason they weren't calling the cops. And that very good reason was putting the keys in the ignition and about to drive off to parts unknown.

"Cops can't get involved."

"Because you killed Anthony and the DJ." Caleb tried his damnedest to sound like he wasn't terrified to his core. "Are... are you going to kill me?"

"Didn't kill anyone."

"How the hell do I know that? The last thing I saw was something ripping my ex's throat out. Then—boom—there you are? How come you don't have a damn hair even out of place?"

It was pissing Caleb off, too, that this big bastard looked even better than he had back at the bar. Sexy and uninterested was one thing to contend with. Now there was the very real possibility that he was some sort of sick twisted killer to boot. And for reasons Caleb had no interest in examining, he still found the bastard hotter than hell.

"You know it because I just told you."

The truck slowly rolled out of the parking lot and peeled out as soon as it hit pavement. For a hot minute, Caleb actually thought about opening the door and leaping to the ground while the truck sped along. And just as quickly as he thought it, he heard the tell-tale click of the power locks being engaged.

Oh, shit.

"I told you I didn't kill anyone."

"I didn't say a word." Caleb really wished he could still feel some of that Fireball buzz right now. At least that would explain the semi he'd been sporting since he'd crawled out from his hidey-hole and realized whose truck he was under. Clearly he was coming unhinged. It was the only explanation he could come up with. Why else would he be thinking indecent thoughts about the man who was more than likely about to be his murderer.

"I can hear your heartbeat. So, either you're terrified of me because you think I'm a killer, or you're part hummingbird."

That deep, husky voice sounded like whiskey and honey to Caleb, which turned him on and irritated him to no end.

"You can hear my heartbeat." Caleb rolled his eyes, despite the fear he was attempting to swallow. "Okay, *Twilight*."

"Name's Marick." He kept his eyes on the road as a smirk crossed his face. "Gevrees."

Caleb was surprised to hear the reply delivered with a low, rumbling chuckle. And, for some fucked up reason, that also sent a rush of blood to his cock. *Get a hold of yourself, Caleb.*

"Whatever." Caleb grunted out in the most noncommittal tone he could muster, and hoped the dark of night hid the fact that he was furtively trying to adjust himself. "Can you at least tell me where you're taking me?"

"My place."

"What?" Caleb knew his squawked response didn't exactly scream confidence.

"My place. Pretty sure I didn't stutter."

"Did you—" Caleb bit back his initial response, then continued despite his better judgment. "I'm sorry, but didn't you tell me to—and I quote, 'fuck off back to wherever I came from'?"

"It's the only place you'll be safe."

"What are you talking about? You're the only threat I can see right now!"

"And I've already told you, I didn't kill anyone. But someone did."

"So, what, I'm supposed to just take your word for that and come play house with the big, bad Daddy who thinks my pretty days are well behind me?"

Marick shot Caleb a dark look.

"Just until I find him."

"What are you, a cop or something?"

"Something."

"What does 'something' mean? And who the hell is 'him'?" Caleb's voice had steadily climbed to a piercing shriek. And since he'd just witnessed the most brazen Fuck You *and* a brutal murder within the span of a few hours, Caleb didn't quite care.

Marick let out a string of words that sounded like cursing, but were nothing but gibberish to Caleb.

"You saw your boyfriend—"

"—Ex."

"Fine. You saw your ex at the club with a guy you didn't know, right?"

"Yeah."

"Odds are he saw you, too."

Caleb had turned sideways to watch Marick's face, hoping that it might give away some clue as to what the hell he was talking about. It was bad enough that with every word the infuriating man spoke, Caleb felt more and more light headed. Rationally, he knew that red flags were being thrown up left, right and center. But logic didn't explain away the almost dizzy sensation—not to mention the traitorous throb in his crotch—that was making him just the slightest bit manic.

"Wait, are you saying the DJ is who I saw tearing Anthony to pieces back there? That makes no fucking sense at all."

"No, it wouldn't."

"Are you high? The guy back at the club was a total douche but he was still just a guy! That... *thing* I saw in the parking lot, that was no human being. Not by a long shot."

"Skakelaar."

"Excuse you?"

"That's what he was. Skakelaar."

"And what, pray tell, is a *sky klar*?"

"Skakelaar."

"You can keep saying it until one of us falls asleep, but it's really not going to help my comprehension any. And if you're trying to explain away what happened back there—and now my *abduction*," Caleb punctuated the word with a pointed glare, "by telling some twisted tale of werewolves, then you are one crazy son of a bitch!" *And I need to get the* hell *out of this truck!*

Marick let out a sigh, then pulled the truck onto an unpaved driveway. Trees lined the long stretch of dirt road that took them further and further away from any chance of Caleb finding his way back home.

The night sky seemed infinitely darker, which really should have been ratcheting up Caleb's feeling of panic. For some inexplicable reason though, what he was feeling right now was frustrated. And horny. And more than just a little bit irritated with himself. This man had already rejected him. More importantly, his ex—his *dead* ex—was in the back of the truck. *Not exactly a seductive situation, here, Caleb.* So why couldn't his damn hormones get on board? Caleb squirmed in his seat in an attempt to rearrange himself, while he mentally berated his traitorous dick. *Not gonna happen, you Judas.*

When they finally pulled up in front of a modest split-level house, Caleb felt like he was about to jump out of his skin. The urge to bolt dueled with the urge to wrap himself around Marick and hump his leg like a damn dog in heat. It was ridiculous, he knew. And the more he tried to convince himself of that fact, the worse it seemed to get.

"So, what now?"

Marick switched off the ignition then pinned Caleb with a nearly hypnotic gaze. "We go inside."

Caleb gave his head a shake and jumped out of the truck. Following a complete stranger into his home in the dead of night probably wasn't the best decision Caleb had ever made, but it was a bit late for caution now.

"Is there any chance you're going to let me in on your master plan anytime soon, *Twilight*?"

The growl Caleb received in response probably shouldn't have sent a wave of heat rushing to his groin. *Clearly, I've lost my mind. Someone obviously slipped me a mickey at the club, and I'm having some sort of psychotic break.*

"Keep your voice down. I don't want to wake Frank."

"No, heaven forbid we wake Frank. I'd hate for all this murder and kidnapping to get in the way of a good night's sleep."

The gibberish Marick had grumbled earlier was being repeated and Caleb was no further ahead in deciphering what any of it meant.

The house lay quiet and pitch black as Caleb made his way up the stairs at Marick's direction. He could feel the hair on the back of his neck stand at attention and if he hadn't already been unceremoniously turned down by the man earlier that night, he'd swear he was being checked out—closely.

A sudden burst of light from the top of the stairs startled Caleb into tripping over his own feet. He didn't have far to fall, however, as Marick really had been right behind him and was now holding Caleb upright, and flush against his chest. Caleb could feel ridges of muscle against his back, and the hard column of flesh that pressed against his ass sent a flood of heat to his groin. As Caleb enjoyed the momentary reprieve from their bickering and his own jangled nerves, a bathrobe-clad woman peered down at them from the landing.

"You found him!" The woman's face beamed with delight.

"Found who?" Caleb cringed at how breathy he sounded.

"Shut up, Frank."

Marick propelled Caleb forward and they climbed the last few steps to join the woman who had backed into a large homey looking kitchen. She was currently filling a kettle, and smiled over her shoulder at Caleb. "I'm Franka, by the way. Grouchy Smurf's sister. Cocoa?"

"Erm, sure? What I'd really like is for someone to tell me what the f—heck is going on."

Franka spun to glare at Marick. "You found your *bestem* and you haven't even told him?"

"Tell me what?" Caleb's voice was starting to do that pitchy thing again, and his filter went on hiatus. "What the fuck is going *on*?"

"Marick, I can practically hear your pulse when you stand next to this one. Who knew your *bestem*—it means destined," she clarified for Caleb, "would be so cute? And don't give me any of that brooding he's-better-off-without-me bullshit, either, Marick."

"We're skakelaar."

"Yeah. So you've mentioned. What is that, Swedish?"

"South African," Franka explained. "It's where our clan is originally from. Well, technically, France. But then that whole Gévaudan thing blew up and we had to leave."

"So your name is Marick Skakelaar. Hang on, I thought you said your name was Marick Gevrees. So, lie number one. And you're still not telling me a damn thing about what the hell is going on. So, y'know—feel free to jump in here anytime with anything resembling the truth."

"Skakelaar isn't my name. It's what I am."

"And that would be?"

"A shifter."

"A what now?"

"Shifter."

"Yeah, no. I heard that. But seriously? You think you're a shifter? I was kidding with that *Twilight* shit, you know."

"You know what you saw back there."

Caleb couldn't deny that he'd witnessed some damn compelling evidence that supported what Marick was telling him. He sure as hell had no better explanation. But it didn't make it all any less insane.

"So your name is Marick Gevrees and you're a shifter. My ex just got ripped to shreds by the dude I caught him having sex with back at the club. And I'm a—what did you call it? *Bestem*?"

"Pretty much."

"From the beginning, maybe, Mar?" Franka set three steaming mugs down on the table and took a seat with them.

"Have you ever heard the story of the Beast of Gévaudan?"

"The fairy tale about French werewolves?" Caleb couldn't help the wary sarcasm that dripped from his words.

Marick snorted, but continued. "That's the one. That's us."

"Who's you?"

"The Gévaudans," Franka picked up from her brother. "That's our family name. But then things went to shit because we had a rogue clan member who couldn't keep his fangs to himself and started tearing apart the villagers. The king sent out hunters, and off we fucked. We landed in South Africa but figured the story would follow us eventually, so we changed our name. We became Gevrees. Although, if we'd known France was going to change the name of the province after the Revolution anyway, we might not have bothered.

"Anyway," Marick spoke directly to Franka. "It sounds like we have another rogue on our hands."

"Shit. Seriously?" Franka sat up straight and reached across the table for her brother's hand. "Is it Jack?"

Caleb's eyes darted back and forth between the two siblings.

"I think so."

"Who's Jack?" Caleb was trying desperately to not sound shrill. "You're telling me you know this freak-show?"

"Jack Porter. His great, great—actually, I don't know how many *greats*—but his ancestor was François Antoine, one of the first hunters sent out by the king to hunt our kind."

"Okay. So, what, he thinks he's like a real-life *Buffy* or something?"

"Not exactly. His father was… one of us. But his mother was human."

"And I'm guessing he's not exactly thrilled with that, or planning any family reunions anytime soon."

"No."

"Well fuck me." Caleb's voice was barely above a whisper. And if he hadn't looked quickly, he'd have missed the heated look his words drew from Marick. "So what do we do?"

"*We* don't do anything. *I* have to go and deal with…." Marick's words trailed off and Caleb realized the man was trying to be as tactful as possible, given the circumstance. "I can't risk Porter being drawn here by scent."

"By scent? Oh." Caleb shuddered as he realized Marick was talking about Anthony, whose body was still in the back of the truck.

Without further explanation, Marick stood and walked out of the room. Not content with being left even *further* in the dark, Caleb followed suit down a darkened hallway. "You can't just—"

"Yes. I can." Marick growled as he turned and grabbed Caleb by the shoulders. One step closer and Marick's huge frame pressed Caleb back and up against the wall. "You're in danger. You don't seem to understand that."

Marick's growl was probably meant to intimidate Caleb, and a part of him was actually pretty damn panicked. His body, however, was totally on board for something else entirely. And Marick noticed. With one swift movement, he reached behind Caleb, pushed them both through a door, then deftly pinned Caleb once again. An overhead light was flipped on, causing Caleb to squint, but his eyes were quick to adjust and focus on the wall of muscle that was currently his captor.

"I get it. There's a maniac out there. But why the hell would he be after me?" Caleb was actually quite pleased with his ability to speak. The heady scent of clean sweat and a natural pheromone Caleb was sure he could bottle and sell for millions, overwhelmed his senses in a way that was absolutely irresistible. He leaned in closer to the broad expanse of chest in front of him and inhaled deeply, burrowing his face up toward the crook of Marick's neck.

A slow, careful exhale followed by, "because you're my *bestem*," wasn't exactly what Caleb expected.

"That makes no sense. And, not that I think any of this *bestem* shit is even a thing, but how the hell would this Porter guy know that?"

"The same way I knew before you even walked into The Garrison." Marick's hands slid from Caleb's shoulders to caress their way down to his hips and around to possessively clutch at his ass. He leaned in closer to speak directly into Caleb's ear, each word a gentle caress on his overheated skin.

"And it's definitely a thing. You've been hard since you met me, haven't you?" Marick slowly pressed his hips against Caleb, granting him no quarter. "Even when you were sure I killed your *friend*—" the word friend sounded like a curse on his lips, "—you still wanted me, didn't you?"

Marick continued to knead his fingers into the muscled flesh of Caleb's ass. As he traced the seam of Caleb's jeans with his index finger and pressed firmly between his cheeks, Marick whispered, "You do still, don't you, my *bestem*?"

"You arrogant prick, what makes you think I—"

Deft fingers working at Caleb's fly effectively stifled any further denial he might have thought to offer. Marick's fingers grazed the heated flesh of his hard, aching cock, and even with a cotton barrier between them, Caleb's skin felt singed. He mindlessly pushed his hips forward, anything that would afford a bit more friction. When Marick didn't move away, he did it again. This time, his movement elicited a deliciously dangerous-sounding growl from the man holding him not entirely against his will.

A low moan escaped Caleb's throat and his pulse raced as Marick ghosted his fingers under the waistband of his tented boxers. "You told me to fuck off," he managed.

"I did." Marick's fingers oh-so slowly wrapped around Caleb's cock with a gentle squeeze, only enough to taunt. That light-headed feeling he'd experienced in the truck was back and Caleb was spellbound.

"Then why are you—ohhh!"

Marick's grip tightened and cut short Caleb's weak attempt at protest.

"Do you want me to stop?" Marick's hot breath teased at Caleb's throat. He glided his thumb over the head of Caleb's leaking cock in a lazy circle and gently tugged at Caleb's earlobe with his teeth. The moisture already formed at the tip of Caleb's dick made for a convenient lubricant, and Marick reached down and started a slow, steady stroke. The merciless rhythm Marick set with his huge hand and unyielding grip short-circuited Caleb's brain.

"God. Please. Don't." Caleb's knew he sounded of complete and total surrender—despite his adamant protestations not ten minutes earlier. *If Marick's a shifter, maybe he's some sort of magician, too?* That would certainly go a long way in explaining Caleb's conflicted state.

Explanations could come later, though, because right now Caleb was doing well to remain upright. Marick was working magic along the length of Caleb's straining cock, while simultaneously worrying the tender flesh behind his ear with gentle nips. Caleb let his head fall back against the door and his eyes fluttered shut. This was madness. It was completely insane. And Caleb knew there wasn't a chance in hell he would stop any of it, even if he could.

Heat spread through Caleb's entire body, his back arched, and hips canted of their own accord. His hands shot out and grabbed on—tightly—to Marick, one frantically grasping at a powerful forearm, the other landing solidly against six-pack abs. As Marick's strokes gained momentum, Caleb found himself uncontrollably fucking into that tight, heavenly grip. He tried to open his eyes, but Marick varied his speed and gave a flick of his wrist that forced Caleb to, once again, hiss and screw his eyes shut.

"So beautiful." Marick growled into Caleb's ear, the low forceful timbre sending a vibration to his brain that only added to his delirium.

Barely coherent, Caleb was aware only of the low hum of electricity surrounding them and of the fire that scorched a path through his veins. His body tensed, toes curling into the soles of his shoes, blunt fingernails digging into exquisitely muscled flesh. Unable to form words at all, Caleb groaned out his pleasure as his hips snapped forward one last time, sending a hot rush of come across Marick's knuckles. He spasmed once, twice more, painting stripes across Marick's black t-shirt.

Marick blinked and slowly licked his lips. Caleb, still trying to catch his breath, could see the evidence of Marick's own arousal and he reached forward to grab at the other man's waistband. When his hand was batted away with a gruff, "leave it!" Caleb's senses returned to him, along with his apprehension.

What the fuck have I gotten myself into?

Marick made a half-assed attempt to wipe the front of his shirt clean, then pulled Caleb away from the door and back into his embrace.

"I need you to stay put."

"What, here? In the—"

"Stay. Put. Don't leave the house." Marick's jaw clenched and Caleb had enough sense to keep any further argument to himself.

"Okay, but what about you? I could just—"

Marick splayed his hands around Caleb's waist and pulled him away from the door, skilfully switching their position. Before Caleb knew what was happening,

Marick dropped a gentle, almost tender kiss to his forehead, then exited the small room, leaving Caleb alone and bewildered.

After a quick wash-up and a much-needed splash of water to his heated face, Caleb made his way back toward the kitchen in the hopes that Marick hadn't gone far. Much to his chagrin, the only person he found was a sympathetic looking Franka.

"More cocoa?" she asked with a knowing smile.

"Um, no thanks. Is Marick.... Did he leave?" Caleb could feel a god-awful blush creep into his hairline.

"He shouldn't be gone long. He needs to...." Franka had the good grace to let the sentence hang and not offer up any detail.

Before an uncomfortable silence had a chance to settle in, Caleb jumped in feet first. Marick was obviously a tight-lipped sonuvabitch, but maybe his sister might be a bit more forthcoming.

"So what do we do now? About this *bestem* thing?"

"Nothing. Unless you want to."

Caleb forced a strained sounding chuckle. "Really? Thank fuck." But even as he said it, Caleb knew his flippant response was far from honest. Sure, the man was arrogant and unflappable, but for some damn reason, Caleb was actually starting to believe the whole bestem-destined thing. He didn't particularly like it, but he wasn't completely opposed to the idea of spending more time in Marick's company—especially after their little grapple against the bathroom door.

"Really. As long as there's been no exchange of bodily fluids, then the bonding process stays dormant."

There'd definitely been bodily fluids, but only Caleb's, and nothing that could be called an exchange.

But Caleb suddenly remembered the beer and his ridiculous attempt at seduction, and he felt the blush return.

"So when you say bodily fluids, do you mean *any* bodily fluids? Or are we talking seed-of-life kinda thing?

"Any."

Fuck.

"Say, hypothetically, I drank out of Marick's beer bottle and caught just the tiniest bit of backwash. I'd be fine right?"

"Oh."

"Oh, what?"

"Then you really do need to stay put."

"Yeah, I don't really see that happening."

"No, really, Caleb. If the bonding process has been triggered, and I'm guessing it has, the pain of separation will be nearly unbearable. With our kind, it's not just a bond of affection or of sexual monogamy, a skakelaar bond is also mystical and permanent."

"Started?" The permanent part had Caleb's hackles up as well, but he was trying to focus on one thing at a time. Panicking wasn't likely to help

"A skakelaar's *bestem* need only a drop of his or her DNA to act as a trigger. But the process isn't complete until you've—I guess *consummated* is the best word for it—your relationship." The look of fear in Caleb's eyes registered quickly and Franka added, "And I don't mean that little hand job in the bathroom earlier."

"How did you—"

Franka's slowly arched brow and an elegant index finger laid aside of her nose gave Caleb more than enough response to the question he nearly asked.

"I'm sure Marick can give you any hands-on guidance you may need, but it's pretty self-explanatory."

"Okay, so what if we don't?"

"Then you have a pretty serious decision to make. If you really don't want to complete the process, then we need to call Aoife. But you need to be absolutely certain that's what you want. I know my brother can be surly and hard-headed, but he's a good man. And he's been lonely a long time. I think he's forgotten how to act around most people. You? You likely have him in a complete tizzy, not that he'd ever admit it."

Caleb let her words sink in.

"I'm probably going to hate myself for asking, but who's *Eeefuh*?"

"She's a witch."

"Of course she is."

"She can reverse the process if no further contact is made. And this time I do actually mean what the two of you got up to in the bathroom. It's too risky."

"Well get *Eeefuh* on the fucking horn and haul her ass over here!"

"You know you curse a lot."

"I think, given the circumstance, that's to be expected, don't you?"

A sudden crash sounded from outside the front door and the house was pitched into total darkness. Caleb ran to the window but Franka quickly pulled him back and blocked him from any misguided notion he may have been entertaining that involved heading outside to investigate.

"I think the power's been cut," Franka hissed. "The yard lights are still on but they're on a different breaker."

"Marick?" Caleb tried to shout out the window, but his voice, tremulous with fear, was barely above a stage whisper.

Only a dim light illuminating part of the yard kept them from total darkness. Caleb couldn't see much beyond the edge of the front porch so he crept down the steps to the front door and reached for the handle. He barely managed to open the door a crack before it was slammed shut from the outside.

"Caleb, if you come out here, so help me I will drag you inside and chain you to a wall!"

"Marick? What's going on?" Caleb knew he sounded terrified.

"Get inside with Franka, Caleb!" Marick's voice was gruff and commanding. And Caleb did as he was told.

Caleb felt his heart pound out a staccato beat as he strained to hear anything that might give him some clue as to what was happening on the other side of that door. Then again, maybe he was better off not knowing. "Come out and face me, Porter!"

"Where's the boy?"

Caleb and Franka huddled together in the kitchen, the voices outside clearly audible from their relative safety. The second voice wasn't familiar to Caleb, but it was a sure bet that this was the man responsible for the carnage he'd witnessed earlier.

"He's got no part in your quarrel, Porter."

"Oh, but he does. He means something to you. And that's all the reason I need to destroy him before I move on to you and the rest of your family."

"You're right about that. He means everything to me." Marick growled. "And for that reason alone, you will never lay a finger on him!"

What the fuck? Caleb shot a questioning look at Franka. She simply smiled, shrugged and mouthed the word, "bestem."

"I never wanted this. Any of this! I never asked to be like… you!" Porter spat. His voice sounded crazed and unstable.

"Doesn't excuse what you're doing," Marick shouted. "That's not our way. It never has been."

"Your way killed my mother!"

"You mother died in childbirth." Caleb could tell Marick was attempting to diffuse the situation before it got even uglier.

"Because she was delivering *me*—an abomination!"

"You can't keep killing out of some misplaced sense of rage against human kind. It won't change who you are."

"My rage isn't against humans. It's against your kind!"

"That boy at the club was human," Marick's snarled words echoed through the night air.

"So is the one I know is in your kitchen. But he's different, isn't he? He's yours."

For some reason Caleb didn't bristle at the statement the way he probably should have. Paralyzing fear did have a way of rearranging a man's priorities.

"Be a man, Porter. If it's me you want, come after me directly. Don't leave a string of corpses along your way."

"The boy at the club wasn't planned, just a delicious bonus. Tearing apart the other one while you watch, that's what's going to make my night."

"Never going to happen." The slow and careful delivery of Marick's words sounded dangerous and menacing. Caleb was grateful they weren't aimed in his direction.

"And who's going to stop me? You?"

A tense moment of silence was broken by a feral snarl followed by a low-pitched threatening growl.

Caleb was frantic to see what was happening. But when Franka whispered, "Oh shit, they've shifted," he was grateful for his woefully human night vision.

The hair on the back of his neck bristled as Caleb listened carefully at the window for some sign that Marick was okay. Instead he was greeted with a terrifying symphony of wild barks, snaps, and roars. Caleb stood stock still for what seemed like hours, hearing only the gristly sound of snapping teeth, and the horrible rumble of fighting animals. He knew it had only been mere minutes, but with every muscle in his body tensed, it felt so much longer.

A formidable howl followed by the heavy thump of a body hitting the ground sent chills down Caleb's spine. Marick could be being torn to pieces and there was fuck all he could do about it. And when a high-pitched yelp pierced the night air, Caleb reached for one of the kitchen chairs for balance. Passing out sure as hell wasn't going to help anyone. The least he could do was hold it together for Franka's sake. It was her brother out there, after all. *She must be twice as panicked as I am.*

When Marick finally walked through the front door, it took every ounce of restraint Caleb had to keep from launching himself at the man and clinging to him for dear life. Marick was covered in blood and dirt, and the shirt he carried was torn to shreds, but he looked no worse for the wear. Caleb let out a sigh of relief so loud that both Marick and Franka turned to look at him. Franka's amused smile was eclipsed by the severe expression on Marick's face, and Caleb shrank back and took a seat in the chair he'd been bracing himself against.

"What happened?" Franka's tone sounded void of any emotion.

"He's in the shed." Marick sounded just as detached.

"Is he...?" Caleb couldn't quite utter the entire question.

"He's alive. I called Aoife, she's on her way over."

"Oh." The lump Caleb found forming in his throat was a bit of a surprise. Of course he couldn't run away and live happily ever after with a man he had just met, a man who also happened to be *not* human. And it wasn't as though he was totally on board with the whole *bestem* thing, anyway. But he could see growing to not hate it quite so much. With Aoife on her way over, though, it was obvious that Marick was ready to be rid of him as quickly as possible.

"How long will it take her to...." Again Caleb found himself struggling to finish his sentences.

"Not long," Marick replied.

A light knock at the door kept Caleb from continuing his line of questioning.

Franka disappeared to let in their awaited guest and Caleb watched as Marick bent to toss his torn shirt into a recycling box next to the sink. The man was built like a damn comic-book hero. Muscles bunched and flexed with each simple movement as he washed the worst of the grime from his face, and Caleb found himself squirming, once again, with the effort to hide his body's reaction. So caught up in worshiping the man with his eyes, Caleb barely noticed that Marick had turned around and was now watching him as he ogled.

Dammit.

Caleb's embarrassment was mercifully cut short when Franka and a tall redheaded woman entered the room in a whirl of chatter and conversation.

"Caleb, this is Aoife. Aoife, Caleb."

"Nice to meet you," Caleb offered as they all seated themselves at the table.

Marick took the chair closest to Caleb and leaned forward, elbows on the table.

"Thanks for coming so quickly." Marick was still shirtless and Caleb had to stifle a giddy giggle when he felt the heat that radiated from his skin.

"Of course. We can't have our community coming under fire because of one loose cannon."

Caleb found himself drifting in and out of the conversation. He hoped the procedure wouldn't be painful. He knew he wasn't exactly the toughest cookie in the jar.

The sight of Aoife unwrapping a syringe that looked big enough to fell a horse, however, caused Caleb to instinctively pull back from the table, his chair screeching abrasively across the laminate flooring.

"What the fuck!"

Marick pulled his own chair closer to Caleb and gently placed a hand on the younger man's shoulder.

"It's not for you, *soet bestem*. It's for Porter." Marick gave Caleb's arm a quick squeeze before casually moving his hand to rest out of sight, on Caleb's thigh.

Despite the soothing—and not entirely unarousing—effect that Marick's hand massaging small circles on his leg was having, Caleb still wasn't convinced.

"It's for my retrogression spell," Aoife added with a look of sympathy directed at Caleb. "A mixture of aconite and althaea leaves can neutralize his skakelaar side and keep him from shifting ever again.

"But it is permanent," she said to Marick.

"It's either that or I end him. And I don't want any more blood spilled tonight."

"Then take me to him. I can stay by his side until the spell takes effect." Aoife wrapped up the syringe and gathered her belongings. And with a raised eyebrow and a pointed look toward Caleb, she added, "I can see you have more important and far more pleasant things to attend to."

"I'll come with you and help you get set up." Franka looked from her brother to Caleb, and back again, before making her exit with the witch.

With the threat of imminent danger now at bay, Caleb let his mind wander. What happened now? Was he supposed to bring up the whole *bestem* thing? It wasn't like it was some minor detail they could just sweep under the carpet, or at least that's how Franka made it sound. But Marick hadn't said a damn word since they'd been left alone. Instead he was standing in front of the sink again, just staring out the window. And he was still shirtless.

Like that's a simple thing to ignore.

"Listen it's stupid late, and I have no idea how to get back to town." Caleb folded his arms over his chest and crossed the room to stand near Marick. "Do you think I could maybe get a lift now that—"

"No." The growled response was a little harsh and a lot unexpected.

"Okay, fine. I'll wait and ask your sister."

Marick turned to Caleb and reached out to encircle his waist, his large hand pulling Caleb close and settling possessively on his hip. Caleb wasn't sure if he believed in the whole destined mate thing. But then, before tonight, he hadn't believed in shifters or witches either. He did know that the magnetic attraction he felt toward Marick was inexplicably powerful. And right now, standing this close to the man, Caleb knew it was something he needed to explore.

"I just found you." Marick carded his fingers through Caleb's hair, and Caleb leaned into the caress.

The touch was surprisingly gentle and, not surprisingly, incredibly arousing. Then again, Caleb was pretty sure Marick could just look at him and he would find it arousing. In fact, that little theory had already been proven hours ago. "Stay. One night?"

"And then what?" Caleb was pretty sure one night wasn't going to be enough. He was also certain that agreeing to the rest of his life measured damn high on the crazy scale. But maybe there was a happy medium?

"I don't know. I honestly didn't expect to find you." Marick pushed Caleb against the counter, his hips pinning him in place. "But here you are." Marick paused and lowered his head, burying his face in Caleb's neck. His nose poked at Caleb's throat as he continued to nuzzle. When Caleb realized what was happening, he was unable to keep a moan from escaping. *Oh, god. He's scenting me. Why is that so fucking hot?*

Caleb rested his hands at Marick's waist and tried to hold himself together, a task easier said than done when standing groin to groin with a man so sexy it made Caleb's teeth itch. A low groan rumbled up from Marick's chest when Caleb tilted his hips just enough to press into the length of hard, unyielding flesh he now desperately wanted to touch.

Marick licked a swath up Caleb's neck and nipped lightly under his ear before taking his face in both hands. He traced a thumb across Caleb's bottom lip and gasped at the touch of Caleb's darting tongue.

Caleb's heart raced and electricity sparked everywhere Marick touched him. His body didn't seem to care that he'd only gotten off a few scant hours ago. And Marick didn't seem to care either as he rocked against Caleb, creating the most tantalizing friction. The sight of Marick licking his lips held Caleb rapt and he only narrowly avoided the kiss that nearly followed.

"No, don't." It was the most difficult *no* Caleb had ever uttered. "I'm not ready for that. Not yet."

"A kiss?"

"No, the—kissing is fine. I mean the bonding thing. Franka told me how it works and I'm just...."

A chuckle rumbled up from Marick's chest. "Kissing isn't what completes the bond, Caleb."

"But Franka said DNA exchange—"

"That's a delicate way to put it. And maybe to ignite the process. But trust me, you and I need to swap a lot more than just spit to seal that deal."

"So what—oh!" Realization dawned on Caleb and he snickered.

"I don't want Aoife to do her witchy thing, either."

"Then she won't."

"But am I not supposed to just *know*? Like, shouldn't I be instantly ready to just drop everything and live happily ever after like some damn fairy tale?"

"Fairy tales aren't real. Well, not entirely real. Humans tend to screw them up in the retelling."

"So you don't mind? That I'm not ready? Not just yet. It's too soon. And tonight has just been so...."

"Insane?"

"That's one word for it." Caleb grinned.

"Let me ask you this: do you want me?"

Caleb thrust his erection against Marick's thigh and beamed. "What do you think?"

"I think I'm glad you didn't listen when I told you to fuck off."

Caleb grinned and rolled his eyes at Marick's teasing tone.

"I do want you, Marick. The minute I saw you in the club I wanted you more than I've ever wanted anyone. And now?" Caleb sighed. "Now, even more so."

Marick lowered his lips and captured Caleb's in a searing kiss. Despite his brain's earlier inclination to panic, Caleb's body took over and he allowed himself to melt into Marick's touch. Liquid heat coursed through his veins and he instinctively responded, allowing his lips to part and give access to Marick's gently probing tongue. Caleb explored the sweet, warm confines of Marick's mouth until a very theatrical "ahem" interrupted them.

"I guess it's a good thing Aoife's not up to any more spell casting tonight, isn't it?" Franka smirked. "I don't know about you two, but I've had about all the excitement I can handle for one night. And I need my beauty sleep. G'night."

And once again, they were alone.

"So what now?" Caleb could see that Franka's interruption hadn't cooled Marick's ardour one iota. "I mean, if we can't... *you know*. And I'm not ready to... *you know*."

"We most certainly can *you know*." Despite a gruff delivery, the gentle tease was still evident in Marick's voice.

"But what about the whole bestem-orgasm-together-forever thing?"

"Ever hear of a condom?"

Caleb felt his head swim once again, and did his best to not stagger and buckle at the knee. The power and sway Marick held over him was undeniable; there wasn't a single imaginable universe where Caleb could ever see himself saying no to the man. And when Marick pinned him with a heated gaze, then started toward the stairs, Caleb wasted no time following close on his heels.

"You seem pretty damn confident I'm just going to tag along after you, no questions asked." Caleb realized how daft he sounded, considering he was doing exactly that. And when they entered a darkened bedroom

Caleb assumed was Marick's, he ramped up his false bravado—or, at least, tried to. "Am I supposed to just drop to my knees when you snap your fingers?"

Marick held his hand aloft, fingers poised to click a response in front of Caleb, as a lascivious smirk spread across his face. Instead he took a step closer and simply lowered his hand to stroke a finger down Caleb's jawline. With his free hand Marick circled one of Caleb's hips and pushed him up against the far wall, the gentleness and the forcefulness of the move seemingly at odds.

Not allowing him time to react, Marick dipped his head down and captured Caleb's lips in a kiss so bone meltingly hot that, once again, Caleb was lost. Any of his previous inclinations to bolt were gone, any fear that might have lingered was a distant memory, and any thoughts beyond touching every single inch of this exquisitely built man in front of him, had vanished.

Caleb opened to Marick's kiss, his hands working their way up across sculpted muscles and to nipples he worried and pinched to hardened peaks. A deep, rumbling groan from Marick sent tendrils of heat to Caleb's groin and he was certain that this time he would, in fact, come in his pants.

Marick, apparently, had other plans. As he broke the kiss and grinned at the desperate whimper that escaped Caleb's lips, Marick took a half pace back and slowly ran his hands down his own chest toward his waist, slipped the button from its confines and unzipped his fly.

Caleb took this as his cue, and without further prompting, he dropped to his knees, taking Marick's jeans to the floor with him. Marick was deliciously commando, and Caleb licked his lips in anticipation of tasting the gorgeous, solid flesh on display. The hooded gaze that Marick directed at him was proof enough that he had made the right choice.

Caleb braced his hands on thighs like tree trunks, and leaned forward to run his tongue across Marick's balls. There was no way in hell he was even going to attempt to dazzle the man with deep-throat skills—he was pretty sure the laws of physics would prevent it, anyway—but it didn't mean he couldn't impress Marick with a few flourishes of his own.

The smell of arousal rolled off Marick in waves and Caleb's mouth watered. He lavished wet, sloppy licks upon every inch of Marick's tightened sac, then took one ball into his mouth completely. The resulting groan spurred him on to repeat his ministrations to the other one, then back again. A glistening pearl of moisture dropped from the head of Marick's magnificent cock, and Caleb had yet to even touch him there.

Caleb glanced up through his eyelashes, flicked the tip of his tongue over the slit, and marvelled at the taste of Marick's arousal. He ran his tongue up the full length of Marick's shaft, then took the fat, mushroom head into his mouth as he firmly gripped the base with one hand. Caleb swirled his tongue around the spongy tip, and started a firm, even stroke. Slow and steady, Caleb slid Marick's cock in and out of his mouth, his lips creating the perfect suction as his hand worked in tandem.

Caleb felt Marick's thighs flex under his fingertips as he growled out, "Stop!"

And, as Caleb sat back on his heels and palmed his own aching erection, Marick grabbed his hand and pulled him to his feet.

"This isn't ending with just a blowjob. I want your ass."

Caleb rummaged through his pockets, but Marick was quicker on the draw and had a condom at the ready almost instantly.

"Please tell me you have lube somewhere, too." Caleb's eyes widened as he took in the size of Marick once more. "Lots of it."

"As much as you need." Marick grinned and waved a bottle in front of Caleb's face. "We do have one more problem, though." Marick's gaze traveled the length of Caleb's body, then returned to his wide-eyed stare. Marick rolled on the condom, then raised a brow at Caleb. "Clothes?"

Caleb shucked his pants and shirt so quickly he nearly tripped over himself in the process. But when he started to tumble forward, Marick grasped his shoulders and kicked the pants aside for him. Marick ran one hand down Caleb's back, while the lube-covered fingers of his other hand trailed purposefully into the crack of his ass.

Caleb gasped indelicately as Marick worked the tip of one finger into his asshole, and when the big man nipped teasingly at his throat with lips and teeth, he nearly came apart. He'd never been this hard in his life. When Marick started finger fucking him in earnest with two of those big fingers, Caleb knew he was in for the ride of his life. And he was more than ready for it.

What he wasn't ready for, was Marick picking him up bodily from the floor. Caleb yelped and instinctively wrapped his legs around Marick's waist, giving Marick ample opportunity to line himself up with Caleb's eager ass. Marick's big hands under Caleb's thighs left him trembling at what was to come. And when he felt the blunt head of that huge dick at his entrance, Caleb forced himself downward.

"Fuck me!" Caleb shouted out as he impaled himself upon Marick. The sensation of being suspended in air—his ass full of throbbing flesh—with only Marick's brute strength holding him aloft, made Caleb's head spin. And as Marick thrust up into him over and over, Caleb could only cling to the man's shoulders and moan incoherently.

Caleb's own cock was trapped between their sweaty flesh, Marick's flat stomach and abs creating an exquisite torture; each thrust a dual stroke to Caleb's leaking dick. There wasn't anything slow or romantic about the way Marick manhandled him, and Caleb was *so* okay with that.

Grunts and growls that weren't quite human sounded in Caleb's ears. Each forceful thrust was countered with a long, slow slide out, and as the animalistic sounds increased, Marick's onslaught grew harder and faster.

Caleb's own groans echoed in his head and he felt the tell-tale tightening of his balls; one more thrust and Caleb howled out his release as his orgasm was, quite literally, pounded out of him. Marick growled and pushed Caleb against the door, his thrusts becoming almost brutal. Caleb wrapped his arms around Marick's neck and held on tightly.

"Come for me, Marick," Caleb panted into Marick's ear.

Marick bellowed out his release with one final ferocious thrust and Caleb was certain he saw stars. Marick's chest heaved and Caleb felt his own lungs screaming from exertion.

"Quick and dirty is definitely your strong suit." Caleb grinned as he slowly lowered both feet to the floor. He winced slightly as Marick withdrew from his tender, abused ass. He'd definitely be feeling that for a day or two. Marick tied off the used condom and tossed it in the trash, then took Caleb in his arms once more, kissing him soundly.

Caleb smiled up at Marick and ran his hands over solidly muscled arms. "You called me *soet bestem* earlier. What does that mean?"

"My sweet destined one." Marick stared straight into Caleb's eyes, almost daring him to mock.

"A bit cheesy, but I can live with it."

"Think you can you live with me being your mate and not your daddy?" Marick laughed out loud at the sheepish expression on Caleb's face.

"Well, I am a little old for that twink shit, after all."

The End

www.ldblakeley.com

7 AUTHOR ANTHOLOGY

TROUBLE

Copyright © 2015

James Cox

Chapter One

I was holding on for dear life. My fingers were curled around a section of windowsill and my bare feet were perched sideways on a small ledge. I was hunched slightly, making sure nothing scraped against the wall of the building. I was also, very, very, naked.

"What the hell are you doing?" That would be Rigele, my would-be lover, yelling in the room I had just vacated.

"I know he's here!" And that would be Rigel's mate, Cam. "I know you're fucking that bastard Tremarc."

You don't have parents and suddenly everybody finds it acceptable to call you a bastard. Of course, I did just have his boyfriend's lips wrapped around my dick.

I stayed silent. It was night, so the shadows hid most of my body. The moon was covered by thick rain clouds. I could probably make the four-story jump, but then I'd pass on the opportunity to hop back in the window and get Rigel's mouth back on me.

"We're not married. I can fuck whoever I want, but no, I was *not* with Tremarc." Rigel's voice filtered through the open window louder than it had been.

Were they edging closer to me? I glanced down. I might have to attempt this jump.

"Tremarc has slept with every fucking bear in our clan. Hell, that's why they kicked him out of the last one. Why would you let him shit on our love?"

"Because you're a limped-dick bully," Rigel shouted.

Okay. My cue to get the fuck out. I shifted my feet so I could kick off the building if I angled my ass out. With a good push, I might be able to land in those green bushes near the front of his apartment. And for the record, they didn't kick me out of the last clan. I left because there was a mob of angry exes that *chased* me out of town. Totally different from being kicked out. I slanted my body for the jump. Too bad I couldn't shift just my hands. I was a Spectacled bear and we could climb like a damn lizard.

"I couldn't get it up one time!" Cam yelled, and it sounded directly in front of the window. "I was drunk...."

Why didn't he finish? I was mildly curious as to his argument. I glanced up. "Ah, fuck it."

Cam was glaring down at me. The angry mate with a thick beard, long black hair, and wild eyes, grabbed my wrist.

My feet slid off the perch, I dangled as my shoulder protested. "Hey, Cam," I tried for casual. I still held on with one hand but my fingers were starting to strain.

"I'm going to kill you!" he screamed. And then the scary mother fucker lifted me to eye level.

I loosened my hand from the windowsill, poked him in the eye and he let go. I heard his roar as I tumbled backward, falling down the four stories in the blink of an eye. I bounced off the apartment canopy, landed in the bushes and the momentum rolled me into the street.

I grabbed my dick, making sure it was unscathed. *Yup, all good.* I shoved to my feet and ran as fast as my legs could take me. Running naked through my new bear clan village got a few glances. Okay, more than a few. Damn, I was going to get run off again. Just how many clans were left on earth?

"Mr. Tremarctos Smith."

I froze. Talk about bad timing. "Hello Alpha Quick." I turned around, keeping my hands over my crotch. "Nice night for a stroll." I could see his full head of black hair and the crinkle of lines at the corner of his eyes. He was the leader of this pack, just passing fifty and still looked like he could rip my throat out.

"I want you in my den at dawn."

"Yes, Sir." I wasn't a fan of submissiveness, but he was the alpha. Showing him up would lead to a fight, which I wasn't sure I'd win.

He grunted and turned to keep walking down the street.

I sighed. No point in even trying to hide now. I closed my eyes and started to shift into my bear form. My skin prickled like pins and needles. I felt the shift of my bones as I fell to all fours. The world around me blacked out for a split second, then I saw everything through my bear eyes.

My fur was a dark black except for my face, which had light brown markings around my eyes and nose. I licked my muzzle and started padding toward home. The den that I called mine didn't have much in it. The way I moved around, it was good to keep it simple.

It's not like I had a home to begin with. I was an orphan, born then discarded , and since then it's been one clan or another. Sometimes I felt a little sad that I didn't have a true place to call home, but who needed a home when you could chase tail all over the world?

My house was partially dug into a rock formation. It was a tiny thing that I had stocked with fresh vegetables. Another thing the other bears looked down on me for. I was a vegetarian—hell most of my species was—nothing wrong with that, but by the way the clans looked at me, you'd think I was the runt of the litter. Which I wasn't. At six feet tall, I was fit with sandy hair the same color of the markings on my face.

I padded on my oversized paws to the front door and sat on the porch that had seen better days. If only Cam hadn't come home. I'd have fucked Rigel, felt amazing, and fought off these depressing thoughts.

I sighed as I stared up at the stars. I could see them better with bear eyes. Each twinkle was brighter, the moon more visible. I could actually see the domes. Each big country had a sheer dome that kept our people safe up there. It was going pretty well too. Taking the strain off Earth. Of course, there was a shifter colony. I wasn't sure if it was mixed or only one species, though.

A wolf howled and my ears perked up. Yeah, I was procrastinating. I didn't want to go inside and start packing. Not that it mattered what I wanted. There would always be another town, another man.

Chapter Two

"I've spoken to several different clans, Tremarctos."

I hated when people used my full name. I was an orphan so they just named me after my species' technical name, Tremarctos Ornatus. Tremarc sounded less... pansy ass. I adjusted my clean black shirt that hugged my upper half. Black jeans were on my legs showing off my ass. There was a hole in the back of the knee, but I made sure to face the alpha so he wouldn't see it.

"Most clans have already had the... pleasure of your company."

I remained silent. We were in his den—the study, to be specific. The smell of old, dusty books made my nose twitch. The desk before me was a thick yellow wood that creaked as the alpha leaned on it.

"There are, in fact, only two clans you haven't been to."

Two? That was it? "Are any of them for Spectacled bears?" I blurted. Since my childhood, I'd never found a clan just for my kind. There were so few of us left.

"No." The Alpha's hard features softened. "I'm sorry." He cleared his throat. "And you can no longer remain here."

Ah, here it came. The leave-or-we'll-chase-you-away speech.

"You've had several illicit affairs which caused...." He glanced at the paper in front of him. "Five brawls in the street, three mated couples breaking up, two men are in the hospital from fight related injuries, and one bear is convinced you're a demon."

I fought the urge to grin. That poor bastard should have listened when I told him not to eat that mushroom.

"Because of this, I have here a ticket to the moon."

"What?"

"There is one bear clan on the moon. This Alpha happens to be the leader of the United States' Dome. He agreed to take you in." The alpha slid the white slip toward me rather than continue. "The shuttle leaves in two hours."

"Not only are you kicking me out, but you're sending me to the fucking *moon*?"

The alpha shot to his feet and growled. The sound sent a shiver down my spine. "I am the alpha here, Tremarctos, and don't you ever forget it. I could let the clan handle you, but instead I'm giving you a chance."

"On the moon."

He crossed his arms over his chest.

I guessed the conversation was over. And I guessed I was heading for the fucking moon.

I picked up the shuttle at the nearest airport. Hundreds of people travel to the moon every day, so I really wasn't nervous. I had one bag of clothes and a picture of my first foster parents. That was stuffed under my only pair of pants without holes. I leaned back in the half-empty ride and closed my eyes. Even as the vibrating started, I kept my eyes closed.

Maybe the moon would be good for me. New asses to conquer. Yeah, that'd cheer me up. Maybe I could find a sexy ass up on the moon. I did men who were already taken. It just made the victory that much sweeter. I opened my eyes to stare out the window as we lifted off the ground, off Earth. Thanks to technology, it only took an hour to get to the moon's surface. The whole time I thought about the possible new conquests. Hey, every guy should have a hobby.

We landed and I felt the floor vibrate as the tube extracted and connected to the dome. It took two minutes to fill the connection with air and then I stepped onto my new home. The city on the moon was all shiny, tall, buildings bunched together with narrow streets. The dome covered everything, including the few trees I saw. It wasn't a dirty place, but it wasn't scenic like Earth. The night and days here lasted two weeks long. And wasn't I lucky, the sun was glaring down. I'd get a hell of a lot of time to tan.

The air was stale from the oxygen generators. It made breathing a little harder. There were small trees flourishing along the inside of the doom. Outside was the dry, dull, white surface of the moon and craters that could hide entire cities. The streets were filled with people, some walking, others cruising in their hover cars. Home, sweet home.

I got in line like everyone else. A thin man with glasses took my papers and handed me a chip. It fit into the palm of my hand. It held my credit information, blood type, and license. I made my way past the horde of newcomers and toward the street. Despite not wanting to appear like a tourist or a lost lamb looking for company, I glanced up at the dome. It was huge, easily high enough to accommodate one-hundred-story buildings. The sky overhead was bright, dotted with stars that were hard to see with my human eyes and... Earth. I could see the continents and the oceans. There was a mass of clouds over South America. It took my breath away, watching it all the way from the moon.

"Hey."

I glanced at the driver that half hung out the window.

"You need a ride. I can take you to the very first moon landing."

I opened my mouth to flirt because the guy was kind of cute, but someone beat me to it.

"He's taken." The voice was behind me and I was pleased when I turned around and saw a very sexy man in a suit. I lifted an eyebrow taking in the way his auburn hair looked mussed from really good morning sex. Believe me, I could recognize it anywhere.

His green eyes were narrowed as I looked him over. He was handsome, fit, and the suit looked delicious on him. "Hello. Do I know you? Can I get to know you?" I smiled wide.

He chuckled. "Does that line actually work?"

"Nope." I stepped up to him. "But it does make people like me. Especially fine looking men like yourself."

"Easy there, bear, I'm already taken."

My smiled instantly dropped. He knew I was a bear shifter. Not many humans knew of our existence. I sniffed the air. My nose was stronger than a human's was, and I could smell he was not one of us. But he did smell of bear, like he had been riding atop of one—naked—for the last few hours. A residual scent.

"Don't start growling at me, big boy." He was still smiling. "I'm Quinn."

Ah, so he was the mate to my new alpha. Interesting and way too dangerous to go for, but you know me, I'm always pushing the line.

"I hear you're our newest member. I'll show you to him." Quinn walked past me to the hover car that pulled up.

I waited to stare at his ass and then followed. "So, what's the leader like?" I sat in the back seat with him.

We took off as Quinn spoke. "Lyon is a great guy."

"Lyon?" I snorted. "A bear shifter named Lyon? Seriously?"

Quinn didn't look offended. "Long story. And if you're nice to him he may even tell it to you."

"Eh, I ain't interested in his story." I leaned so I was clearly on his side of the hover car. "What makes you live on the moon and mate a bear name after a kitty cat?"

"Well, what makes a smart man like you get kicked out of so many bear colonies?" He countered.

I smirked. "I just love to make love and I'm real fucking good at it."

Quinn didn't respond as the hover car stopped. He thanked the driver who just waved and then we both exited. I stared out at a large building, nearly one-hundred-stories high, I estimated. The outside was shiny with reinforced glass and the large arched door had two men on either side. Both shifters. I winked at the cuter one and followed Quinn inside.

The hover lift could fit at least eight people, but I stood as close to Quinn as I possibly could. "So, how did you handle the shifter thing?"

"I...." He paused. "I kind of passed out."

I snorted. "Hey, at least you didn't run screaming."

"I ran, then passed out." He smiled. "Took some getting used to, but I love Lyon. He really is an honest guy. Bear."

"So you never get bored sleeping with just one man? He must have a hell of a mouth."

Quinn lifted an eyebrow. "No I don't, and yes he does." The doors opened.

We walked into a foyer that lead to a large living room. "How long you two been together?" There were lots of browns and beiges, even a lamp with wooden bears climbing up it. I rolled my eyes.

"Two years."

"That's a long time chewing the same meat," I muttered. There were huge windows here that displayed the city below. The door to my right, the one with the cubs carved into it, opened, and I was momentarily stunned. This was the alpha? This was the guy Quinn fucked? He was so much older. Quinn was a few years older than my twenty two but this guy had to be at least forty or older. He had dark brown hair that brushed his shoulders and there were strands of grey sprinkled in there. Some hair was pulled back to show off his face. He had brown eyes, with abundant lines near the outer corners. He had a neatly trimmed beard and a scowl on his face. His shirt was off, showing his muscular chest splattered with dark hair.

"Tremarctos?" Lyon's voice was deep. A rumble of sound before an earthquake.

"Everybody calls me Tremarc."

He pulled his shirt over his head. "I'm Alpha Lyon."

I smiled, that was just too weird.

"Yes, I've heard all the jokes before, so you can wipe the smug look off your face."

I rolled my eyes. All these alpha types were the same.

"You're a new member of this community. Until we have a home for you, you'll be staying here where I can watch you." He narrowed his eyes, making the age lines stand out. "Any trouble from you and I'll shoot you out the dome airlock. You understand that?"

"Yes, sir," I said with completely no gusto.

He pointed to the door on the left. "You sleep there. That the only bag you have?"

I nodded.

"Good. Go put it down, we're eating together tonight."

I spun on my heels like a good boy and went to put my things away. When I closed the door, I leaned against it. He seemed like more of a hard ass than usual—and why was he named Lyon? Stupid fucker.

"You could have been a little nicer." I heard Quinn's voice.

"I am being nice," Lyon replied.

"You're being an ass. He's hurting, he's lonely, can't you see that?"

"The only one who's hurting, is me. My fucking pants get any tighter over my dick and there'll be permanent damage."

I snorted. Their voices moved away until they were just muffled sounds. I looked out the large window. It faced the dome, showing off the plain, pale moon and empty craters. Home, sweet home, but for how long?

Chapter Three

"So do you have any hobbies?"

Fucking. "Not really." We were sitting at the small wooden table made for four in a large kitchen filled with browns and more bear stuff then was sane. I was across from Lyon waiting for food. Apparently, Quinn cooked.

"You good at anything?"

Fucking. "Nothing in particular."

"What kind of jobs have you had?" He asked.

Escaping and evading angry mates, usually naked. "Not many."

Quinn came toward us. "He's not very talkative. Reminds me of you." He smiled at Lyon then placed three plates down.

I frowned. There was a huge piece of meat and a helping of asparagus with butter melting over the top of it. I picked up my fork and started with the only thing I could eat. It didn't taste bad either. Soft, buttery, that unique asparagus flavor underneath with a sprinkling of pepper.

"You don't eat steak?" Quinn asked with the fork of meat halfway to his mouth.

"I'm a...." I paused and prepared myself for the usual laughter. "I'm a vegetarian."

"Nice!" Lyon instantly leaned over the table, shoved his asparagus onto my plate and stole my meat. He sat down with a hardy smile. "Best news I've heard all day."

"You big brute," Quinn said but chuckled. "You should have told me, I would have made something else."

"This is fine," Lyon answered. "He gets the green bits and I'll take the meat." He popped a piece in his mouth and chewed.

The smile looked good on him. Or maybe it was just that most shifters laughed at me. These guys didn't— hell, Quinn was talking about rearranging the meals for me. I wasn't expecting that. It made me take another long look at them. "Thanks."

I dug into my food, feeling a little guilty about having tried to steal Quinn.

While we ate, I learned about the moon, and Quinn and Lyon. Apparently, the alpha owned the only bank in the United States' Dome. Quinn was working for him as an accountant when they found out they were mated. They mention something about overcoming exes, but were seriously vague.

I left the table feeling completely awkward. Look at how happy they were. Two years they'd been together and they still smiled at each other. I had a boyfriend for all of one week and that was only because he wouldn't leave me alone. But hey, crazy sex is always amazing.

I made my way back to my new room. It was sparsely furnished: a bed with bears carved into the post, a dresser, a desk with more bears, a large window and me. My bag was on the floor. It wasn't like I had a lot to unpack. I lay back on the bed and stared at the ceiling until sleep claimed me.

Chapter Four

"You've been a bad boy." Lyon's deep voice was low, but I heard it clearly.

I slipped off the bed, rubbing my eyes as I walked to the door. We were in the sunny phase of the moon so I had no idea what time it was.

"Very bad," Quinn spoke. "I think I need to be punished."

My eyebrows lifted. This was getting interesting. I placed my ear to the thick wood. It sounded like they were kissing or someone was sucking dick. *And I was missing it!* I slowly turned the knob and opened the door an inch at a time.

They *were* kissing. I watched as Lyon and Quinn sucked at each other's mouths. There was a hint of tongue as they stood in the living room before the big window. "Get your tight ass in the bedroom," Lyon ordered.

Quinn obeyed, looking giddy as he made his way into the bedroom across the way. He began to undress as Lyon marched toward him. Quinn had pierced nipples. I saw the shiny rings and nearly drooled. They were gorgeous against his freckled skin. His stomach was flat, flexing as he bent over. I saw the line of his back and heard the rustle of his pants. Then Lyon walked into the bedroom and closed the door. Damn it!

I toed my boots off and rushed across the living room as silently as I could. My dick was growing firm between my legs as I stopped at the door. I pressed my ear to it and closed my eyes.

"Take my cock out," Lyon's growled out.

Holy fuck. His deep voice sent a shiver down my spine. I wasn't sure if I was lusting after Lyon or Quinn.

Usually I picked the sexiest of the pair and worked my seduction magic. Now, I couldn't really choose.

I heard a soft whimper. With as much stealth as I could muster, I touched the knob and inched it open. When the door parted from the frame, I held my breath. *A little bit more....* It opened a few inches. I stopped when I could see them. Lyon was standing tall and so very naked. The long, muscular line of his back met up with his gorgeously tight ass. His thick thighs flexed, legs spread shoulder width apart. Then I saw Quinn on his knees before him.

He was still wearing boxers of a creamy-beige color. His knees dug into the carpet as his body shifted back and forth. I heard the loud slurping sounds and had to bite back a moan. What did Lyon's cock look like? Was he cut? Foreskin? I needed to know.

I shoved my buttons open, popping one and sending it careening toward the large, sunny window. My pants fell to my ankles and my shaft bounced free. I grabbed my balls first, cupping them and soaking in pleasure.

"Deeper, Quinn." Lyon's voice was breathy.

I wrapped my hand around the base of my dick. I was shaved so it was just skin on skin. My cock was fully erect now. The flesh was tan with a pink tip, void of foreskin. I slid my fingers to the curved end, swirled the cloudy drop on my palm and then eased back down.

"Hold it," Lyon spoke with a gasp. "Hold it."

I was breathing heavily, my hand frozen on my dick as Quinn deep throated.

"Keep holding. Don't you dare come up for air."

Fuck me! I pumped my dick, watching as Lyon stared down at Quinn. I'd love to witness his cock disappear down the sexy man's throat.

"Release."

Quinn gasped as he fumbled to his feet.

"Good boy." Lyon pushed him back onto the bed. "You want me to make you feel better?"

"Yes, please, sir." Quinn pulled off his boxers, revealing his shaft.

Damn, I wanted a close up. From here I could see his long length and cut tip. I started stroking my dick. Up and down, my ass muscles flexing, my free hand moved to cup my balls. I watched as Quinn moved to all fours. Lyon started fingering his ass. I could see as he slid two fingers between Quinn's cheeks.

My pleasure doubled, I felt it crawl up my spine like a shiver. I stroked faster. I was so close to coming that it was getting hard to stay quiet. But there was no way I'd miss Lyon and Quinn fucking. I pulled my hand away from my dick long enough to stave off my pleasure for another few minutes.

Quinn grabbed something from the side of the bed, probably lube. Yeah…. He dripped some on his erect cock, which was still out of my sight. Then he turned and the giant weapon came into view. That fucking thing was a god among men. He was huge, long and wide with gorgeous foreskin that shimmered in the light. I may have drooled. Just a little.

He pressed his tip to Quinn's hole. I watched, rubbing my hands along my thighs, aching to rub my shaft again. Quinn hissed out a breath.

"Push back. Force me into you," Lyon ordered

Quinn started to thrust back, inch by inch as he hissed and groaned. Lyon remained still, hands on his hips as he made his lover do all the work. "You're so fucking tight." Lyon grunted then grabbed Quinn's hips and started pounding in earnest.

I grabbed my dick and pumped. Quinn cried out. He started chanting Lyon's name. The big bear slammed inside over and over again. I felt my pulse racing as I squeezed my cock harder. The orgasm was so close.

"Yes, *please!*" Quinn screamed. "Fuck me, Lyon. Harder, harder!"

Sweet fuck, he was begging. I jammed a hand over my mouth as the orgasm tore through me. Long streams of cum shot out of my slit and sprayed the door. It splattered as my eyelids closed. I savored the trembling muscles, the urge to groan but not being able to.

I heard the intense moan from the other room. It had to be Lyon. The sound was followed by a gasp and a shout. That would be Quinn. I opened my eyes, standing with my cum now covering their door. I did not think this one through. How the fuck was I going to wipe this away without them noticing or smelling—

"—The fuck!" Lyon yelled, then growled. It wasn't from pleasure. That resonance was the roar before the battle of our animals. He sniffed the air. My eyes widened. In three strides, he had his hand on the door, shoving it open.

I fell back, tripping on my pants that were still around my ankles. And there I was, with my knees spread, ankles trapped in pants, cock dangling satisfied between my legs, when Lyon glanced down at me.

"Are you fucking spying on us?" His voice went deeper. I heard the soft growl at the end, his beast fighting to get out.

"Baby, his dick's out. He wasn't spying on us, he was masturbating watching us." Quinn had a towel around his hips. He looked... amused.

"Like that's any better!" Lyon shouted. He hovered over me, looking like a demon about to create a new hell.

"Could be worse." Quinn was watching Lyon.

"And how the fuck could it be worse?"

"He could have shot your nuts off, which I'm about to do if you don't stop yelling at me!" Quinn narrowed his eyes.

Lyon finally stopped looking at me and glanced at his lover.

I quietly tucked my dick away and lifted my hips so I could pull my pants up. "I was not spying," I said, which made them both glance at my mostly naked body. "I just… heard you guys, and I was horny. You're both hot."

"You didn't think I'd smell your release?" Lyon asked. At least he wasn't yelling anymore.

"I didn't really plan that far ahead."

Lyon grunted.

"Like you've never been caught up in the moment." Quinn rolled his eyes and held out his hand.

I took it, feeling better now that my pants were on and I was standing.

"We got banned from visiting the first moon landing site because Mr. Badass Bear couldn't keep his dick in his pants," Quinn admitted.

"You weren't complaining when I was shoving it in your ass." His tone had lightened.

Quinn grinned. "Very true." He looked at me. "Now, what are we going to do with him?"

"Kick him out," Lyon said immediately.

"*No*," I shouted before I could think. What the hell kind of reaction was that? I'd been through dozens of clans, although usually I wasn't kicked out this quickly.

"I think he likes us." Quinn smiled.

"I think I don't give a fuck," Lyon growled out.

"Listen, it's almost midnight. Let him clean up our door, we go to sleep, then figure this out in the morning," Quinn suggested.

"You're being awfully calm about this," I muttered. Usually there was a lot more shouting and a few fists thrown, maybe even a shift or two.

"I just had sex. The endorphins haven't faded yet." Quinn grabbed Lyon's arm and started tugging him back toward the bedroom. "Come on, big guy."

I stood there like a fool as they went into the bedroom and closed the door. That was… odd. I shook my head and went about finding something to clean my cum off the door with. After, I would lie in bed and try to figure out what the fuck was wrong with me.

I should have been packing, not trying to find a way to stay on the moon.

Chapter Five

"I talked to several other Alphas. Apparently, you like breaking up mates." Lyon sat across from me. The three of us were on the rooftop of his building. From here, the dome seemed much bigger. I stared out at this amazing city on the surface of the moon and kept my mouth shut.

"Nothing to say?" Quinn sipped on his expensive cup of coffee. He closed his eyes like he was savoring each drop.

"I didn't break them up on purpose." Which was true. "They were hot, I flirted, we had sex, and their mates had issues with it." I didn't force anyone to do anything.

"Why would you do that?" Lyon fisted his hands on top of the table as the sun shone down on us.

I felt its warmth like a weight as I tried to answer the question. "Honestly, I don't know." It was just what I did.

"Maybe you're looking for that match, the mating," Quinn suggested.

Lyon snorted. "Because *that's* the way to do it. Steal a mate from another shifter." He crossed his arms over his massive chest. "Is that what you planned to do with Quinn and me?"

"I didn't plan anything." I stood up and walked to the edge of the roof. There was a half wall here. From this height, the noises of the city were just as loud. The sounds seemed to echo off the dome. "I heard you guys fucking and got caught up with my hand on my dick."

Quinn sipped his drink and stood up too. "Tremarc, maybe you're subconsciously trying to find your mate. You see someone else's happiness and go for theirs instead of finding your own."

"When did you become a fucking psychiatrist?" Lyon blurted.

Quinn narrowed his eyes at the big man. "Was I talking to you? No, no I don't think I was. But since you know everything, Alpha fucking bear, you tell me why he sleeps his way through entire clans?"

Lyon wisely remained silent.

"What's that?" Quinn cupped his ear. "Nothing?"

Lyon scoffed and uncrossed his arms. "His past is his own fucking problem. We have to figure out what to do with him now."

"And... I don't want to leave." I spoke quietly. The moon felt right for me. I know it sounded crazy, maybe I was losing my mind from the air filter runoff. "Let me stay. I'll work for Lyon. I'll keep my dick in my... well, I won't fuck anyone's mate." There was no way I'd be able to keep my dick locked up in my pants for days, let alone weeks.

Lyon frowned but Quinn gave me a reassuring nod.

"One screw up...," Lyon warned.

I held up my hands, palms toward him. I don't know what made me think I could pull it off. Maybe it was seeing how much Lyon and Quinn loved each other. Maybe it really was the oxygen. Either way, I was going to give this a try.

The next morning Lyon put me to work in his bank. I did menial shit that nearly bored me blind. Hell, the only thing that kept me sane was masturbating in the empty office on the top floor. I did stay away from other shifters. Several worked there. I smelled them when they passed and smiled.

Quinn really took me under his wing. We'd have lunch together. It became a habit as the week wore on.

He'd teach me accounting and skills that I hadn't used since high school. Lyon kept a watchful eye but he softened more around me. He started joining our lunches. It was nice. I felt like I was really carving out a place for myself. And that was just the first week.

When the weekend came, I was almost nervous to leave work and head home. There was an entire two days without dealing with office bullshit. I'd be left thinking of them fucking in the next room or Quinn's plump lips around Lyon's cock. I groaned and closed my eyes. I was in that empty office. There was only a desk so I was sitting atop it in my borrowed suit looking like a fool. The pants were too tight and I opened the button on my shirt so my chest could get some air. It wasn't exactly comfortable, but working here—being with Quinn and Lyon was helping. I think a small part of me expected it all to fall apart by now.

"Tremarc." Quinn's voice startled me.

I hopped off the desk and grabbed it to keep from falling backward. "Hey." Shit. My gaze darted around the room. I didn't think there was any evidence of what I did up here. The window was clean from this morning's masturbation. I smiled, trying to look casual.

"You like this spot, huh?" Quinn sat on the desk and stared out the window.

"Um, yeah. It's a nice view." I joined him, scanning the glass but finding no smudges. The view was of the city, with splotches of green trees sprinkled about. A park was going up, something to create less work for the air filters. The land had been flattened. Right now, it was a grey stain surrounded by fallen trees that weren't planted yet. "Park's going to be nice to shift and run in."

Quinn nodded. "You look sad."

"Nah." I smiled but was sure it didn't reach my eyes. "I'm good. I've been really trying to stick to the rules. Working."

"Looking for your mate?"

My smile fell. "Yeah, that too." I took what Quinn and Lyon said to heart. What if the reason I couldn't settle down was because I needed my other half? I never really thought about that before I met them.

"No luck?"

"Not one shifter or human I meet makes me want to…."

"Clutch your berries?" Quinn chuckled. "Bears, berries… get it?"

I shook my head but grinned. "Yeah, no berry clutching going on. How did you know Lyon was your mate?"

Quinn glanced out the window again. "I came here running from someone, he found me, Lyon saved me then I learned about shifters and mates. It was something to get used to." He blushed slightly. "It helps that Lyon's as… persuasive as he is."

"Yeah, I saw it when I was looking through the door." I snorted. "He is both wide and long." I licked my lips.

"It's not just his size. Lyon is… he's very dominant. He likes to be the alpha in bed and it makes me feel complete. When his hand is around my throat…."

The bulge in my pants grew firmer.

"When he's holding my wrists and pushing into me. Even when he kisses me, it's like a force of nature. It's a storm that batters me on every side." Quinn chuckled. "I sound like a fucking poet."

A grunt sounded behind us. "Have you told him?" Lyon came from the lift with a frown. Nothing new there. He walked toward us with long determined strides.

"What's going on? Told me what?"

Quinn tried to fight a smile. "Lyon got a few calls about a man who keeps masturbating in this window."

"Really?" *Oh, fuck.* "That is just disgusting. I mean, how could someone do such a thing?" I put as much conviction in my voice as possible and knew it didn't work by the small grin on Quinn's face.

Lyon lifted a dark eyebrow. "So no confession?"

"What? Me?" My voice was pitchy. I went silent. Pleading the fifth is always the plan in an awkward situation. "Well, I'll get back to work while you figure out who the culprit is." I clucked my tongue and walked toward the lift. I didn't make it two steps before Lyon stood in front of me.

"You're that hard up, you have to spray all over the windows?"

"It's not my fault it's daylight for so long!" I glanced at the ground. "No one would have seen me if it was night. Besides, I needed an orgasm and since I'm doing this being-good shit—" I let my sentence end there.

Lyon crossed his arms over his chest.

"Oh, come on." Quinn hopped back on the desk. "Like we've never been caught up here."

"Quinn," Lyon growled his name. "That's not the point. I'm the alpha."

"He's just pissed he had a sex dream about you," he said and rolled his green eyes.

"*Quinn!*"

A miracle just hopped off a cloud and landed in my lap. "You did?"

Lyon blew out a breath and walked to the desk. "Thanks, Quinn."

He smiled smugly.

Lyon faced me. "I may have been… dreaming of you the past couple of nights."

"Sex dreams?" I wiggled my eyebrows.

"No."

"Oh."

"But... you may have been... somewhat, clothing challenged."

"The fuck does that mean?" I closed my mouth promptly when he snarled at my tone.

"It means you were naked," Quinn supplied. "He thinks you're our mate."

My lungs stopped working. I stood before them with wide eyes and a sharply increasing pulse rate. "I'm a... you're my... what? How is that possible?" A three-way mate bond was very rare.

"It's not common," Lyon supplied. "We can't tell until you shift."

A mate? *A real mate?* "Yes. I mean, sure. When?" How could they be my mates? Was this why I felt the urge to stay here on the moon and stay out of trouble?

Quinn chuckled. "Easy, baby bear."

I glared at him. "I'm only a year or so younger than you."

"Now," Lyon spoke.

I jerked my gaze toward him. "Now, now? Like right here?"

"It's nearly ten in the evening. Everyone should be sleeping and if not, we'll give someone a show. So, undress, shift and let's find out if my dreams are right." He didn't look happy about this.

"Okay." No pressure. My entire life had been spun around this week and this moment was when it was cresting. *What if I wasn't theirs? What if I was?* I wouldn't be able to tell because we weren't the same species, but Lyon being an alpha might be able to. Suddenly, my past felt foolish. I think Quinn was right, maybe seeing happy couples made me jealous. I was looking for my own happy ending and I didn't mean an orgasm.

"Take your clothes off," Lyon said.

"Oh, he's starting his orders." Quinn looked positively giddy as he switched spots to sit next to him. He grabbed Lyon's hand and watched me expectantly.

Well. Here goes nothing. I unbuttoned the fancy shirt Quinn had given me. Fuck, but my fingers were stiff. I slid the shirt off my shoulders. I wasn't exactly ripped like Lyon but more smooth and toned like Quinn. Muscles took patience and work. I preferred sex in my spare time.

I toed off my shoes and shoved them under the desk. Then I worked on my pants. My hands were shaking. Why the fuck was I so anxious? Oh, yeah. My potential mates were watching. *Come on, Tremarc, get a grip. You're a fucking sex god in bed, standing, or on tables.*

The pep talk helped. I pulled my pants open and let them fall to my ankles. I then stepped out, showing off my thighs with scattered hair, and my thick calves. I did a lot of running. My dick was stuffed behind a pair of blue boxers. It pressed against the material. I stuck my thumbs in and then tugged them down.

There. Naked.

My cock bobbed free. It wasn't the biggest thing on the moon, especially since I'd seen what Lyon was packing, but I could still make him scream my name.

"Mmm, very nice." Quinn winked at me.

Lyon stayed silent.

I took a deep breath and started to shift. Instantly, I fell on all fours. My skin tingled, bones shifting, sending shards of stinging pain through my body. I felt the fur grow through my skin and a moment later, my bear self was there. I padded around on all fours, my claws scratching up the wood.

"Do you feel anything?" Quinn asked, glancing at Lyon.

He frowned again. "Yeah, trouble is ours."

I shouted, loud and long before I realized it was a roar.

"He's really nice looking. How come he has those markings around his face?" Quinn hopped off the desk. For a human, he was ridiculously calm. Maybe because he'd been living with shifters for years now.

"His species. There aren't too many Spectacled bears left." Lyon leaned against the desk. "Change back."

I closed my bear eyes and focused on my body. The fur retracted, my bones returned to their natural form and I was panting when I was human again. On all fours, with my ass in the air I took heavy breaths. My shaft was hanging between my legs as I moved to kneel before them. My mates.

Lyon muttered something. He seemed pissed off.

What did I do wrong? All I had to do was get my mouth on him and he wouldn't be frowning so damn much. Quinn knelt before me.

"I felt it, you know. This weird, crazy attraction the first time I saw you." He smiled. "I've only been able to get hard for Lyon since we mated but here you come and boom, hard as an Earth rock." He leaned close. "Lyon? Can I kiss him?"

I glanced at our alpha with excited anticipation. *Please, for the love of shifting, say yes.*

Lyon kept frowning, but said a gruff, "Fine."

Quinn didn't waste a second. He closed the distance between us and pressed his mouth to mine. We were both hesitant. Our kiss was all lips and no tongue. When we parted, I was smiling like a fool, staring into

Quinn's green eyes. A shadow fell over us. Lyon. I glanced up at my alpha, my mate, and shivered.

"No more trouble from you, Tremarc," he growled my name.

I nodded.

"No fucking anyone but us."

I licked my lips. "Yes."

"No more running," Lyon said softly.

I hadn't realized that all my life I was running until I fell into their arms.

"Your place is here now. With us. Under me." Lyon pulled on the buttons of his shirt.

"It's a good place to be," Quinn said with a grin. Then he kissed me again. This time our mouths opened and tongues met. We truly kissed. He was gentle, timid, and it made me want to take care of him. I pulled his shirt over his head, checking out the shiny nipple piercings. The rings made me want to lean down and suck on them.

Lyon threw his shirt on the floor. "I am the alpha. I am the dominant. I am the one making the rules." He tugged on his pants. "Can you handle that, Tremarc? Can you handle being the submissive?"

I was sure as hell going to try. He shoved his pants down. *Damn*, Lyon was fucking beautiful! From the streaks of gray in his hair to the firm ab muscles and his gorgeous dick. I was practically drooling. His balls were tight and big. He was long and hard with his foreskin pulled from his tip.

"I want you to kiss me first, Tremarc, while Quinn sucks on my cock."

Quinn groaned.

I stood up to the side of Lyon and felt this nervous twitch run through my body. With Quinn, it was all pleasure, but with Lyon I felt intimidated. He gave off this aggressive intensity with every breath. I licked my lips and leaned close. I could make out the lines at the corner of his eyes showing his age. There were a few gray strands in the stubble on his face.

"Tremarc," he whispered.

"Yeah?"

Lyon shoved his fingers into my hair. It was just long enough for him to grip. "Open your mouth." Then he descended.

It was like a damn out-of-body experience. Lyon instantly took control. His mouth ruled mine. I became the weak one, the submissive, the innocent. He sucked on my lower lip. His tongue slithered into my mouth and traced my teeth. Our breaths and saliva mingled as he took complete control of me. I felt... ravished. Then Lyon tilted his head back and let out a soft growl. I glanced down to see Quinn's handsome face as he sucked on Lyon's balls. At this point, I might come all over Lyon's leg.

"Join him." Lyon didn't suggest, he ordered, and he expected obedience.

I was more than eager to taste him. I fell to my knees, wincing as I landed too hard on the wood. Quinn was sucking on Lyon's tip, probing the foreskin with his tongue. I opened my mouth on the left side of Lyon's shaft. Quinn did the same on the right. Our mouths slid down his length in an almost matching rhythm. The big man let out a loud groan. "That sound," I mumbled.

"Perfect," Quinn said before cupping Lyon's balls.

We licked him from base to tip. When Quinn sucked on the skin around his sacks, I used my tongue on his foreskin. We teased and tasted until a spurt of pre-cum filled our vision. Like sharks around blood, we attacked. Our tongues touched as we shared Lyon's taste.

"Quinn, get your clothes off." Lyon's voice was raspy. He pulled Quinn to his feet, then me. Our lips met. The lingering, salty taste was shared during the kiss. I heard clothing rustle as we parted. Quinn was naked. It made me groan. How was I ever going to get enough of them? My mates. The title made me smile.

"On the desk. Tremarc, on your back."

I rushed to comply. Lyon liked to be in control and he was damn good at it. Sunlight streamed through the large window as I lay on the desk. My cock flopped onto my stomach as I lifted my legs and presented my ass. I was flexible when it came to being a bottom.

"Quinn on top."

Quinn moved atop me. His skin was smooth, beautiful, warm. Our bodies touched and then our shafts pressed against each other. I groaned. Quinn started to thrust. It had been too long since I had any kind of fun with another man. My head fell back. Quinn leaned down for a kiss as he rubbed against me.

Wet fingers touched my crack and glided toward my hole. Quinn lifted slightly, just so he could hold my legs up and make my ass more presentable. "Fuck yes," I cried out when Lyon's finger pushed into me. He pressed it deep then added another. "Lyon!" Three fingers. I was stretched, feeling the need to be penetrated.

"Quinn is going to hold onto you while I fuck your ass, Tremarc."

"Yes!" I wanted this so bad. I wanted them.

"Then you're going to take Quinn deep into your mouth and suck him off."

"I am good with my mouth," I muttered.

Quinn chuckled.

I heard the snap of a condom. Lyon pulled his fingers out and replaced them with the head of his cock. I felt the pressure. *Oh, please, yes.* It had been an entire week since I found any pleasure that hadn't come from my hand. I closed my eyes and savored every second. Quinn rubbed his shaft against mine. Lyon pushed his huge dick into me. I hissed out a breath as he stretched and forced himself inside me. "Please." Damn, I usually made my lovers beg, not the other way around.

Quinn moved upward, presenting his pierced nipple before my face. I greedily took it, sucking on the flat bud and tasting the metallic ring. Lyon thrust hard and I gasped. I lost hold of Quinn and jerked, trying to get more of Lyon's length inside me.

"More."

"Is that a fucking order?" he yelled and grabbed my hips. Lyon jammed himself deeper.

The sting soared through me, pushed my pain into pleasure unlike any other.

"I am the alpha." He pulled back then in. "*I* am in control. You will obey me, Tremarc." He stopped talking and started a rhythm.

His fingers dug into my skin as his cock pushed my limits. "Lyon!" Quinn placed his mouth over mine, swallowing my shout. His body slammed into me. The desk beneath us creaked. Quinn started rubbing against my shaft, adding to the stimulation. Then there was a deep, loud roar that made the hair on the back of my neck stand up.

I squeezed as Lyon shoved deep. My ass was sore as he came. He held me in his powerful grip until his orgasm began to fade. Then I felt him pull out, leaving me empty and breathless. Quinn climbed down my body and wrapped his hand around my dick. He squeezed me just under my tip and started stroking. Fast, tight tugs and I was screaming his name.

My body seized up. Cum shot from my slit like a fountain. The white liquid bubbled up, splashing us and dribbling over Quinn's hand. I was gasping when I lay back. My head fell over the edge and I was staring at the city on the moon with the sunlight shining in. When my heart stopped beating like it was going to burst out of my chest, I sat up. Quinn and Lyon were kissing. I hopped to my feet and walked toward them.

"Tremarc." Lyon glanced at me. "That was… fantastic."

I smiled. "Yeah, it was." I moved to my knees. "Now to show you how talented I am with a full mouth." I crawled the short distance to Quinn then kneeled. I was faced with his impressive erection. He was as long as I was, but thinner. His balls were tight and heavy—I knew, because I reached up and cupped him. His shaft was on the pale side with a cut, red-tinted head. The tip was smeared with shiny pre-cum. I grabbed him and lowered my head. I swiped my tongue over his slit, savoring his flavor. He was sweeter than Lyon, less salty. I placed my lips over him and sucked on his tip.

Quinn whispered my name.

Lyon shifted behind me. I felt his hand in my hair, fingers stroking my scalp as I sucked harder. "Take more of him inside your mouth." I could hear his heavy breaths over Quinn's moans.

I opened wider and took more of him in. Lyon increased the pressure on the back of my head. I had nowhere to go but deeper. I took a breath and let them guide me. My mates. I stretched my mouth more, my lips stung as I took all of Quinn. He slipped down my throat making me gag, and I was forced to retreat. I took a moment to catch my breath. Lyon kept stroking my head. Then he pushed me closer to Quinn.

"Tremarc. Lyon. Please." Quinn hissed out a breath when I touched him. His gorgeous shaft was shiny with saliva.

I spread wide again. Lyon eased me slowly forward with the pressure of his hand. I took a giant breath and let Quinn slide back down my throat. My eyes began to water. I held as long as I could, fighting the urge to breathe as Lyon held me in place. Then he let go. I pulled back quickly, coughing and gasping.

Quinn and Lyon began kissing over me.

Lyon pushed me forward again. Another breath. I held it. Quinn forced his dick down my throat and he began to thrust with short pulses of movement into my mouth. I tried holding the spot. My body locked into place. My lungs burned as Quinn fucked my mouth and Lyon kissed him. Then there was a jerk, a jolt. Quinn pulled back so his cock head was lying on my tongue and I tasted his orgasm.

His jizz filled my mouth. I savored the cloudy, sweet flavor and swallowed every single drop. Perfection. I was kneeling there catching my breath when Quinn lowered to me. He kissed me briefly, pulling me in for a hug.

"Thank you... mate."

Lyon moved to my back. He pulled me to him, wrapping his arms around me and Quinn. "That was perfect."

"We're going to get a hell of a complaint for that show," I said with a smile.

"You're a bad influence." Lyon pressed his lips to the back of my neck and bit down, pressing his teeth into my skin. The sting made me feel the mark, his mark. Mated.

"He's pure trouble," Quinn added and kissed me.

We sat there for a few minutes and my gaze drifted out the window. The sunlight was so bright it made me wince. I didn't know what the future held, but I think I might have actually found a clan to call my own.

For right now, I was the happiest man on the moon, kneeling between a naked Quinn and Lyon. "How did you get your name anyway? Who names a bear Lyon?"

Quinn chuckled. He untangled from us and stood up.

"That's a long story." Lyon stood and pulled me to my feet by my hair.

"I'll tell it to you when I get you both home and in my bed." He growled and nipped at my lower lip.

Quinn winked at me.

I watched as they both padded naked around the room collecting clothing. It was a nice view. One I was content to watch for the next hundred years or so.

The End

Lyon and Quinn's story: *Dipping His Pen in the Office Ink*, is a free read at Evernight Publishing.

www.authorjamescox.weebly.com

OUTLAW WOLF

Copyright © 2015

Elizabeth Monvey

Chapter One

Although the bar was loud with the sound of pool balls clacking together, people talking, and the golden oldies screeching from the archaic jukebox, the unmistakable sound of breaking glass had Dekker wincing. He hadn't even needed his superior hearing to know someone had thrown a tumbler. He glanced from where he stood stacking clean glasses, to see two women cat fighting in the corner over a man who, in Dekker's opinion, didn't seem worth it—if the paunch belly and yellow teeth were any indication. Then again, he wasn't a chick, so what the hell did he know?

Dekker was a lot more selective in his desires. Handsome, being the foremost. Strong. Loyal. All of which the bar patrons most definitely did not provide. Instinctively, his mind shied away from the one man who owned his heart and soul, because it just wouldn't do to travel down memory lane.

Dekker had left that life behind the day Grey had slain the old Alpha of the pack to become the new one, knowing there was no room for their secret relationship. Alphas couldn't be gay, especially those who were the president of a feared outlaw motorcycle club, one that also happened to be full of werewolves.

"Don't just stand there, you fucking nitwit," the owner, Hoss, bellowed at him. "Go clean that shit up!"

"The glass or the two women?" Dekker mumbled to himself, ignoring the cankerous man. He hadn't wanted to hire Dekker until the former bar help hadn't shown for his shift, and by then Hoss needed help desperately. He'd told Dekker to get to work and it'd been fucking drudgery ever since. He had half a mind to permanently shed his human form and live out his days in the wild. The only thing that held him back was his mental connection to his pack.

He longed for Grey. His heart and body still pined for the man, the addiction still just as sharp and potent after missing the man for six months.

Dekker sighed, grabbed the broom and pan, and headed over into the corner to clean up the mess, literally and figuratively. People had given the two women a wide berth to continue their little hair-pulling spat, mainly ignoring them as they continued their Friday night partying. The man they fought over seemed to have grown bored of being the center of attention because he was playing at his phone.

It took him a few minutes to separate the two females and send them on their way in opposite corners of the bar, before sweeping up the glass fragments. Cleaning up messes was nothing new to him. He'd been doing that for the Bone Crushers Motorcycle Club most of his life.

Once the broken glass had been cleaned up, Dekker resumed his duties of collecting dirty glasses and throwing away empty beer bottles. Hoss was a stickler for recouping revenue, so every Monday they recycled. Dekker was careful to separate the dark colored beer bottles from the lighter. He didn't mind. It was good for the environment, plus it kept his mind occupied.

The night began to wind down. The bar wasn't a biker bar. It was a hillbilly place that served cheap whiskey and even cheaper beer. Moonshine was even on the menu. So mostly the people left inside were the regulars who usually had too much to drink. Dekker knew from past experience each of the people would have rides waiting for them because Hoss had already taken their keys.

It was near closing time and Dekker swept the floor as the cool night air swirled around him. Wondering who could possibly be walking in so late, he looked up. The first thing he saw were the cuts, leather jackets worn by two muscular bikers that had caused everyone to turn their heads and stare at the newcomers. Shock washed over him, turning his body to ice. Cold. Unable to move, because he recognized the men.

His past had just come strolling back into his life like a tornado. He stared at Grey as the big man moved to the bar. Dekker couldn't think, even if the smart thing to have done was leave. He'd run away from Grey—from the pack—in an effort to save them both, but damned if his feet would cooperate this time with common sense. He seemed rooted to the ground.

It had been six months since he'd seen the man he loved, and Dekker couldn't tear his gaze away from him. The saliva dried up in his mouth and his heart thundered painfully in his chest. It wasn't until that moment that Dekker realized he'd only been half alive since leaving the pack, and he wondered how he was supposed to make his heart go back to being numb.

Awareness suddenly coursed through him, the same feeling just before lightning struck. The anticipation of something momentous just about to happen. In slow motion, Dekker saw Grey stiffen. Saw the biker raise his nose and sniff the air. Like a deer caught in headlights, Dekker was unable to turn away as Grey scanned the room, and then their eyes met. Locked. The world disappeared around them. He'd been a fool to think time and distance would've been enough to sever the bond that arched between them. In a mere instant the electrifying tangent that had always existed between them snapped tautly into place.

The second biker leaned into Grey, and Dekker dragged his gaze from Grey's to glance at the other man. Stones, the club's enforcer, and the pack's most vicious wolf. He was older than them both by about twenty years, but Stones' age had never been a liability. He was the only person Dekker truly feared.

Grey shook his head sharply and walked away from Stones, heading directly toward him. Dekker took a deep breath, unable to move or even look away. Fury darkened Grey's face, turning his golden eyes into cold flecks of amber. The premature gray in his hair, responsible for his name, glowed in the dim lighting. Dekker waited, gripping the broom handle tightly. He couldn't save himself. There would be no turning and running away like last time.

Grey came to a stop in front of him, glaring at him from his superior height. They'd known each other their whole lives, having grown up in the club and pack. Grey had always been taller. Stronger. Bigger. Dekker hadn't minded. That had been one of the things that had drawn him to Grey.

"You've been here all this time?" Grey demanded.

Dekker shrugged, unable to form words past the lump in his throat.

"No," Grey said harshly. "You don't get to shrug this off. We searched everywhere for you. *I* wouldn't give up, even when they told me to."

Dekker looked around, knowing that everyone was listening avidly. The last thing he wanted was to air their past to gossip mongers, which was exactly what the small backwoods community was. Small-town life seemed to thrive on swapping stories of what went on behind closed doors.

"Let's not hash this out here, Grey," Dekker said, leaning closer to keep his voice down.

Grey folded his arms. "I'm not leaving."

"Fine. Could you at least wait until after my shift? I only have half an hour left."

Indecision warred through Grey's eyes, but finally, he gave a stiff nod. "Fine. But I'm not leaving this bar without you."

"I sleep upstairs, so we'll talk out back. In the alley. Okay?"

"Don't even think about leaving," Grey warned.

He turned and headed back to Stones' side, taking a seat at the bar. A second later, Hoss placed two beers in front of them. Dekker wondered how the hell he was supposed to concentrate on finishing up his chores when the love of his life sat not but ten feet from him.

****

"I can't believe we found the fucking whelp," Stones muttered.

"Don't call him that," Grey said sharply. He was still reeling over the fact that he'd finally found Dekker. He'd been tracking the smaller wolf for the past six months, keeping feelers out all over the state. One of his informants had said they'd sniffed a new wolf in their territory, and on a hunch, Grey had gone, not expecting to find anything.

Stones stared at him angrily. "Really? You're still defending him after he betrayed us?"

"I'm saying we don't know his story," Grey replied. "Now drop it. I'll have a talk with him. Discover why he left."

Stones shook his head. "You're Alpha. You should rip his throat out and ask questions later. A deserter to the club, to the *pack*, deserves nothing less than the ultimate restitution."

Grey grabbed Stones' jacket and yanked him close. "I said drop it. If there's any restitution to be made, I'll be the one to take it. Understand?"

Stones gave an angry nod and Grey let him go. The pissed off biker grabbed his beer and downed half of it in angry protest, but as long as he shut up about hurting Dekker then Grey didn't care if Stones never talked again.

He hadn't wanted the enforcer to come along in the first place, thinking this trip would be just another dead lead. His gaze landed on Dekker through the bar mirror, watching as he worked quickly around the area, and his dick hardened behind the fly of his jeans. Damn it, it wasn't the appropriate time or place to get a hard on, but he'd always been helpless to control his body around the smaller wolf.

They'd grown up together, and once they'd grown up, their relationship had moved from simply friends, to lovers. It hadn't been something he planned, and yet it was as natural to him as breathing. The past six months had been excruciating and he couldn't imagine the rest of his life without Dekker by his side.

Now he had to convince Dekker to come back with him as well as get the pack to accept that his mate was a male.

Chapter Two

Dekker waited in the alley behind the bar, knowing that Grey would come to him. They had a lot to talk about. He knew Grey wanted answers. Was he supposed to tell the truth? He sighed and his shoulders slumped a little. Of course he had to tell the truth. He owed that much not only to his Alpha, but to their relationship. They'd been friends first, lovers second, but the pack was always paramount.

The smell of pine and male floated through the night air and Dekker swung around to stare at the mouth of the alley a second before Grey appeared. His dick hardened at the enticing aroma, which still made his mouth water. No one else smelled as good as Grey did, and Dekker wondered how the hell he was supposed to fight the feelings of love and desire coursing through him, knowing he had to say good-bye. All he wanted to do was bow before his Alpha... his lover... and show just how sorry he was for leaving.

"Is there any reason you want to talk out here?" Grey asked.

"There's nowhere else," Dekker said. "Hoss closed the bar and unless you want people at the twenty-four-hour diner to hear our business, then this is as good as it's going to get."

Grey's mouth tightened. "You owe me an explanation."

"Why?" Dekker demanded. Maybe if he stayed on the offense he wouldn't succumb to Grey's intoxicating presence. "It's not going to change anything."

Anger flashed through Grey's eyes. "You didn't even say good-bye, Dekker! Didn't I at least deserve that?"

Dekker hung his head. "Yeah."

Grey lifted his chin with a finger. Their eyes met, and Grey searched his face, trying to find something.

"What?" Dekker asked.

"I was trying to find out why you left me."

Dekker pulled his face away. "Don't."

"What the fuck, Dekker!" Grey exploded. "What made you turn from me? What made you start *hating* me?"

"I don't hate you," Dekker said, appalled he could think that.

"Then tell me why the fuck you left me! I thought we had a great thing going. I thought you loved me."

Dekker closed his eyes. He couldn't stand the confusion, anger and censure in Grey's voice. "I *do* love you."

Grey grabbed his shoulders. "Then why did you leave me?"

"It's *because* I love you that I left," Dekker replied softly. "Don't you understand? The pack won't accept you being gay. Not their Alpha."

"That's bullshit," Grey said. "They would get past it."

Dekker shook his head. "No, Grey, they wouldn't. I overheard a few members talking. They suspected our relationship had deepened because our scents had mingled." He gave a self-depreciating laugh. "Can't keep a fucking secret within a wolf pack, you know."

Grey cocked his head. "What did they say?"

"They said... They said if their Alpha turned out to be a fucking fag, they were going to kill you."

He didn't add that his life had also been threatened, but that wasn't why he'd run. He couldn't be the one responsible for Grey getting hurt.

Grey studied him. "Who said that?"

"It doesn't matter."

"Yeah, it fucking does," Grey said harshly.

"No. Not anymore. By me leaving, you're safe now. All you have to do is pick one of the bitches to have a pup with and you'll—"

"Shut up, Dekker," Grey muttered. "You left out of some misguided hero notion? Is that what you're telling me? You were protecting me?"

Dekker didn't answer those questions. He didn't need to. He knew that Grey understood.

"Son of a bitch!" Grey hollered. A menacing growl underlined the words. "Do you know how I found you, Dekker? I put out your scent to the surrounding wolf packs and one of them caught a faint trace of you. If I hadn't done that, you'd have disappeared from my life forever, wouldn't you?"

Dekker looked away.

"Oh no, you're going to answer me," Grey stated. "You said you loved me."

"I do," Dekker replied. He didn't add that Grey had never once, in all their time together, admitted he returned the feeling.

"Wolves mate for life," Grey told him.

Dekker shook his head frantically. "We're not mates. There's still hope for you."

"We most certainly are mates. I don't want anyone else." This time, when he placed his hands on Dekker's shoulders, they were gentle. "I've wanted you since we were sixteen and went skinny dipping in farmer LaGrange's pond. I took one look at your skinny body and knew one day you were going to be mine."

"I hadn't gone through the change yet," Dekker defended.

"I had," Grey reminded him. "My wolf knew you. He wanted you then and he wants you even more now."

Grey always used the word *want*, never love. Dekker knew he wasn't that lovable, especially as an omega in the pack. He was one step above a pup, which wasn't saying much.

Dekker knew he should walk away, but when Grey pulled him into his arms, all of Dekker's resistance melted away. He could no longer deny what was in his heart and what his own wolf wanted, which was Grey.

"Grey," he moaned.

"Yes, Dekker."

Their lips met in a blinding clash of passion, almost furious in its intensity. They'd become lovers when they were teenagers, and they'd never been apart. After hearing the threats against Grey, it had taken every ounce of strength Dekker possessed to leave, knowing he would never see Grey again. He had still done it to protect the man he was in love with. Now he poured all the heartbreak he'd felt into the kiss, showing without words how much he loved Grey, how much he had missed him.

Grey broke the kiss with a groan. Dekker heard him panting and smelled how turned on he was. Dekker wanted that cock, wanted once more to feel it sliding into his body, claiming him. He'd been strong once, but he knew he couldn't walk away again. He didn't have it in him to deny his love a second time.

"Have you fucked anyone else these past six months?" Grey demanded.

Dekker shook his head. "No. You?"

"There's never been anyone else for me. There never will be."

Grey spun him and pulled Dekker's ass against his pelvis. Grey bent his head and sucked on the back of Dekker's neck, using his teeth to nip the skin, marking him. Large hands gripped his hips to hold him in place. Just the thought of where his cock was going to end up had him squirming even more.

"Hold still," Grey murmured in his ear, just before he fell to his knees.

There was something primitive in having his Alpha kneeling behind him. When Grey tugged at his pants, Dekker hurried to unbuckle his jeans. They slid down his legs a second later, followed immediately by his boxer briefs. Dekker felt Grey's breath on his backside. A shudder of excitement shot through him. Teeth brushed over the skin and bit—gently—but it was enough to know Grey was there and dominating his ass. Hands palmed the fleshy mounds. Fingers dug in, spreading him.

"What a beautiful sight," Grey said. A feather-light touch ran over his perineum. "You want my dick in your ass?"

"Yes," Dekker breathed. "Please. Fuck my ass."

A tongue licked around his anus, causing a jack-knife reaction. Precome ran in a steady stream from the tip of his cock. Grey reached around to collect it, only to bring it around to his puckered hole. A finger slipped in, and Dekker forced himself to relax. Another finger joined the first and the burn traveled up and down his spine.

Dekker loved the slight bite of pain. It was only a second later that Grey withdrew and stood. The sound of a zipper only heightened his anticipation. Grey's engorged cockhead brushed over his rosette. His big hands held his waist as he slowly, inch by inch, pushed inside Dekker.

"Oh, God," Grey muttered. "Seeing my dick buried balls-deep in you is so fucking hot. You're never fucking leaving me again, Dekker. You hear me? You belong to me."

"Grey!" Dekker gasped. He wanted so desperately to agree, but he knew by saying yes Grey could lose everything. He loved him too much to see that happen so he just moaned and thrust his ass more forcefully into Grey.

Grey groaned and his fingers dug into his skin to move him faster back and forth against his cock. He eased back, spat on the area they were joined, and slid back inside Dekker. Then it was no holds barred. Grey fucked him fast and hard. All Dekker could do was grunt and try to keep up with Grey's furious fucking, working his cock deeper, harder, until he found that sweet spot inside Dekker, each push hitting his prostrate and making him writhe. He wasn't going to last much longer. Grey reached down to jerk him off. They moved as one, stroking, kissing, moaning their rapture as they spiraled higher and higher.

Dekker fell first, flinging back his head with a shout as wave after wave of satisfaction coursed through him. Grey then swelled inside him, planting himself as deeply as he could get before spasms raked his big body.

They held each other up, panting through the aftermath. Dekker had never felt so happy in his life.

That was, until the moment Grey whispered in his ear.

"Who threatened me?"

Dekker stiffened and pulled away, bending to pull up his pants. "Why do you want to know?"

"Because I'm going to challenge them," Grey replied. "I am Alpha and no one threatens me."

Dekker felt trapped. If it were just one wolf, Dekker had no doubt that Grey would be able to take him down easily. He was Alpha after all. There were none other in the pack who could match him in strength and integrity. But it *wasn't* just one wolf, and Grey had an obligation to think of the whole pack rather than his own wants and desires. An Alpha *always* put the needs of his people first.

A few minutes ago, Dekker didn't think he could say good-bye to Grey a second time. He thought he didn't have the strength to rip out his heart again, but all the reasons why he'd run in the first place came rushing back. This time, however, he knew he had to make the ultimate sacrifice.

"I think you should go, Grey," he whispered achingly. Already, he was dying inside.

Grey narrowed his eyes. "Well, then you're coming back with me. Right now. Back to the club."

"No, Grey. I'm not. I'm done with the club. I'm done with the pack."

"What? We've talked about this."

Dekker squared his shoulders and lifted his chin. He had to do this. He had to be brave and strong. He had to put Grey and the pack first. "I have to. I no longer claim—"

"No!" Grey shouted. "Don't you dare! Don't you *dare*, Dekker."

"I renounce you as my alpha. From this day forward, consider me a lone wolf, without pack."

Silence descended between them. How Dekker held it together, he didn't know, but it was crucial that he maintained eye contact. As part of the pack, he'd lower his head, give obedience and servitude to his alpha. But as a lone wolf, he didn't have to hold to that rule.

"Damn you, Dekker!"

Grey spun on his heel and stormed away.

Chapter Three

Mere seconds later the sound of a motorcycle filled the deafening silence. A heavy heartache settled in Dekker's bones and he bent over, placing his palms on his knees as he tried to suck in deep breaths, hoping to stave off the need to vomit. He knew instinctively that Grey would not come back, not after Dekker had renounced him as his alpha. It was a decision that was absolute and unbreakable.

For the first time in his life, Dekker felt completely isolated. Just speaking the words had made the moon not quite so bright, the night sounds dull and muted.

And this was all he had to look forward to for the rest of his life. No pack and no Grey. The pain was unbearable and all he wanted to do was howl out his grief, but the tread of a footstep behind him had him spinning.

"What are you doing here, Stones?" Dekker demanded. He silently berated himself. If he hadn't been mourning all he'd lost, he would've easily smelled the other wolf's threatening scent which now overwhelmed him.

Stones smiled at him, but there wasn't any amusement in his eyes. "I came back to take care of the problem you've presented to the pack."

Dekker shook his head. "You don't have to worry about me anymore. I'm not coming back. I'm a lone wolf now."

"You don't understand," Stones said. "Nobody leaves the pack. There aren't any lone wolves that come from the Bone Crushers."

Fear sliced through Dekker and he took a step back. "What are you talking about?"

Stones cracked his knuckles. "You don't think I can't smell Grey on you? That I don't know you two fucked? I've suspected for some time but the disgusting little display I saw earlier confirmed it."

Dekker took another step away. "Whatever Grey and I had is over, Stones."

"Oh, I know it's over," Stones drawled mockingly. "And I'm gonna guarantee that it stays over."

Dekker knew exactly what Stones meant just as the enforcer grabbed hold of him. Panic exploded through him. Self-preservation had him shifting, letting through enough of his wolf to attack with his jaws. He snarled as he snapped at Stones' arm in an effort to escape, but Stones counteracted with his own wolf, and Dekker wasn't very strong. He certainly wasn't stronger than the beta in front of him who outweighed him with sixty pounds of muscle.

If anyone could see them, they'd be nothing but monsters, half human and half wolf. Stones managed to subdue him, but Dekker reined back his wolf in order to turn and run. However, he found himself flying backward as Stones grabbed the back of his shirt and yanked. He fell with a thud onto the ground, slightly winded. He stared up at the night sky and then blinked when Stones appeared in his line of vision, back in his human form.

"I'm sorry, Dekker," Stones said. To his credit, he did sound regretful. "This is how it is. How it's always been. How it will always be."

"You mean... Grey approved this?" Dekker managed to gasp.

Stones shook his head. "Grey doesn't know this policy of the pack yet. He's still a new alpha, after all.

But we can't have someone running around who knows us. And we especially can't have a fag inside our pack."

Dekker shook his head fearfully. "I'll... I'll disappear. I'll go away!"

"I'm sorry, Dekker," he said again and brought his fist back. "And unfortunately I can't make it quick. You need to be a warning to all who want to desert the pack."

All Dekker could do was watch, his gut clenching as he braced for impact. When Stones' fist connected to his jaw, pain detonated through his skull, racing over every nerve ending and lighting up like a firecracker. Dekker groaned and spat out the blood rapidly filling his mouth. His teeth had cut the inside of his cheek.

"Wait," he gasped and threw up a hand.

Stones paused, his fist poised over his head. "Don't beg for mercy."

"Not for me," Dekker muttered around his swelling jaw. "Don't hurt Grey. Please. Do what you gotta do with me, but leave Grey alone."

Stones studied him for a long moment, but he didn't say anything. Instead, he simply punched him, again and again, and pretty soon, Dekker couldn't feel the blows. His body simply gave up the struggle to care that he was being beaten to death in an alley. Images of Grey drifted through his mind, and the only regret he had was not having the chance to tell the man he loved good-bye.

Then a loud crack reverberated through the air. The blows stopped, but Dekker couldn't even open his eyes to see why. He felt himself float away from the destruction of his body. *Perhaps it won't be so bad. Perhaps death was simply going to sleep in one world and waking up in another.*

It was the last coherent thought he had as he succumbed to the darkness.

Chapter Four

Hoss fired his shotgun in the air and then leveled it at the big man beating up his employee. He may think Dekker was an idiot but he wasn't about to allow him to die, especially not on his property. The biker paused with his fist in the air and looked over his shoulder, glowering at him. For a moment, Hoss could've sworn the man's eyes flashed gold, like a canine.

"I'll put the next shot in you," Hoss warned. "Let him go and get the hell out of here. I never want to see you around these parts again."

His aim never wavered, even when the biker dropped Dekker and turned his big-ass self to fully face him.

"I can kill you with one blow, old man," the biker snarled.

"Not before I fill you with buckshot," Hoss promised.

The big man studied him for a long moment before glancing over his shoulder and giving a shrug. He gave a sarcastic chuckle. "He's dead anyway."

Hoss didn't relax until the sound of the man's bike was long gone, and then he hurried over to the prone body. Dekker lay on his back, his face a bloody mess. Labored breathing whistled from between swollen lips. Pity moved through Hoss. He was afraid to move him, but he didn't want the young man to bleed to death on the dirty ground.

He slung his shotgun around his shoulders and then as carefully as possible, hefted Dekker fireman style. It worried him when the passed-out kid didn't make a sound. He hurried to his car, fished the keys out of his pocket, and opened the back door. He laid Dekker across the back, closed the door, and then raced around to the driver's seat.

The small town of Gate City didn't have a hospital so Dekker would have to make due with the urgent care center. As soon as he pulled up, he hopped out and rushed inside to grab someone for help. The two of them moved Dekker inside where he was placed on a gurney and taken into the back, leaving Hoss to answer questions.

"What happened to him?" a nurse asked. She held a clipboard and a pen.

"A patron beat him up," Hoss replied.

"Who?"

Hoss shrugged. "Some asshole I hope to hell was only passing through."

"But why?" she asked, bewildered. "I've been in your bar. I know Dekker. He's a sweet guy."

"I think... well, don't think bad of the kid, but I think he was beat up because he's gay."

The nurse shook her head sorrowfully. "I just don't get people. It isn't anyone's business what goes on behind closed bedroom doors."

"Can you make sure Dekker gets the best care?" Hoss asked gruffly.

"Of course," the nurse said with a gentle smile. "I'll call you if... when... he wakes up."

Hoss nodded his thanks and then turned and left. No reason for him to stay. Looked like he was going to have to find a new bar helper.

****

Grey sat at the local wolf clubhouse, nursing a whiskey. He'd called ahead of time to get approval for him and Stones to stay within the pack's border, so he'd come back here to cool his anger. Already he regretted storming off, but he had needed space away from

Dekker's illogical reasoning of why they couldn't be together.

And of him renouncing his allegiance.

He'd give Dekker the night but come morning he was going to take his wayward lover back—kicking and screaming if necessary—to their home. The past six months had shown him a life without Dekker, and Grey wanted no part of it.

The door to the clubhouse opened, and Grey knew without looking that it was Stones. Only one wolf he knew walked with such a gait. Truthfully, he didn't much care for the enforcer of his pack, but Stones had been the last member of the old regime, and still a mean-old son-of-a-bitch despite his years. His keen hearing tracked Stones' heavy footfalls across the clubhouse heading for the stairs, but the whisper of blood tickled Grey's nose and he set his glass down sharply as he turned.

"Stop!" he ordered loudly.

The men in the clubhouse paused, including Stones, who didn't turn to face him. Grey tipped his head up, scenting the air as he walked toward his enforcer. With each step, the unmistakable smell of Dekker's blood grew stronger.

Grey stopped in front of Stones. "What did you do?"

Finally, Stones looked at him, and the flash of hatred in the older man's eyes was unmistakable.

"I did what I had to do," he sneered.

Fury exploded through him and Grey grabbed Stone's jacket, forcing the man up against the wall. He pressed his elbow into Stones' neck to hold him in place.

"What the hell does that mean?" he demanded, practically screaming the question. The members from the other pack simply stood and watched them. "Why is Dekker's blood on you?"

"He was a traitor," Stones wheezed. He pulled at Grey's elbow, trying to dislodge it. He was strong but Grey was stronger. He only pressed harder.

"I didn't give the order to harm him!"

"Didn't need to," Stones muttered. "This is the way of the packs. Not only did he abandon the pack, he's gay. Aberrations to our culture must die."

Shock poured through Grey and he turned his head to look at the other pack. Each man crossed his arms and stared at him defiantly. Grey couldn't believe what he was hearing, what he was seeing. He loosened his grip on Stones enough for the man to push him away.

"Aberrations? Preferring men for sex doesn't make anyone an aberration. Wolves have been known to engage in—"

"Save your fucking biological speech," Stones said mockingly. "We don't tolerate it in the club or pack."

"Stones, you've known me and Dekker our whole lives," Grey said, trying to reason with him. "We're just as much part of the pack as anyone."

"Not anymore."

Anger boiled through Grey. He didn't have time for this bullshit right now. "I want you to go back home."

Stones rubbed his neck and laughed. "I don't think so."

"I am your alpha," Grey said in a low, tight voice.

Stones leaned in to whisper in his ear. "Do you think I would take orders from a man who fucks other men?"

Grey didn't even consider his next action, he just hauled back and punched Stones across the jaw. The enforcer's head snapped to the side and he half fell against the wall. Blood oozed from the cut on his lip.

"Get up," Grey ordered in a cold voice.

Stones chuckled as he wiped his mouth. "What, you going to end me? In front of all these witnesses? You don't have any ground to stand on, Grey, but that's okay. The little fag is dead."

The world suddenly narrowed in on him, and Grey shook his head desperately, denying what he saw on Stones' face. He glanced at Stones' knuckles, covered in blood, and Grey felt like he was going to be sick. His heart thudded painfully in his chest, crumbling into a thousand pieces. He was too stunned to do anything except back away, from Stones and his words, as well as from the local pack who watched him stoically. This fight wasn't their business so they offered no help. Grey stormed out of the clubhouse and headed for his bike. He had to find Dekker.

He *couldn't* be dead.

He would know, wouldn't he? He'd have felt it if his mate had passed from this world.

Dekker wasn't your mate….

The words taunted Grey. Haunted him. No, he'd never officially claimed Dekker, never sunk his teeth into his neck so their scents could merge. Grey always thought that was just a formality. His wolf knew who Dekker was.

He just couldn't be dead.

Grey lifted his head and howled mournfully at the moon as he sped back to the bar.

Chapter Five

Grey drew his bike up at the mouth of the alley and turned off the engine. The sudden silence after the roar of the bike echoed with a painful finality and he threw out the kickstand before dismounting. He hadn't bothered to put on his helmet when he'd left the clubhouse so he immediately caught the thick scent of blood. Dekker's blood.

Bile churned in his gut and he wanted to run away. Never before had he had such a cowardly reaction, but Grey didn't know what he would do if he found Dekker's lifeless body.

He took a deep breath and pushed forward. He may want to bury his head in sand, but he was an alpha. Running wasn't in his nature. As he walked, recriminations poured through him. He shouldn't have tracked Dekker down. He should've just accepted Dekker's decision, no matter what his own feelings were on the matter.

He should've realized there were wolves who would never accept having a gay alpha. He and Dekker were close friends, then lovers, long before they had even known what being gay meant. For someone to come along and place such an ugly connotation on their feelings was shocking. Stones had been cast, and he hadn't even had time to battle them.

The scent of blood became stronger and Grey stopped, looking around. His wolf's vision allowed him to see the obvious signs of what had happened, but then again, the smears of blood weren't that invisible in the dark even to the naked eye. They were dark ink stains upon the concrete. The only thing Grey could relax about was the fact that Dekker's body wasn't there.

"You come back to finish the job?"

So lost in his thoughts, Grey hadn't heard anyone behind him. He spun and saw the bar owner, Hoss, at the mouth of the alley, pointing a shotgun at him. Slowly, Grey held up his hands.

"I'm not here to cause problems," he said. "I just wanted to find Dekker."

"Your friend already found him," Hoss said angrily.

"That man wasn't my friend. Where is he?" Grey asked softly. "Where's Dekker? He's not... he's going to be okay, isn't he?"

"Why the hell should I tell you that?" Hoss demanded.

"Because I love him," Grey admitted softly. He'd always held back the words, knowing once he uttered them he'd be completely bound. But not saying them didn't make it any less true, and it gutted him to think that Dekker might have been killed not knowing his real feelings.

Hoss studied him, then the gun barrel lowered slightly. "He's not dead, but he's not good either."

For a moment, Grey's shoulders slumped with relief and happiness zinged through his soul. His wolf calmed upon hearing their mate was alive.

"Where is he?"

"Urgent care center," Hoss replied. "We don't have a hospital here so I drove him there."

"Much obliged," Grey said and walked toward Hoss. The bar owner moved out of his way and Grey headed toward his bike.

"You were the one he was with, before the other fellow beat him up," Hoss stated.

Grey nodded. "Yes."

"Did that man beat Dekker up because he's gay?"

"I think so," Grey murmured. That was the easiest answer to give.

Hoss shook his head. "That's not right. The boy may be slow cleaning a bar, but no one deserves to be beat to death."

Grey nodded his thanks and then revved up his engine, flipping the kickstand up before punching the throttle. He drove away without looking back.

****

Dekker's wolf lay still inside him, licking his wounds. He'd always been on the small side, which had often left him ostracized from the pack. The only reason he was still admitted into the club was because his father had been a sentinel in the pack, chosen by the previous alpha to take reins in case something happened to the leader. Grey had always been high up the ladder, a natural born warrior who had ascended until he'd fought for—and won—the alpha title.

He wondered how he could still be alive when there wasn't anything to live for. Grey was gone and he'd renounced his pack. There wasn't anything worse for a wolf than to be forever alone. Tears leaked from his closed eyes to run down his sore face. Voices murmured around him but he couldn't seem to focus on any one conversation.

Words like crushed cheekbones, broken nose, and deep lacerations drifted through the fog in his head. He knew they were talking about him because hands were examining his wounds, but he didn't care. Not anymore. He was actually sorry he hadn't died. That had to be better than the soul-tearing emptiness that resided in him now.

He felt a tiny prick in his arm and moments later succumbed to the darkness reaching for him. Sounds tried to pry him from sleep's embrace, but he ignored them. Now that he knew he was going to live, the only way he would heal quickly was by letting his wolf take over. He'd rest for a little and regain enough strength so he could change. He'd worry about how to escape when he'd slept enough.

****

How long Dekker drifted in and out of limbo, he didn't know. It wasn't until the low growl of a wolf nuzzling his ear had him fighting against the sleeping medicine dripping through his IV. He cracked open his eyelids to see Grey bending over him in the darkened room.

He opened his mouth to say something, but Grey placed a finger over his lips, keeping him silent.

"I'm going to get you out of here," Grey whispered in his ear. "You can only heal properly when you shift, you know that, right?"

Dekker gave a single nod, groaning a little at the pain slicing through his head. He slipped in and out of consciousness as Grey unhooked his machines. He gave a stifled groan as the IV slid out of his arm. Free from the medical trappings, his wolf surged up, wanting out.

"Not yet," Grey muttered. "Don't change until we get you outside. There are cameras outside this door and no one needs to see a wolf walking out of here."

Grey draped his arm around his shoulder and then helped him off the bed. The door eased open silently and they made their way out of the darkened medical facility.

Grey led him out the back door where Dekker noticed the alarm wires had been cut. The area behind the building held a huge dumpster and several parked cars, but Grey didn't lead him to a vehicle. Instead, he went straight to the woods located on the other side of the clearing. Once they reached the tree line, Grey stepped away from Dekker and yanked off the ugly cotton gown.

"Go on, shift," Grey ordered softly.

Dekker concentrated and felt the change tingle deep within him. It took a little more effort because pain wracked his body and all he wanted to do was curl up and whimper tearfully, but he also knew that the only way to fully heal was to let the wolf come out. So he sucked in a deep breath and relaxed. Moments later, he stared at Grey through his canine gaze.

Chapter Six

Grey stood watch over Dekker as the smaller wolf healed from his wounds. Dekker mostly slept, but as the days passed, his strength gradually returned. Through it all, Grey could do nothing but provide his mate with food and drink, either in animal or human form.

Grey would stare at Dekker as he slept, scared something would happen if he relaxed his guard. It had taken him almost losing Dekker, twice, but it finally sunk in how much he stood to lose. Being alpha meant being the strongest, being the mightiest. But it also meant he felt the most love, hungered for it with every beat of his heart.

He couldn't embrace one aspect of his nature without embracing all of it, and he came to a decision late one night, as the crescent moon hung high in the sky. He wouldn't have to kill all who opposed him taking a male mate. He would just have to kill the beta that had stood by his side during his ascension to leader of the pack.

He was going to have to kill Stones.

And he would have to do it in a way to ensure no repercussions would revisit him. The best way to achieve that was through the Challenge. He had to get Stones to throw down the gauntlet.

Dekker stirred and rolled. One minute Grey was staring at a wolf, and the next there was a naked human man lying in the pale moonlight. Grey's heart thumped heavily in his chest, because if the wolf disappeared, that meant Dekker had healed. He traced a finger over Dekker's hip, the area where the skin curved toward his buttocks. There were faint white lines where Dekker had a growth spurt at some point, stretching the flesh suddenly. Or possibly from all the shifts he'd done through the years. Grey bent and placed a soft kiss against the pale scars.

"What are you doing?" Dekker asked in a low, rumbling voice, rough from disuse.

"Kissing away all your pain," Grey murmured.

Dekker rolled onto his back so he could stare Grey in the eyes. "I should've died."

"Don't say that," Grey snapped, anger causing his mouth to tighten. "You almost did. It was Stones, wasn't it? The member you overheard."

Dekker nodded. "I just want to protect you."

"*I'm* the alpha," Grey said. "That means it's my job to protect *you*. Although I could compromise and say let's protect each other. Dekker, I love you."

Dekker's eyes widened. "You... love me?"

"Why do you sound so surprised?"

"Because you've never said it before."

"Doesn't mean I didn't feel it," Grey told him. "I choose you as my mate, Dekker."

"You can't! An alpha—"

"An alpha embraces all facets of his strengths," Grey said. He cupped Dekker's face. "And you're my greatest strength, Dekker. You always have been."

Dekker opened his mouth, probably to argue, but Grey was tired of hearing excuses. He was over having his mate doubt his ability to defeat their enemy. There was a reason why he was alpha and it was damn time he demonstrated just how tough he was.

Grey sat up and took off his shirt. Dekker's eyes were glued to his chest, and Grey felt his gaze tracing over every tattoo he had decorating his torso. They were all depictions of wolves, all the symbology to their bloodline and his allegiance to the pack. Plus, there was a new one. Right above his heart was the letter D.

Dekker reached out with a trembling hand and traced over the letter. "Is this…. Is this for me?" he asked hesitantly.

"Yes," Grey replied. "Wolves mate for life."

Dekker smiled. "Yes, they do." He cupped the back of Grey head. "Kiss me, Grey."

"I'm going to do more than kiss you," Grey said. His fingers slid through the softness of Dekker's hair and clenched a handful to bring back his head. "I'm going to claim you."

Before Dekker could say anything else, Grey covered his mouth to shut him up.

****

The kiss was not gentle. It was rough, raw. Grey pressed his mouth open and his tongue slipped inside, seeking his, twisting with it, dancing. Any protest that Dekker might have had, evaporated. He pressed his body more firmly into Grey's, needing to feel every inch of him. Grey's hard cock pressed back, pulsing.

Dekker's hand roamed over Grey's hard body, over the tightly defined shoulders, down a corded back. Sweat slicked his skin and Grey licked his way down his neck to suck on the erect nipples. Dekker was moaning this time, loving the almost too intense way Grey devoured him as the alpha wolf kissed and nipped his way down his body.

Then, in the blink of an eye, Grey flipped him onto his stomach and pulled his hips up until he had full access to Dekker's tight hole. Dekker's breath came out in a harsh rush when he felt Grey's tongue enter him, working the puckered sphincter lose, using one, then two fingers to open him up. At this point Dekker was panting, his hard on almost painful.

Dekker heard the rustle of clothes as Grey disrobed. Finally, Grey was pushing into him. It was heaven. The slight burning sensation eased little by little with each small jab of Grey's cock. In and out he pistoned, each thrust going deeper, spreading him wider. Only when Dekker pushed back did Grey impale himself fully, filling him up.

"Dekker," Grey moaned. "Are you okay?"

"Yeah," Dekker panted. "Don't stop."

"Never," Grey vowed.

Over and over Grey pumped, grabbing hold of Dekker's cock and pumping it in time with his own hips. The moonlight bathed them as they made love.

"More." Dekker gasped. "Harder!"

Grey moved deeper still, pushing on the center of Dekker's back to make him bend his head down, allowing Grey's cock to sink further. *There!* With Grey touching the spot that drove him crazy, Dekker released a cry of undisguised pleasure, pushing back into Grey's pelvis.

"Yes! So good, so good," Dekker panted, withering as the pressure built. "Grey!"

It was too much. Dekker exploded in a kaleidoscope of colors as Grey milked his cock for every drop of cum. Seconds later, Grey's teeth sank into his neck, claiming him as Grey climaxed, shuddering uncontrollably. He drank Dekker's blood as he came deep inside him, branding him. Grey thrust his forearm under Dekker's mouth and out of instinct, Dekker allowed his canines to elongate and bite the muscled flesh. Their scents mingled, combining as one as the mating bond took root. Grey's teeth ultimately retracted as he collapsed on top of Dekker.

Both their bodies spasmed as they tried to catch their breaths. Grey's body was heavy, but Dekker welcomed it, liking the feeling of being covered. He could have easily fallen asleep, but Grey's tender kiss on his shoulder had him glancing behind him.

"We are mated," Grey whispered.

"Yes," Dekker agreed.

Chapter Seven

They stood on the outskirts of their territory, and Dekker raised his nose to smell that the pack wasn't too far away. They had been waiting for their alpha to return. Dekker had promised Grey not to let fear overwhelm him, but it was a hard promise to keep. He had run to keep Grey safe, and yet, he was right back at the beginning.

"They know we're here," Grey said.

"Yes," Dekker replied.

Grey took his hand and led him into their pack territory. Dekker wished they were back in their own little world, even if he had still been healing from Stones' attack. After Grey had initiated the mating bond, they had spent another three days cementing their claim on each other, loving the days and nights away. Dekker had healed fully, but the trauma and stress of the beat-down still haunted him.

"Who else did you overhear talking about hurting me?" Grey asked.

"Claw." Dekker saw Grey wince. Yeah, it was bad enough having the enforcer for the club and pack be against you, but to have the leader of the Elders was even worse. The pack relied on the Elders for wisdom and the alpha relied on them for advice. The hierarchy within the wolf pack ranks was absolute, with the alpha being first and the Beta being second, followed by the Sentinels and then the Elders. But that didn't mean an alpha didn't need guidance from time to time.

When they reached the clearing where the entire pack was waiting, Grey tightened his grip on Dekker's hand and strode boldly out so everyone could see them. All the men wore the Bone Crusher's cut, designating their place within the pack. Dekker took courage from Grey's strength and determination.

Grey focused on Stones and Claw, who stood shoulder to shoulder.

"I see you've brought a welcoming party for us," Grey said sarcastically.

Stones pointed at their joined hands. "Your deviance is not welcome in this pack."

Dekker saw several members shift uncomfortably, and it dawned on him that Stones didn't have full backing of the whole pack. Hope surged. Perhaps they would live through this night after all.

"You know, I've heard you use words like deviance and abomination to describe Dekker and me," Grey said. He released Dekker's hand and stepped forward, toward Stones and Claw. The rest of the members formed a circle around them. "I've been part of this brotherhood all my life and I don't remember the old alpha using such derogatory slurs. Is there a reason why you've decided to threaten my life and that of my mate?"

He looked pointedly at Dekker and a murmur swept through the assembled people. Dekker looked at each person, meeting their gazes, trying to convey with his body language that he was just like them. Just another wolf who belonged to the pack.

"I see he survived," Stones said. Dekker stared coldly at him. "Why don't you tell everyone the passionate declaration you made to the... *alpha*. You know which one I'm talking about. The one where you—"

"Where I renounced my allegiance to the pack," Dekker finished. Another shocked murmur went through the crowd. Gathering his courage, he took a step toward Stones, ready to fight back. Ready to fight for his mate. "But I should also tell them the reason why I was forced to run away. Why I took such a drastic measure in becoming a lone wolf. Or would you like to tell them how *you* were the one who threatened to kill Grey? You had the suspicion that his and my relationship had deepened. Changed. And you couldn't stomach that, could you? Maybe you wanted to be alpha yourself. Maybe Claw desired that position."

At his name, Claw bristled next to Stones. But the sudden stench of excitement that surrounded Stones let him know that he'd hit the nail on the head.

Stones took a threatening step in Dekker's direction and Grey growled. Stones stopped and gave him a furtive glance.

"As your alpha, I order you and Claw to retire," Grey said.

Stones looked at Claw and then around to the people. He shook his head. "No."

"No?" Grey asked sharply. "I am your alpha. You will do as I say."

Stones threw his shoulders back. "Then I challenge you as right to be alpha."

Grey's smile reminded Dekker of the Cheshire Cat.

"So be it," Grey murmured. He pulled off his shirt and dropped it off to the side, waiting. Stones did the same and it was immediately apparent the difference between the two men. Although Stones still maintained his physique, age had begun to take its toll. His skin wasn't as tight, or his muscles as defined. Grey was in his late twenties, in prime condition. And while Stones might have experience on his side, the burning anger shining through Grey's eyes wouldn't have Dekker betting against him.

Grey and Stones circled one another and hatred poured off them in buckets. They each used their animosity for the other to charge with a savage cry. Fists flashed out from both men, fighting bare knuckled in a test of strength and will. Stones was able to get in a few good shots, but from the onset, it was clear who the victor would be. Grey outmatched his opponent in every way, from tactical attack to his calm demeanor.

In between breaths, Grey kicked, hitting Stones who moved forward and thrust him away. In Stones' disorientation, Grey quickly reached out and grabbed Stones' arms, bringing up his foot and catapulting the older man over his head. The flip impaired Stones long enough for Grey to straddle him and hold him down.

"Why would you betray me like this?" Grey demanded.

"Because I wish to be alpha," Stones hissed, spitting the blood at the corner of his mouth over Grey's face. "I'm more powerful than a Beta. I should not have to bow and scrape to a whelp."

"You've already admitted your weakness," Grey taunted. "Do you yield?"

"I'll never yield to an alpha I think is wrong for this pack," Stones stated.

Grey didn't say a word. He let his wolf through and his features changed. The snout elongated, whiskers sprouted, and the canines came down long and sharp. With a snarl, Grey clamped on Stones' throat and sank his incisors into the flesh. Then he ripped out the windpipe and blood sprayed in a fantastical red arch.

Grey stood up from the lifeless carcass, and his features went back to human form. Blood soaked the lower half of his face and dripped onto his muscular torso, obscuring some of his tattoos, including the D over his heart.

"Will there be anyone else who opposes me as the alpha?" he asked, projecting his voice so all could hear. He waited. Dekker looked around and saw only acceptance in the faces of every pack member.

Grey pointed to him.

"Dekker is my mate. Accept him as the wolf beside me, or meet Stones' fate." Grey walked up to Claw. "This is *my* pack. *My* club. And I am alpha of all. Are we clear?"

Claw bowed his head, showing his submission. One by one, each member fell to one knee, giving their oath and loyalty. Grey held out his hand to Dekker.

With happiness and love filling his heart, he grabbed hold and squeezed tightly.

The End

Evernight Publishing ®

www.evernightpublishing.com

54005852R10157

Made in the USA
Charleston, SC
22 March 2016